Witchlight

Also by J.S. Watts

A dark magical realism novel from Vagabondage Press

Praise for A Darker Moon

"A new twist on the Adam and Cain story, but it's a fresh and interesting take ... very thought-provoking. Watts has a knack of writing just the right words that I was entranced, pages flying by, I was so immersed in the story. So, if you're looking for a new author to try, or you like mythological fantasy, pick up *A Darker Moon*! It's well worth every cent!"

— *Minding Spot*

"Watts peppers her writing with exquisitely imaginative imagery, making this a wonderfully poetic novel, as well as a great read. *A Darker Moon* is a book that will delight both hardcore fantasy fans and newcomers to the genre."

— *Literary Ely*

"One of the best modern-day gothic mysteries you've ever read."

— J.P. Lowe

"The writing ... is lush and beautiful."

— Harriet Goodchild for *Heroines of Fantasy*

Witchlight

J.S. Watts

Vagabondage Press

Witchlight

ISBN: 978-0-692-40690-8

Vagabondage Press
PO Box 3563
Apollo Beach, Florida 33572
http://www.vagabondagepress.com

First edition printed in the United States of America and the United Kingdom, May 2015

First digital edition released in the United States of America and the United Kingdom, March 2015

10 9 8 7 6 5 4 3 2 1

Cover art by Serazetdinov and Naum. Cover design by Maggie Ward.

Witchlight

Chapter 1

The cat was studying the mouse with considerable interest. Only a few seconds before, it had had its claws hooked into the soft flesh, but, being a cat, its mother had scrupulously taught it to play with its food before eating. So, it had released its trembling prey in order to watch it run and squirm some more before the final and inevitable conclusion to the age-old game of cat and mouse. The mouse ran, the cat leapt, sharp claws once again sank into the mouse's flank, strong teeth closed around skin, flesh, and bone, and the mouse, with an almost relieved sigh, plunged into the eternal blackness of the final mouse hole. The cat licked its lips and wandered off in pursuit of further feline gratification, thus missing out on a truly startling event, at least as far as the mortal human world was concerned. Then again, it was a cat, so perhaps the event would have been less surprising than failing to catch the mouse, had that happened, which of course it hadn't; it was a cat, after all.

Twenty seconds after the cat vacated its spot in the darkest and most secluded part of the field, a blob of pale turquoise light appeared a metre or so above the grass, expanded in volume and brightness, and then disappeared with a barely audible *poof!* leaving in its place a short, dapper man in well-washed blue jeans and an extremely bright and ever-so-slightly twinkly turquoise shirt. He patted himself down, smoothed his already immaculate auburn hair, and walked across the closely cropped combination of grass, thistles, and nettles towards the back of the houses overlooking the field. His intended destination was the somewhat rampant looking garden at the back of number sixty-six Basingfield Lane in which Holly Jepps, the owner, was currently attempting to tame some long-untended grass.

Holly remained unaware of her impending visitor until he leaned over the back fence, coughed politely, and in distinctly over-emphatic tones said, "Hi Holly, good to meet you. How's it going?"

Holly looked up with a start, a look of puzzlement on her face, and a handful of grass cuttings in her left hand.

"Erm, hello? Can I help you?"

"Oh, no, no, no, no, no! It's me who's come to help you, girlie." And with that, he jumped over the fence—or to be precise, he levitated over it—but Holly, being a pragmatic, levelheaded woman, saw it as a jump. To be honest, as a woman two years or so off the milestone of forty, she was rather more surprised at being called girlie than by the pseudo leap. Though, as she was also fairly short and was used to being patted on the head, both metaphorically and literally, by people of more extended height, her initial reaction was actually an internal "Heightist, patronising git!" She revised this slightly as she realised he was little taller than she was and then further revised it when it occurred to her that both her garden and her personal space were being invaded by an unknown and unduly familiar man. She reached for the lawn rake, just in case.

"No need for that, girlie," said the small, twinkly man. "I really am here to help you. I'm your fairy godfather."

The silence that followed this announcement was dense enough to cut with a lawn mower. More explanation was clearly needed.

"Although, to be precise and, leaving out the issue of sexual preference, I'm actually a witch rather than a fairy."

Holly briefly debated whether to hit him with the lawn rake before legging it to the kitchen door, or just run as fast as she could for the door prior to locking it firmly behind her. The man seemed to sense her thought processes and eyeballed her pointedly before clapping his hands and releasing a sizeable charm of goldfinches from between them. Holly remained rooted to the spot. He clapped his hands again, and Holly found herself sitting at her kitchen table with a mug of hot coffee in her hands. Opposite her, the man was juggling yellow coloured gemstones, which turned into canaries, flew upwards, and disappeared.

"I think, young Holly, that we need to talk."

* * *

In summary, his name was Partridge Mayflower, he was a witch, and he was Holly's eldritch godfather: every young witch had a mentor from birth, and he was hers. The obvious problem with that was that Holly was thirty-eight years beyond her birth, and for all of those years it had never occurred to her, even once, that she might be a witch.

"Never?"

"Trust me, never."

Okay. I am prepared to concede that we might, therefore, have something of a problem."

There was a long pause. Their relatively short conversation had already been seasoned with a number of quite notable long pauses. This time it was Holly's turn to break the silence.

"So, have you ever come across this sort of problem before?"

"Not really… I've had some late starters from time to time, that's why I was chosen to godfather you, but I'll admit I've never had anyone as late as you, or as ignorant."

"What do you mean, 'ignorant'?"

"Okay, okay, wrong term. Sorry. Not ignorant. How about unknowing?"

"I guess I can live with that."

Another long pause unwound itself and stretched. Holly stood up to get some more coffee, but found her mug was already full. She sat down again, heavily.

"So how come these other mentees of yours weren't as unknowing?"

"I like to call them my fairy godchildren."

"Mentee works fine for me."

"Well, with the other mentees, there might have been some advance signs; little incidents, odd occurrences; but mostly their mothers had already told them about the family trait, or they at least knew of their mothers' powers."

"Why just their mothers? Don't the fathers ever get involved?"

"Ability is passed down the maternal line. That's how it is."

"But you're a man, aren't you?"

"Yes I am. Well spotted." A tint of sarcasm had coloured Partridge's previously effusively jolly tones. "Men can be witches too, you know. They inherit their witchlight from their mothers; they just can't pass it on, is all. It's a genetic thing linked to the female chromosome. We call it the Abracadabra gene, and only your mother can pass it on; in effect, only your mother can make you a witch."

"Really?"

Yet another silence had started to pile up. Holly guessed things weren't going as Partridge had envisaged.

"So what about your mother?"

"What about her?"

"She never said anything to you, or showed any magical ability herself?"

"No."

"When did she die, if I might ask?"

"She didn't. She's alive and remarkably well for seventy-seven and living in Croydon with Dad. Fair dos, some people might call Croydon a living death, but I'm not one of them. I do so hope you're not one, either."

There was a further silence. This silence was starting to spawn little silences of its own. Eventually those silences would grow up to have their own silences.

"So, which of the two of them do you most take after?"

"The two of whom?"

"Your parents, Mum and Dad down in Croydon; which of them gave you your hazel eyes and quaintly natural mid-brown hair?"

Holly self-consciously ran a hand through her short, bobbed, and rather tousled hair.

"Neither. I was adopted."

Partridge exhaled sharply. "Now, why didn't you say that before?"

"You didn't ask."

"Holly girl, we're not exactly making progress here, are we?"

"I guess not."

"Do you know anything about your birth mother?"

"No. I was abandoned shortly after birth in a cardboard box."

"Seriously?"

"Seriously."

"Is there anything at all you can tell me that might help?"

"Like what, for instance?"

"I don't feel we're really engaging here."

Holly stared at Partridge fixedly and without blinking. Her hazel eyes were not exactly radiating warmth. She reminded Partridge of an irritable owl that was being kept from its supper by an increasingly annoying creature that was itself almost small enough to be dinner.

"Look, I've already apologised for calling you girlie. It usually goes down well with the younger godchi…mentees. I said it without thinking."

"That's not the problem."

"So what is?"

"It's this—the whole bloody thing: you, me, magic. I don't believe it. I don't believe you. All this talk of witches, you might as well tell me you're Father Christmas. I am sure your girlies believe in him, too, but I'm not so much of a girlie any more, as I believe we have already noted."

"Look, I'm sorry all this has come as something of a shock. What more can I do to prove it to you? I've shown you some real magic, haven't I? Filled your kitchen with canaries and cleaned up afterwards, as you wanted. Isn't that proof enough?"

"No, because, despite the bird shit, I'm just observing you allegedly doing those things. I'm seeing stuff that might not be real. It could all be trickery. A big scam. Derren Brown and David Blaine do it all the time. I've seen it on TV. You don't need to know how it's done to know it's a con."

"So what will make you believe? If I get you to do something yourself, something tangible, will that convince you?"

"Maybe. Depends on what it is."

Partridge paused and thought. He convinced himself that this time the silence felt a tad more positive.

"If I suggest something for you to do, you'll only accuse me of another trick set up, so I think it's best if you choose what you are going to do."

"How can I choose? I've got no idea. I don't do magic, remember?"

"Think of something simple that you couldn't do by any means other than magic."

"Like turning the cat into a canary?"

"Sort of, only simpler and less disrespectful of the cat."

It was Holly's turn to pause and think.

"Floating a pencil in mid-air and making it spin. That's what they do in all the cool movies."

Mayflower nodded his agreement. Holly got up to get a pencil. She placed it on the table between them. It lay there unmoving, not even the slightest twitch, let alone rising or spinning. Holly stared at it and then at Partridge.

"Nothing's happening. Do I need a wand or something?"

"Good grief, no. There's no such thing. Harry Potter has such a lot to answer for. Same with spells. Only the really strong Old Magic needs to be contained by words. Normal magic is just a matter of deciding, willing, and directing: decide, precisely, what you want to do; will it to happen; and direct your will to where it's going to happen. If you've got ability, and you do have, your will prevails."

Holly stared at Partridge, stared at the pencil and tried again. Nothing.

"Perhaps I don't have the ability. Perhaps this is all a big con. Perhaps you're just barking."

"No. It's not, I'm not and you do have. Take it from the top, but slowly. Decide what you want to happen and tell yourself clearly."

"I want the pencil to rise and then spin."

"No. More precise. How high will it rise? When will it start to spin and in which direction? Plus, you don't have to say it out loud. It's like reading—you can do it without moving your lips."

Holly began again, but this time in her head. *I want the pencil to rise three inches above the table.* She pictured it doing just that. *At three inches, it will pause and then start to turn in an anti-clockwise direction, rotating around the axis of its lead.* The mental image of the pencil correspondingly obliged. *It will spin faster and faster until it is just a blur.* The pencil image accelerated. Holly focussed on willing it to happen as she had imagined it and directed her will at the pencil itself, which slowly, but surely, started to rise. At three inches above the table, it paused and then started to rotate in an anti-clockwise direction. The spinning grew faster. Holly looked at Partridge in wordless amazement and then hurriedly refocused on the pencil. It carried on getting faster.

"You'd better stop it now."

The pencil carried on spinning.

"How?"

"Exactly the same process as before: decide, will, direct." Partridge waited. The pencil carried on spinning like the world depended on it. "Sometime now would be good."

The pencil was an audibly spinning blur. Holly started to panic.

"It's not working. I can't make it stop. You stop it, please."

The pencil appeared to be smoking. Small blue flames started to dance along its length. Partridge rolled his eyes with a pained "oh God" expression on his face.

"Oh fucking hell. This is going to hurt… both of us."

He stared at the pencil, which stopped spinning abruptly and fell to the table, just as a searing pain ripped through Holly's skull. Partridge winced simultaneously, then produced two aspirin and a glass of water from thin air and gave them to Holly, whilst producing another glass and a couple of pills for himself, which he downed rapidly.

"Right. Now do you believe me?"

Holly looked quite shaken.

"Yes. I guess I have to, don't I?"

"Good. Some progress at last. So, what have you learnt from all this?"

"Learnt? Oh, you mean decide, will, direct, and I don't need to move my lips."

"And…?"

"Stopping a spell hurts?"

"Stopping someone else's magical intention with your own hurts both of you. It's like head butting someone, so don't do it unless you really have to. So what else?"

"Else?" Holly examined her empty glass. "Um, I guess magic can't fix headaches."

"Normally it can, but in this case you'd be trying to fix something with the very thing that needs fixing. Aspirin is quicker and more reliable. What else?"

"There's more?"

"Yup."

Holly just looked puzzled. Partridge tried again.

"What went wrong?"

"The pencil wouldn't stop spinning."

"But why not?"

"I got it wrong."

"Yes, but what did you get wrong?"

"I didn't make it stop."

"You never decided it needed to stop, did you? You envisioned it spinning, you willed it to spin, you directed your will at the pencil and made it spin, but you didn't envision it stopping."

"I didn't believe it would actually start to rise, let alone spin, so thinking about it stopping was neither here nor there."

"And now you know different."

"…And now I know different."

"You need to be precise when deciding what you want to happen. Say you choose to make yourself look a bit younger. If you aren't precise in deciding how much younger you want to look and when you want the youthing process to stop, you risk getting younger and younger until you end up unborn. You need to make sure there is a clear conclusion, a full stop, built in to what you are doing."

Holly nursed her head in the palms of her hands. "Lesson learned."

"Good."

The kitchen was once more silent, but the silence did not seem as spiky as before, just thoughtful and a little hung over.

"Is there anything else I should know?"

"Lots. That's why I'm here. Think of me as your driving instructor in magic, if you prefer it to fairy godfather. We have quite a few lessons ahead of us, but I think you've had enough introductory session for one day. Anyway, you've got some explaining to do."

"I have?"

"Too true. You need to make sure you tell Barny what's going on."

Right on cue, Barny, Holly's black and white cat, made his entrance, tail held high and a dead mouse dangling from his mouth. He dropped the mouse at Holly's feet and walked round her three times in an anti-clockwise direction, then rubbed himself against her legs and purred loudly.

"Oh, looks like he already knows: a familiar that's very much on the ball. That's good." Partridge nodded approvingly.

"He's not a familiar, he's a cat."

"Same difference, if a cat's worth his biscuits. They're born with an innate understanding of the magical world and can be very helpful if you involve them properly. Very good at directing focus, cats."

Barny's focus currently centred on getting his ears scratched by Holly. So far, his focus was working quite satisfactorily.

"I'll leave you two to talk things through. Barny's more than ready to do his bit."

Holly was about to ask what doing his bit meant and how her visitor had known Barny's name, but Partridge Mayflower had already disappeared with a small implosion of ever-so-slightly twinkly turquoise light.

Chapter 2

Almost exactly thirty eight years previously…

A warm August night. Little or no breeze. The smell of warmed tarmac and paving stones, sunset heated grass and soil: a city getting on with urban life, while pretending to remain in touch with its rural roots.

Dull, yellow street light shines patchily through the heavy leaf coverage of the trees lining Kew Road. A young woman is making her way discreetly alongside the high wall that surrounds Kew Gardens, attempting to keep within the shadows wherever possible, but every now and then being obliged to step into a pool of thick, yellow lamplight.

She is not in a hurry, but she is not going slowly either, and her heels echo a steady *click click* as she makes her way along the pavement. She notices this, and suddenly the sound disappears, although her shoes continue forward at exactly the same pace as before. Despite the warmth of the night, she pulls her light-coloured raincoat closer around her, concealing the pastel pink and yellow of her summer dress. Drying water stains on her cheeks indicate she has been crying until only fairly recently, but her eyes display a focused determination that seems at odds with past tears. Or perhaps not.

Checking to see if she is being observed, she waits until there are no late-night vehicles within sight and then swiftly crosses the road. As she does so, a brisk wind chases after her, causing the leaves on the nearest trees to rustle and disturbing the already mottled glow of the adjacent streetlight, which drapes her in camouflage patterning.

The wind follows her down the front garden path of a small house facing onto the Kew Road and the severe wall of Kew Gardens. It causes stray leaves to scuttle along the ground and a large black tom, crouched under a lavender bush in the front garden, to lower its ears and defensively fluff up its tail.

The woman approaches the front door of the house cautiously. The night seems somehow denser where she is, and it is difficult to see what it is she is doing as she pauses briefly by the locked door that is suddenly unlocked and ajar. She leans forward and whispers through the gap,

"Mother? Are you here?"

Satisfied, or not, with the silence that absorbs her hushed questions, she slowly opens the door wider and steps through into the house, shutting the door softly behind her. The sound of a key turning decisively in the lock is audible in the still, wind-free silence of the garden. The cat raises its ears, slims down its tail and resettles itself.

Out in the garden, there are probably four minutes of silent, uninterrupted darkness before the cat's patience is rewarded. A small mouse scampers into line of sight. A large, black paw descends like the hand of God and with a swift, instinctive reflex, pins the mouse to the ground. Before nature can take its course, though, there is a flash of blinding white light from within the house, as if a bolt of raw lightning has been released within the domesticity of the downstairs front room. The entire front garden is briefly illuminated. Then, as the sharp brilliance fades, a fierce fire can be seen and heard burning inside the house, the crackle and hiss of the flames audible to the cat, along with what could be human screams; but these are consumed within the cascading roar of the conflagration.

A human observer would, by now, be frantically calling 999, but the cat gazes on with wide-eyed dispassion until the flames, and the agonised noises within their searing core, die down. Darkness returns to the house and the front garden. Where, minutes before, there was a savage inferno, there is now only nocturnal calm: no traces of fire, heat, or scorching, no charcoal-blackened evidence, just suburban predictability.

The cat continues its motionless vigil until, with a faint click, the front door starts to swing open. The cat's ears flatten back down to its head. Its tail flares up once more into an expanded brush. The bedraggled mouse, snatching its once-in-a-lifetime chance, wriggles free and darts away. The cat, now running as if his own life depends on it, disappears into the black edges of the darkening night.

Chapter 3

Another morning. Holly woke up with a start. She had been waking up with a start every day now for the last four weeks, ever since Partridge Mayflower had twinkled his way into her life. Each morning, she viewed the world afresh, pinching herself to test it was still as she had dreamed it: filled with magic and witchcraft like a children's fairy story. Automatically, and without actually touching them, she drew the bedroom curtains with a flourish—it invariably was.

The hardest part was not being able to tell other people, but Partridge was adamant this was a secret she had to keep to herself, at least until she was proficient in handling the basics of her new-found ability. So, although she ached to tell her best friend Sarah or her parents, though the latter would come with added complications, the only one she was able to talk to was Barny. Fortunately, Barny had proved a good listener and in recent weeks had become particularly attentive. Whenever she was home, or in the garden, he was rarely far from her heels. He had also become a regular participant in Holly's training sessions with Partridge.

Every day after work and sometimes at weekends, she met up with Partridge for an hour's magic practice. He had her repeating the same basic exercises over and over again to the point of frustration. When she remonstrated with him and asked for at least a little variety, he tartly told her that magic was like some forms of Tai Chi and related martial arts, in that you did the same moves slowly, over and over again, until they became second nature and as unthought of as breathing. The point being, that when you needed to call upon your ability in earnest it would be there without a second's thought.

Holly was not sure she could ever envisage a time when she would want to levitate spinning pencils, make empty coffee mugs disappear, or create paper aeroplanes out of thin air at a moment's notice, but whenever that time came, she would be ready. Her paper planes were really quite nifty, too, even if she thought so herself.

Moreover, with Barny next to her and intently studying whatever it was she was doing, the effort required to do whatever it was seemed a lot less than when she was on her own. Partridge had said that was because Barny had the makings of a really good familiar. Holly, who for a reason she couldn't quite eyeball directly, still wasn't comfortable with the thought of her pet cat as some form of magical accomplice, put it down to practice on her part and a cat's natural fascination with moving objects, but she wasn't complaining. Whatever Barny was or was not doing, he remained a very fine and affectionate cat. She was concerned, however, that her own newly discovered magical abilities meant she was less of a fine human being than she had always previously thought, and she wasn't too sure what that made her anymore, other than uncomfortable.

In her heart of hearts, magic didn't feel natural—not part of a credible day-to-day reality. Routine domestic life was the norm, was how things were supposed to be. Deviating from that made Holly feel somehow guilty, as if she was intruding on something or someplace she wasn't supposed to. Like the time she was three and had crept into her parents' bedroom without them knowing, all excited, and had tried on her mother's clothes and make-up. It was a big thrill, but had made her feel not quite right. Then, when she had looked at herself in the mirror, all dressed and made-up, she saw someone who was no longer her. Scared, she had cried for her mum, but when Mum came and tried to comfort her, she couldn't tell her why she was crying, because what she had done had to be kept a secret, even if the outcome was still plastered all over her face.

Holly couldn't help thinking she was too mature a woman to be feeling like a three-year-old, let alone left doubting her own humanity. When she raised the subject with Partridge, he spluttered into the coffee he had just produced.

"Holly girl, you are all too human, I can assure you. Prickly and awkward and human, because that's what witches are—human, that is. Not necessarily the prickly and annoying bit. That's just you."

"But how…?"

"Our power comes from the Abracadabra gene which, I would assure you yet again, has evolved as a natural part of the human condition, albeit a relatively rare one, occurring in much less than one per cent of the human population and one that hasn't been discovered yet by anyone beyond witching circles or, more accurately, one that has been successfully concealed from anyone not part of a witching circle."

Holly was temporarily reassured by Partridge's comments and produced an entire squadron of paper planes, which she flew round the room in a semi-triumphal flypast, much to the fascination of Barny, who tried to swat them with his paws until she relented and landed them in tight formation on the kitchen table. At least these days she knew to ensure her magical activities concluded with an appropriate full stop.

So, here she was, about to embark on another day of magic and amazement and, if she was honest, ever so slightly growing boredom. Holly had initially thought witchcraft might involve rather more fun and self indulgence than it currently seemed to, or at least the odd broomstick ride, but so far there had been no joy on that score. It appeared most of her preconceptions about magic, based on childhood tales and fantasies, were hopelessly wrong. Moreover, for all of his superficially twinkly ways, Partridge was a firm, no fun until you are competent, teacher. Still, today was a Saturday, and he had promised Holly longer than the usual one hour of his time to explore things in more depth and had hinted at something for today beyond the usual routine exercises. She had even put back her weekly lunchtime get-together with Sarah in order to make sure she had a reasonable amount of time with Partridge.

At one minute to ten (Partridge was always extremely punctual), there was a faint popping sound outside the back door, followed by a brisk knock on the kitchen window. Partridge walked straight on in, accompanied by a very large ginger cat. Holly lunged at Barny, who was not known for his hospitality as far as other cats were concerned, particularly when they turned up unannounced in his kitchen, but was surprised by Barny's calm response. Once he had squirmed and wriggled free from Holly's grip, he wandered over to the marmalade interloper and greeted him with a soft *miaow* and a friendly sniff.

"Knew there wouldn't be any problem with these two," said Partridge. "Both of them are highly professional chappies, aren't you boys?"

Two pairs of feline eyes glanced briefly at Partridge before their owners circled one another widdershins and sat down opposite one another in mutual contemplation.

"Now the boys have completed their own introductions, may I do the honours on behalf of the ginger lad here? Holly, this is Grindlebones, my long-term partner in crime, so to speak. He's going to spend some time with Barny today to show him the ropes from a feline perspective."

Holly was rather non-plussed. Given that she wasn't totally convinced by the role of a familiar to begin with, she couldn't for the life of her begin to fathom what Partridge's cat was going to share with a run-of-the-mill domestic moggy like Barny.

"Is it compulsory to have a familiar?" she asked.

"No," said Partridge, "but the majority of witches do have one. They don't have to be cats, though. There are quite a few dogs who fill the role admirably. Birds are invariably good at it, and I know of at least one chinchilla. They do make things easier for a witch, a bit like making a cake with a food mixer compared to the slightly more arduous process of baking by hand."

Barny and Grindlebones both gave Partridge an old-fashioned stare, as if being likened to an electric food mixer wasn't in keeping with a feline sense of personal dignity.

"So, is Grindlebones the promised added extra for today?" Holly tried not to let her disappointment show, but the extremely sedentary demeanour of Grindlebones and Barny so far did not promise a more exciting tutorial than normal.

"Partially. We'll see, but first we need to get cracking on your exercises whilst the boys sort themselves out."

Partridge must have noticed the look that briefly passed over Holly's face, because he at least allowed her to materialise the pencil from thin air, rather than making her retrieve it manually from the kitchen drawer as he usually did. Holly was secretly relieved it appeared whole and in clear air at the first attempt. Barny and Grindlebones just looked self satisfied, but then, they were cats.

Holly went through her routine exercises perfectly. She felt she would be able to do them in her sleep, if called upon to do so. When she mentioned this to Partridge, all she got was a brief, "Good. That means the exercises are working."

At the end of their standard training session however, Partridge unusually produced two mugs of hot chocolate and a plate of what looked like homemade biscuits with a wave of his hands and settled himself down on Holly's plumply upholstered lounge sofa with the biscuits and one of the mugs. Holly retrieved the second mug of chocolate from where it hung suspended in mid-air above her coffee table and joined him.

"Okay," said Partridge, "there's still room for improvement with the exercises, but I think you are getting there." Wherever *there* was. "It's therefore probably about time I told you a few more things about your ability and about you, yourself; babies abandoned anonymously in cardboard boxes were too much of a good thing to leave uninvestigated."

At which point, there was a sudden loud knock on Holly's front door. Both the cats looked up, startled, and Holly looked questioningly at Partridge.

"Nothing to do with me, though I like the dramatic timing," he said.

Holly wished whoever it was at the door would go away, but they knocked again, even more loudly.

"Shit!" She got up hoping this wouldn't mean too long an interruption. She wanted to know what Partridge had been about to tell her, but she was hoping in vain. Her friend Sarah stood at the front door clutching a bottle of red wine.

"Thought we could have an early pre-lunch drink," she said, craning her neck to see if anyone else was in the house. She didn't have to peer for long because Partridge emerged to stand behind Holly.

"Oh sorry, didn't realise you would still have a visitor," Holly thought her tone of voice rather indicated the opposite, "but I'm sure the bottle will stretch."

"Sorry to be a party pooper, ladies," responded Partridge, "but I'm afraid I'm just leaving."

Holly looked surprised, whilst Sarah managed to look disappointed and intrigued at the same time.

"Oh, do you have to?" Sarah said. "Well at least Holly can introduce us properly before you go."

Holly was trying very hard not to imitate a gaping goldfish, although Sarah's brazenness was making this very difficult.

"Er, Sarah, this is Partridge. Partridge, this is Sarah, an old and at times extremely irritating friend, who I was supposed to meet in town in about an hour and a half's time." Holly grimaced at Sarah. She knew Sarah was waiting for an explanation as to who Partridge was, but she didn't fancy introducing him as either her fairy godfather or her witchcraft instructor and had absolutely no idea what else to say. Fortunately, Partridge seemed rather better than her at deception.

"Hello Sarah, I'm teaching Holly to speak Mandarin," he said, followed by something incomprehensible that was supposedly meant to be Chinese and may well indeed have been Chinese, for all Holly knew. Sarah looked impressed.

"Ooh, Holly, I didn't know you were learning Chinese. That'll make ordering a takeaway fun. What can you say in Mandarin?"

Bugger Partridge. Now what was she supposed to do? Partridge nodded encouragingly at her and Holly, to her surprise, found herself opening her mouth. A stream of unfamiliar words, with even more unfamiliar intonation, poured out.

"Not bad," affirmed Partridge, "but you need to do some more work on those tones. I suggest we have a go at it next lesson." And with a cheery wave, he walked down the front garden path and off down the road.

Holly went back into her house with Sarah following close on her heels. Holly was half expecting to find Grindlebones still hunched down on the kitchen floor, but it was a solitary Barny who greeted Sarah with a none too subtle demand for attention.

"You secretive sod, you," exclaimed Sarah, as she proceeded to open the bottle of wine and pour the contents into two rapidly seized glasses. "Not only didn't you tell me about the Chinese lessons, but you totally forgot to mention that you have a personal tutor who is not far removed from gorgeous."

Holly was still somewhat stunned by the abrupt interruption to her session with Partridge just as it was getting to the interesting bit and at her sudden and unexpected ability to spout something that at least sounded like Chinese, so several seconds ticked by before it dawned on her what Sarah had actually said. When it finally registered she spluttered in disbelief.

"Partridge? Gorgeous? When are you off to the opticians?"

"I'm not, but you clearly need to go: thick auburn hair, trim figure, cute butt—really cute butt—our age or a teensy bit younger. What's not to like? No wonder you postponed me for an hour."

"Yes, and look at the good that did." Holly frowned at Sarah in mock condemnation, still internally struggling with the loss of Partridge's promised revelation and the thought of the somewhat fey Partridge as gorgeous. Plus, he was a lot older than she was, surely?

"Well, I had to know who you were delaying our lunch for, and you hadn't exactly been forthcoming yourself, so I brought into play my subtle and unobtrusive powers of enquiry and investigation and turned up on your doorstep. Shame he had to go so suddenly, though. I wouldn't have minded a bit of private tuition from him."

Holly spluttered again. Sarah carried on regardless.

"So go on, spill the beans. How long have you been having lessons, why have you been having lessons, and what's the low down on the mysterious and rather beddable Partridge?"

Some of Partridge's innate ability at deception must have rubbed off on Holly because she managed to come up with a convincing tale of winning the lessons in a charity raffle a few weeks previously. She also assured Sarah that Partridge was gay and far older than he looked, although Sarah seemed less convinced by this than the tale of the raffle win. Fortunately, by the time they had had lunch and discussed a hundred and one things other than Partridge Mayflower, Sarah appeared to have become less obsessed with finding out all there was to know about the man and went home content with her earlier coup of having found out about the Chinese lessons in the first place.

Holly, however, was left feeling somewhat disconcerted. For starters, there was the matter Partridge had been about to tell her when Sarah first showed up. Did he actually know something about the question of her birth—a question she had always been unable to answer? On a different and more perplexing note, she had really been taken aback by Sarah's response to Partridge. Holly had always considered herself a good judge of people. How could her assessment of Partridge have been so different from Sarah's? Had she really never noticed that Partridge was fanciable and if not, why not? Alternatively, had Partridge performed some kind of magic on Sarah, making her see him as somehow hotter than he actually was, or had the trick been on Holly all this time, duping her into seeing him as avuncular and fey rather than desirable, or even as a potential predator? If she was honest with herself, she had never found Partridge as easy to read as she found other people. Was that because he had blinded her in some way? It rather belatedly dawned on Holly that the introduction of magic into her life might mean that life was no longer as straightforward as she had once thought and, as a result, the world had become a much less certain place than it had used to be.

Chapter 4

Holly had next arranged to meet Partridge on the following Monday, but at the agreed time, it was Grindlebones, and not Mayflower, who materialised in Holly's kitchen. A folded note was stuck into his elaborate leather collar. Holly extracted the note and read it:

Meet me at St. Pancras Station in a couple of minutes. When you are ready, stand perfectly still beside Grindlebones and I'll bring you on over.

Part of Holly was excited at the thought of being transported down to London on nothing more than a waft of magic; part of her wished she could just waft herself there (but had the sense to recognise it was too major a step for her to take on her own without prior practice) and part of her wondered why Partridge was suddenly and without warning changing their previously agreed arrangements. This third part was immediately tense and suspicious. Nevertheless, she dutifully got herself ready, positioned herself beside Grindlebones, and awaited Partridge's summoning. There was a brief flicker, like a fluorescent light misbehaving itself and Holly found herself emerging from the ladies toilets onto the white columned and glass shopping concourse at St. Pancras. Grindlebones was nowhere to be seen.

Partridge was seated drinking coffee at a café table across the concourse. He waved at Holly, and she wandered over to him. She was debating why he'd chosen to meet in such a public place, but given her recent, if belated, realisation of the uncertainties of a magic-fuelled world, she wasn't that unhappy to be meeting him in plain view of other people.

"Thought a change of scenery was in order," Partridge said, as Holly sat down opposite him, "plus there'll be less risk of interruption by friends bearing bottles." He grinned.

"Sorry. I didn't know she would turn up like that."

"No problem. Your friends and family are bound to notice a change in you eventually, however subtly you mask it. At least we now know to be careful around her. At some stage you'll have to decide what, if anything, you can tell her about your new skill set, but not just yet. It's still early days, and we always recommend a planned coming out, if that's what you choose to do."

"Sarah not knowing, I can live with, but I do feel really uncomfortable about not telling Mum and Dad."

"That's only natural. The time will come when it's right to tell them. In the meantime, it's all about maintaining appearances."

Holly looked at Partridge. Today he was dressed in skin-tight black jeans, an open-neck white linen shirt, and black boots. He was draped in assorted silver chains, and she thought he might be wearing eyeliner.

"Did you know that Sarah saw you differently from me?"

Partridge looked surprised. "In what way?"

"She thought you looked hot, in a very masculine, down with the ladies sort of way."

"And you don't?" Partridge did not seem unduly perturbed by this.

"I guess I don't see you that way. You're my tutor and you're older and… I wondered if you had used magic on her… or on me?"

"No. Why should I?"

"Because you can."

"I always try to get across to my tutees that just because you can, doesn't mean you should. Lack of restraint can make the difference between good magic and bad magic."

"So have you?"

Partridge tensed. He did seem perturbed by this particular question.

"No! I would consider it to be very unethical. Haven't you ever found the way you see someone can be changed by the context you see them in?"

"Yes of course, but…."

"No buts. I haven't used magic on you without letting you know, and I didn't use it on your friend. End of story. If you want, I'll show you how you can detect that sort of glamour and then you can see for yourself. Okay?"

"Possibly."

"Bloody Nora, Holly, you are so untrusting! Perhaps that's a good survival trait, who knows, but it would be nice for once to be trusted. I promise to show you how to detect a glamour at our next session, but in the meantime I didn't drag you all the way down here to talk about cosmetic magic. Now, are you alright meeting with me, or are you going to twitch like a sparrow that's just caught sight of Grindlebones for the rest of our session?"

Holly was feeling surprisingly agitated. "I'll try not to. I am trying. It's just that magic can make things seem false once you know things can be changed by it. Nothing is quite as certain now as it was before you came along, and I look at things and I don't bloody know any more what's real and what's not. I don't trust things—anything. How do you ever fucking well know what's real and what's fake once you know magic can change it?"

Partridge looked concerned.

"This looks like a case of late onset shock to me. I thought you'd adjusted remarkably quickly for someone of your age. Obviously a case of too well, too soon. Sorry. Hang on in there. It's all bound to be a bit uncomfortable, but the only way to deal with it is to work your way through it."

"I'm not in shock," Holly snapped. "It's just that I don't bloody know…." At which point, and for no reason she could figure, Holly burst into tears. Partridge discreetly produced a box of man-size tissues and let her get on with it.

By the time she had reached for her seventh tissue, Holly had pulled herself together sufficiently to become aware that St. Pancras was a very public place in which to be having an emotional collapse and that, by now, she must be looking quite a fright. She glanced up briefly and was surprised to find no one seemed to be paying her the slightest bit of attention, not even those relatively close by. She also noticed the air around both her and Partridge seemed ever so slightly darker and perhaps a tint bluer than the rest of the surrounding space. Her interest in this barely discernable difference distracted her from her tears and her eighth tissue was her last. She looked at the changed air again and then at Partridge, who looked back with his head on one side and said nothing.

"Have you put a spell on us?"

"I've covered us both in a glamour, just like we were talking about earlier. It seems you can detect one without having to be shown, doesn't it?"

Having concluded that Holly had returned to some form of emotional stability, Partridge went on to explain that a glamour was a falsification, light magic that made people see what was not. Most magic changed things for real and therefore made people see a different, but concrete, what was. The glamour he had cast over them made people see Holly and him drinking coffee and chatting without an apparent care in the world rather than Holly bawling her eyes out whilst building a model of the Eiger out of soggy tissues. He was impressed she had detected the magic without being shown what to look for.

"A sign of natural aptitude, that. The next time you want to accuse me of pulling a fast one on you, you can check it out for yourself."

"And there's really no way to make people see things that aren't real without leaving that sort of trace?"

"Not if you are making people see things. Hearing and smelling glamours don't leave a visible join like a sight glamour, but cats and dogs can detect audible or olfactory distortions in the same way you saw a visible one. The only way to deceive someone without leaving a trace is to change things for real or to make them think they can see something that isn't there, rather than making them see it, i.e. changing their thoughts inside their head. But that's Old Magic and rarely performed because it's so difficult, particularly in relation to another witch, and it drains the witch who's doing it."

Holly honed in on what, for her, was the really interesting part of the explanation. "So it can be done by Old Magic? What's Old Magic, then? You've mentioned it before, but haven't explained it yet."

"It's a topic for another day if I am ever going to get around to telling you what I had intended to say last time, before your lady friend of the bottle turned up."

"Something about my birth?"

Judging from Holly's suddenly rapt expression, Partridge knew he had her complete focus again, and that the lure of Old Magic would keep for another day.

"Yes, a possible something about your birth."

"So tell me."

Holly had no problems with being adopted. She loved her Mum and Dad dearly and, remarkably early in life, had come to terms with the fact that she would never know who her birth parents were. Now that Partridge had raised the matter, however, her curiosity had been sharply pricked. The discovery that her witching abilities were inherited from her biological mother had started to play on her mind more than she really wanted to admit to herself.

Partridge, it turned out, had also been curious about Holly's heritage, particularly once he had learnt of Holly's arrival in the mundane world in a cardboard box. He had researched one or two things via mundane routes and then had pursued one or two other things amongst the witching community in relation to unexpected pregnancies, missing children, and sudden and relatively short-term absences of women of a particular age round about the time of Holly's birth.

"I think I may have a couple of possible candidates for the role of your birth mother."

"It's not a frigging role, like in a play," Holly snapped back, feeling more like her usual self. "It's who she was—is—maybe."

"Okay. Sorry. Wrong word, but there are a couple of possible contenders."

"So, who are they and what have you found out, then?"

Partridge hesitated, "It's not like it's conclusive. Much of it is just gossip."

"Fine, but you have found something, haven't you, or you wouldn't have spirited me down to London? Come to think of it, why have you brought me down to London?"

"I've been perusing the official Witchery records."

"Witches have official records?"

"Some. We are human, after all, and need our quota of bureaucracy as much as the next man or woman, but mostly we rely on the official mundane records of the time, where they exist. For things purely magical, however, we have our own separate records down in the bowels of The British Library."

Holly wasn't sure which train of query to pursue first: what sort of things were deemed to be purely magical and, if witchcraft was such a well-maintained secret, how come it had official records publicly available in the British Library? She therefore chose to bombard Partridge simultaneously with both questions.

Partridge raised his eyebrows in exaggerated exasperation and stood up. All at once, the signs of the glamour around them disappeared.

"Girlfriend, for someone getting over a case of shock, you ask an awful lot of questions. I suggest we walk and talk. That way, you'll get your answers, and we may stand some chance of getting to the library before it closes."

Holly was going to say something else, but Partridge beat her to it.

"In some instances, it really will be easier if I show you the answers to your questions, rather than simply tell you."

Holly grudgingly saw the sense of this and allowed Partridge to guide her out of the station and along the Euston Road to the British Library. He talked at her the whole of the way.

At the library, they went in via the main entrance and initially followed a flow of signage-compliant people across the foyer, down a corridor, and into a darkened exhibition area. Whilst others stopped to look at the manuscripts on display in the illuminated cases, Partridge pulled Holly towards a very dark corner of the room behind a couple of unused computer display monitors. Even in the gloom, Holly could see the telltale signs of a glamour. Partridge marched up to the supposedly plain wall and put his hand on it as if there were a door with a handle there, which suddenly there was. Partridge pushed the door open and dragged Holly through.

"As I was saying on the way here; there is publicly available and publicly available. Witchcraft's official records are only available if you know where to look, can see through a glamour, and happen to have enough magic about you to open the door and deal with what comes after. We had a witch on the architectural design team, but only those who need to know will have remembered there is a sub–basement in this part of the building."

As Partridge finished talking, Holly realised they were both floating gently down what looked like a lift shaft, but without the usual clutter of cables, lift mechanisms, or, indeed, a lift. The bottom was surprisingly carpeted in a thick, deep-red shag-pile, but otherwise seemed like an enclosed lift shaft pit. Then Partridge walked through one of the enclosing walls, pulling Holly after him.

"I hope you're taking this all in, girlie, in case you need to come back here on your own."

Holly was too busy with the taking-in process to complain about Partridge's use of the word "girlie."

They had arrived in a reception area not especially different from that in the main part of the library, except this one was staffed by a large man with a small blue budgie on his shoulder, the budgie appearing all the smaller because of the bulk of the man he was sitting on.

"Brother Mayflower. How are you?" the man said, "and this must be Sister Holly. If you could both just sign in here, the records you have requested are in Reading Room Two."

They dutifully signed in and were about to make their way to the indicated door when the budgerigar fixed them with one beady, black eye and clearly said, in surprisingly human-sounding tones, "Please remember this is a library. Respect other users by keeping any noise to a minimum and refrain from using all non-essential magics until you have vacated the building. Thank you for your co-operation."

The bird then nonchalantly proceeded to preen its wing feathers, whilst Holly stared at it in open-mouthed amazement. Partridge mouthed a silent "come on" at Holly and pulled her into the reading room. Shutting the door quietly, but firmly, he said,

"There was no need to stare quite so obviously. You were bordering on rude. Insult a familiar, you insult its witch."

"But the bird talked."

"I thought that's what budgerigars are supposed to do."

Holly decided that, for once, this wasn't an argument she wanted to pursue, even though she felt, in relation to budgies at least, there was talking and then there was *talking*.

Partridge was already studying a pile of yellowing files laid out on the table, and Holly moved over to join him.

On the way round to the library, Partridge had explained in, as far as Holly was concerned, unnecessary detail that the world of witches had only succumbed to organised bureaucracy from 1952 onwards. Prior to then, records had been a pot luck affair with witchcraft-related information gleaned from letters, diaries, books, and any other written matter that seemed to offer a relevant fact or possibility. Post fifty-two, records were regularly and automatically kept by Witchery officialdom to augment mundane records and provide a clear and organised view of Witchery in Great Britain.

Holly was now studying the fruits of the Coven's bureaucratic ripening. From May 1952 onwards, the Grand Coven of Great Britain, Ireland, and The Etheric Isles in their Domain (Holly inwardly winced at the pompously wordy title) issued an "Addendum to Birth Certificate Document" when so requested by the birth mother and one other eldritch adult to confirm the birth of a child with witchlight. Holly could not imagine how you decided whether a newborn had witch powers or not; did it change its own nappies or pee canaries rather than infant urine? ABCDs were also issued for older children, when so requested by three eldritch adults, none of whom had to be the birth mother. These confirmed the child's witchlight status and stated why the child had not been registered at birth. Here, if you read between the terse, unemotional lines of bureaucratic phrasing, lurked tales of abandonment, death, abuse, and heartbreak, along with incredible eldritch ineptitude: "the birth mother forgot to register the child until prompted to do so by the transformation of a little friend into a Golden Labrador puppy."

There was yet another series of documents known as DEAs, DECs, and DEFs, respectively; someone had clearly had a love of the alphabet or a strong sense of humour back in the Grand Coven of the 1950s. These documents applied to adults like Holly.

The first, a Declaration of Eldritch Ability, was the adult equivalent of an ABCD and officially confirmed that the adult was recognised as having witchlight. The Declaration of Eldritch Competence confirmed the holder of a DEA had reached a basic level of witchcraft skill, and the Declaration of Eldritch Familiarity permitted the holder of a DEC to practice magic unmentored or, as Partridge put it, "Is a scrap of coven stationery confirming the stabilisers can come off."

It was all rather banal and not what she had expected. Where was the mystery and the magic? As she stared, with a sense of growing frustration, at the reams of paper in front of her, Holly found her thoughts unexpectedly dragged via half-heard echoes of history to the vast, impersonal bureaucracies that had accompanied the Third Reich and Stalinist Russia not that long before the Coven had set up its own extensive paper-pushing systems. All this categorisation, labelling and record keeping: what if it wasn't as mindlessly harmless as it appeared?

All certificates were signed by a Coven official and the relevant Mentor. Holly noticed that one such mentor happened to be a certain Partridge Mayflower. His signature appeared on a good many of the documents, including those dating back to the start of the system he was so obviously a key part of. Even if Partridge had only just turned twenty-one when he signed his first DEA, it still meant he was considerably older than his mid-thirties physical appearance suggested. Holly was pleased her gut reaction to Partridge's age had proved correct, but was surprised, if not actually a little alarmed, that his physical appearance was so out of kilter with his likely chronology. Her previous qualms started to resurrect themselves and merged with her more recent ones. Whilst she was trying to deal with this, Partridge placed a file of contemporary DEAs in front of her. There were only a few, and the third from the front of the file was made out in the name of Holly Jepps, signed by Partridge Mayflower and the Coven representative and dated six months previously.

"I was registered six months ago?"

Partridge nodded and grinned.

"So, what happened to the intervening five months?"

"I kept an eye on you. Watched what you did and how you did it. Verified we had been right to issue a DEA and that you had enough potential ability to be developed."

"In other words, you have been stalking me."

"I wouldn't put it like that." Partridge unexpectedly found himself on the defensive again.

"Would you prefer the term 'Peeping Tom'?"

There was a glint in Holly's eye that Partridge was beginning to recognise all too well.

"It's strictly official procedure, Holly. When we get a tip off, we check out the subject and issue a DEA as soon as possible. But if necessary, we continue to keep the subject under surveillance in order to get a proper feel for them and their abilities before we decide to come out to them."

"And what, Mr Undercover Tutor, or should that be Secret State Inspector, did you decide in my case?"

"What do you think? I showed up at your house, didn't I? All the practice we've been doing over the last month hasn't been so you can become a children's entertainer. You've proved yourself to be a quick learner, and I reckon you'll be ready to take your DEC within another couple of months."

Despite her distaste at the thought of being studied without her knowledge, Holly was secretly chuffed to hear she was a quick learner. Her ego couldn't help but preen itself momentarily.

"So what will the DEC mean in terms of how good I have become?"

"That you have achieved the basic levels of competence we would normally associate with a four-year-old witch who has been trained from birth."

"Four!" Holly's ego went into a spontaneous moult.

"Four years' experience compacted into three or four months is pretty good going, you know, particularly for someone of your age."

Holly was not especially convinced.

"So, what age does the DEF equate to?"

"Holly girl, I didn't bring you here to review the finer points of Coven bureaucracy. Don't you want to know what I've found out about your potential witch line?"

"I do, I do, but everything's all so new, and I need to understand what I'm seeing. There's so much background I don't know and every time you show me something new, I see even more I hadn't even known existed. I'm simply trying to make sense of it all. Please."

"Okay, okay, I'll explain briefly, but then we are moving on to more important matters." If Partridge was surprised at Holly's lack of eagerness to hear what he had found about the possibilities of her birth, he didn't let it show. "DEFs are less directly age-related than DECs. The DEF recognises the average level of competence at the stage a born and raised witch can expect to be released from family control; roughly anytime between sixteen and nineteen."

"And how long before I get one of those?"

"Let's concentrate on the issue in hand, eh?"

"But how long, roughly?"

Partridge seemed uncomfortable at being put on the spot.

"I'd say at least a year, but probably no more than three."

Holly was crestfallen.

"Thanks."

"You asked for an estimate, and you can only rush things so far, but that's really not why I brought you here. Can we please focus on the important issues or we'll only end up getting side tracked again."

"Sorry. I'll try to stay focussed. Tell me about the parade of possible mothers you have found for me."

It was Partridge's turn to look taken aback.

"We're not talking about a couple of new frocks to be tried on for size, you know. I am trying to help you find your birth mother and the source of your witchlight."

"I know. I didn't mean to be flippant. It all seems a bit unreal, is all. I'm not one of those people who has ever felt a strong need to find their biological parents, and I can't quite believe that, at this late stage, it might be a real possibility."

Partridge looked thoughtful. "Haven't you ever wondered?"

"From time to time, but not enough to fret about, you know?"

Partridge didn't seem to, but changed tack.

"So, let's start with the bureaucracy you are so fascinated by: your DEA."

Holly looked at the certificate again. For once, she saw the attraction of regimented paper processing. It was an attraction that had previously eluded her, but here, on paper, officially written down, authenticated and signed, was proof that the last four weeks had been real; she was truly a witch. Even while part of her continued to struggle with the shock of this, a large proportion of her was excited and slightly drunk with it all. She basked happily in the psychological glow from her proof of existence.

"Well?" said Partridge.

"Well what?"

"What do you think?"

"Of the certificate? Well, it's kind of nice to have it, but also kind of scary at the same time."

"And…?"

"And?"

"Look at it. You've seen a number of these already today. What's unusual about yours?"

Holly looked at the certificate made out in her name and thought back to the other DEAs she had just read.

"There's no explanation given as to why I wasn't registered at birth."

"True, but that's hardly surprising given your unconventional arrival in a cardboard box."

"There's also no real reason given for the certificate itself. The other certificates had stiffly formal wording like 'based on the testimony of X and official observations,' or 'from evidence provided by Y and ratified by official observations.' Mine simply reads 'based on official observations.' There's no reason why those observations were carried out in the first place."

"Good girl."

Holly squirmed, but was at least grateful he hadn't used the offensive 'girlie.'

"It surprised me a little at the time, but I didn't dwell on it, and it wasn't until I started thinking about the hereditary line of your witchlight that the anomaly hit me again. I tried to speak to Malcolm Williams, the Coven representative who co-signed your DEA with me and who had asked me to observe you up front, but he died three months ago. He was very old and tired and I knew he was thinking of retiring some time soon, but...."

"Dying is a pretty extreme way to retire."

"Depends, but we're in danger of getting off the issue again. The question is, who was it thought you had witchlight potential in the first place? I never knew, but Williams must have done. The complication is his death. I asked to see his records, including his diary for the three months before I was sent to observe you. There's nothing of assistance in the records, which in itself is odd. The diary is, of course, full of appointments and meetings, but the purpose of most of them is written down and appears to have nothing to do with you. Only three appointments did not have a recorded purpose: two women and a man—Esme Beldam, Belladonna Luxborough, and Appledore Ashwell. The two women also cropped up in my separate trawl through the gossip and rumour mill. Do any of those names ring any bells?"

"No. Should they? I've never heard of these people and with names like that, I think I'd remember if I had."

"Oh well, shame. It was just a chance. The next stage is to get you to look at the records for these three people to see if we can find anything to indicate a connection to you." Partridge produced three files seemingly out of thin air and plonked them on the table in front of Holly.

Esme Beldam's file was remarkably slim. Born in 1944 at the tail end of the war, she lacked early eldritch certification, given there were no ABCDs issued at the time. The file contained a copy of her 1944 birth certificate and a brief statement made by Esme herself in the early 1960s to the effect that her mother and mentor was Ninanna Beldam, a witch powerful enough to practice Old Magic. Holly couldn't work out the purpose of the statement.

Belladonna Luxborough's file was a little thicker. She was born in 1952, and her file therefore contained one of the first ABCDs, which was a fairly underwhelming affair in Holly's opinion. There was a signed letter from her, dated 1969, confirming she wished to be known as Donna Luxborough on all official Coven documentation from here on out and a copy of a police arrest sheet stating that a Miss Donna Luxborough had been arrested on 18th May 1970 for being drunk and disorderly. A hand-written note attached to the arrest sheet recorded that all official records of the arrest had been erased, and the related memories of those non-witches involved had been clouded. Holly shuddered at the implications of this. So much for not being able to dupe people by magic. A second, but separate, hand-written note asked for Sister Donna Luxborough to be invited to a formal meeting to discuss her recent magical activities while under the influence of alcohol. The file also contained a copy of an ABCD issued in December 1970 to a Baby Luxborough and a letter from Sister Belladonna Luxborough to the Grand Coven dated 2007 requesting official assistance in tracking down the boy child she had put up for adoption without their approval in February 1971.

The file for Appledore Ashwell was empty.

"Well, there's nothing there to cause me to have a eureka moment and in the case of Appledore Ashwell, there's nothing there."

"Are you sure? No names or places you recognise, or dates that are significant?" urged Partridge.

"Nope, except giving birth to a boy in December 1970 almost certainly rules Belladonna out as a potential mother suspect. I was born in June 1970, so unless witchcraft can hurry things along, it seems unlikely I'm hers. Plus, she only seems to be looking for a boy."

"I guess that leaves Esme Beldam. Interestingly enough, when I looked into women of the right age range who were pregnant about the time of your birth, or who disappeared for a while about that time, Esme's name came up as someone who did a disappearing act in the early spring of 1970. Although, from what I picked up, hers was supposedly a three decade disappearance rather than a nine month flit."

"Oh. So where do we go from here?"

"One or both of us goes to visit Sister Esme and perhaps Brother Appledore, too. Just because he can't be your mother doesn't mean he couldn't be the person who first drew our attention to you. Assuming they're willing to see us, of course." Partridge suddenly looked concerned. "You do realise, don't you, that this could be a total waste of time? It's just they are the only possibilities we have right now and, if nothing else, we need to eliminate them from our search."

Holly hadn't realised she had been searching, but entered into the spirit of things.

"There's nothing else we can do in terms of these records?"

"Not really, if nothing you've seen so far strikes a chord, and that was always a long shot anyway. I'll request the last known addresses for Sister Esme and Brother Appledore, and then I suggest we visit Esme first, seeing as she has the potential to be your mother, as well as your original referrer. You want to come with me, right?

Holly paused while she thought about it.

"I guess so. I have to say, it would be good to meet some other witches, regardless of outcome, but I'm surprisingly nervous. What if one of them is connected to me? What if they're not? What if Esme turns out to be my mother? It's a big step."

"If I'm honest, Holly, for all Esme's name came up as a possible contender, I'm not expecting to find your birth mother immediately. I'm simply aiming to track down the source of your referral in the hope they might know of a connection we can follow. So, what do you say?"

Holly thought some more. At the end of the day, it was yet more stuff she didn't know.

"Yes, I'll come with you. I'd like to get out and about in the witching community anyway, and if you do find out anything worth knowing, I want to be with you to hear it with my own ears."

"That's the spirit, Holly girl."

Holly winced again, but said nothing.

On the way out they stopped to talk to the receptionist with the blue budgie in order to request the two addresses, but they had to wait as he was already dealing with another witch, a tall blond man in his late twenties with a glowing tan, the body of a super-fit athlete, and a pair of very tight trousers. Holly caught herself admiring him surreptitiously, but Partridge was openly salivating.

"Wow!" sighed Partridge under his breath. "Get a look at him. He sure is packing. Wonder if I can get his address too, while I'm at it?"

He moved casually towards the man, who was continuing to chat to blue budgie guy. As Partridge got up close to the blond Adonis, Holly noticed the now telltale signs of somehow disconnected and darker air, but Partridge seemed oblivious to the warning signals. Holly assumed lust was clouding his faculties. Now that she had seen the glamour for what it was, any sexual interest on her part in Mister Perfect had waned, but she was curious to know what the glamour was concealing.

Focussing on the gorgeous-looking blond in front of her, Holly decided she wanted to see the truth behind the glamour and willed herself to do so. To her surprise, the visual signs of the magic disappeared immediately, along with Blondie. In his place stood a short, skinny man with unpleasantly sallow skin and apparently at least twenty years' more baggage than his alter-image. Partridge, however, remained oblivious to this unhappy transformation and continued to be deeply engaged in chatting up the man of his sexual fantasies.

Holly pondered how she could get Partridge to see who he was really coming on to. Focussing on Partridge, she decided he would see the object of his lust as he really was and then willed him to do so. This time, there was a subdued bang as the darker air around Mister Perfect imploded, revealing the scrawny source of the glamour in all his unglory. The man clutched at his head with a loud moan, just as Holly felt a slight dull ache creep into the back of her skull, though it was nothing whatsoever like the searing pain she had felt when Partridge had applied the etheric brakes to her spinning pencil. Partridge and the blue budgie man looked momentarily shocked as the still moaning and dramatically transformed little witch realised his veneer of beauty and sexual allure had vanished and rushed out of the reception area, scarlet with embarrassment and other unnamed emotions.

Partridge and the receptionist exchanged glances. Then Partridge turned round to glare at Holly and, in a tone of voice no one had used to her since she was in the fourth form at school, said, "Holly Jepps, what have you just done?"

Chapter 5

Holly had managed to get away early from work for once and was in her bedroom at home, getting ready for a night on the town with Sarah, Sarah's partner Mark, and a blind date Sarah had set up for her. She'd initially been a bit ambivalent about the evening, but now was looking forward to it as an opportunity to have a few drinks and forget about the dressing down she'd had from Partridge that lunchtime.

He'd been too angry with her at the library to do much more than tell her she was grounded, which seemed so inappropriate given her age that, by way of response, she had sniggered. This had only served to make him angrier. He'd instructed her to make time to see him at midday the following day and sent her back to her kitchen with an impatient clap of his hands.

Holly was still not totally clear what she had done that was so wrong, but guessed it had much to do with interfering with someone else's magic and specifically with embarrassing Partridge in public. At midday the following day Partridge, had been waiting for her outside her workplace to clarify the full extent of her sins.

He had calmed down considerably since she had last seen him, but was obviously still very annoyed and gave her the whole nine yards of, "Just because you can, doesn't mean you should," "lack of restraint can be the difference between good magic and bad magic," and an extremely long monologue on how rude it was to stop someone else's magical intention with your own unless you really, really needed to.

"And you didn't bloody need to."

"But, I could see he had a glamour around him and that he was fooling you, and I just wanted you to see who you were coming on to before things went too far. I didn't mean to hurt or embarrass him, or you. I didn't think it would. I just thought you'd see what I was seeing."

"And I did, but you didn't think things through and in the process, you didn't just show me, you interrupted his magical intentions and that's just not done, Holly, at least not without really good cause. Saving my face, if that's what you meant to do, is not really good cause, particularly when you end up rubbing it in the dirt as a result. I'm old enough and powerful enough to take care of myself, and if I'm also stupid enough to be taken in by a simple glamour, then that's my issue and, by the way, how did you manage to detect what I failed to?"

"I don't know," Holly sounded sheepish. "I just saw it."

"Well, next time you just see something, don't try to change it without a bit more thought," snapped Partridge and then in a more conciliatory tone, he added, "Did you manage to deal on your own with the aftershock and headache?"

"Um, I didn't really get a headache," Holly admitted, "just a dull throb at the back of my head for a few moments. It cleared up as soon as I got back home."

"Bloody typical," muttered Partridge. "Looks like you're packing more witchlight than I originally gave you credit for, girlie. You and I have got some serious work to do and soon. Take a couple of days' leave either side of a weekend, and we'll combine the work with the visits to Sister Esme and Brother Appledore, but in the meantime..."

There had then followed a long list of dos and don'ts for Holly and a string of what seemed pointless and tedious magic exercises, that Holly felt certain were a punishment rather than a necessity. Partridge, however, insisted they had to be done. He concluded the conversation with yet another lecture on the etiquette of magic and then disappeared in a clearly rather irritated puff of faintly turquoise light. Holly hoped no one had been watching.

She went back to her afternoon clients in a rather subdued state of mind and was very pleased when the time came for her to hurry home and focus on the less guilt-inducing task of getting ready for a night out.

She had just come out of the shower when the phone rang. It was Sarah checking to see if she was in the process of getting ready.

"You want to look good tonight, Holly. Jake's quite a catch."

"If I'm going to look good, I'll look good for me, thank you very much. I'm not aiming to catch anything tonight; I'm pretty well inoculated by now."

"Well, inoculated you may well be, given your track record, but Jake's a lovely guy and remarkably fit for his age. You don't want to miss out, sweetie, unless, of course, you're still panting after your cute-arsed personal tutor?"

"What? No. I'm not. I haven't ever. I'm fond of him, sort of, but not like that. In fact, it's just so wrong, I couldn't begin to explain. Now, are you going to let me get on?"

Sarah agreed to hang up in order to let Holly get on with getting ready, but fifteen minutes later she was on the phone again, calling to see how Holly was progressing and checking on which dress she had chosen to wear. Having verified that Holly had chosen the right one (a soft, deep-red wool number with a flatteringly low neckline), Sarah hung up again. By now, though, Holly was running behind, and she had yet to feed Barny, who was wiping himself around her legs in anticipation. Then the phone rang again. Holly snatched at it, but this time it was her mother, down in Croydon, making a catch-up call. Holly hadn't the heart to tell her she was really too busy to talk, particularly as she was starting to feel guilty about the search for her birth mother, which she hadn't, couldn't, let her Mum know about. By the time their chat had concluded, Holly was on the point of being seriously late and still had her hair and makeup to do. As she started to rush round trying to do the impossible, she caught herself muttering one of her mother's pet phrases, "I could do with a magic wa…" and stopped herself in mid-sentence. This wasn't a children's fairy story; she didn't need a wand. She had herself.

Why not finish her getting ready preparations by witchcraft? Partridge's earlier lecture re-played in her head. She was certain he wouldn't approve of her trying some new magic in a rush and so close to her recent debacle, but it seemed like a simple enough thing to do and without consequence for anyone else. She knew exactly how she wanted her hair and makeup to look. All she had to do was look at herself in the mirror and...

Her thought flow stopped in mid-sentence again. The image in the mirror looking back at her was already exactly how she wanted to look, but she hadn't consciously willed or directed it, had she? She raised a hand to her hair. It was smooth and properly styled. Her makeup was perfectly applied. How had she managed that? Yes, she'd decided what she wanted it to look like, but she knew she hadn't focussed or concentrated or consciously willed anything: she'd gone through none of the processes that Partridge was so keen on her practising. She needed to think about this, but now was not the time. She stuffed the incident to the back of her mind for the time being, scooped up her handbag, and hurried out of the front door.

Sarah's Mark was already waiting at the top of the road in his car, but he assured her he'd only just pulled up. Sarah was still at their house getting ready, but had promised that she'd be finished by the time Holly and Mark got back. Indeed, she was putting the finishing touches to her makeup when the pair of them arrived.

From Sarah and Mark's house it was a fairly brief walk into the town centre for the three of them. The restaurant was conveniently located, and they arrived just as Jake Wortham, Holly's "date" for the evening, was turning up. He was a pleasing-looking man in his early forties: dark hair just beginning to be feathered with filaments of white, and a pair of twinkling blue eyes. His body was lean and discreetly muscular and decidedly fit in all senses of the word. Holly checked him out for signs of a glamour just in case, but he seemed clear of magical interventions and, from what Holly could make out, had both feet planted firmly in the mortal world.

The evening proved to be a very convivial one. All four diners got on well together, and Jake turned out to have a very entertaining sense of humour. Holly should have been having more fun than she actually was, but every time she tried to enjoy the moment, she found her thoughts getting sucked back to Partridge's earlier lecture, or blown forward to the as yet unplanned trip to see the two witches who might be able to help her track down her birth mother.

"So, what do you think?"

"Eh, sorry?"

"What do you think; which one?"

"Um, Appledore Ashwell?"

"No, can't help you there. I rather think it's a case of raspberry or mocha, unless you are hoping to go off menu?"

"Oh," Holly turned slightly pink, "I'm so sorry. That was really stupid. I was—"

"Miles away?"

"Yeah, I guess so."

"Well, I hope he's worth it."

"Worth it?"

"Missing out on a fantastic pudding because you're so wrapped up in thoughts of him, this Appledore Ashwell character."

"Oh, it's not a 'him' as such. It's just…I've got a lot of stuff on at the moment."

"Work?"

"Not really, but in another way, sort of." Holly realised she wasn't being a hundred per cent coherent, but Jake didn't seem to mind.

"So, what do you do?"

"I'm a counsellor. You probably wouldn't be able to tell from tonight, but, allegedly, I'm rather good with people."

"Ah huh? So am I, that's why I'm a vet." Jake grinned. "That's a joke, by the way: good with people, so I work with animals."

Holly grinned back. "Just as well you're not a comedian."

"That bad, huh? I genuinely am a vet. Mostly farm animals, because of the locale and the founding nature of the practice, but I have a few domestic pets on my books, too. Sarah told me you have a cat?"

"Just Barny. He's a black and white mog, nothing special." Holly paused. Barny *was* special, because he was hers and now because he served as her magical familiar, but she could hardly explain the latter to Jake. Life had become seriously unsimple.

"All pets are special to their owners."

"Oh, bollocks!" Holly suddenly remembered she had forgotten to feed Barny in her rush to get out.

"Did I say something wrong?"

"No, sorry, you just jogged my memory. This supposedly loving owner has forgotten to feed her special cat this evening, and I'm meant to be staying round at Sarah and Mike's after here. I'm going to have one very hungry cat on my hands tomorrow morning, and I had been planning on going straight into work from Sarah's.

"Well cats are nothing if not flexible. Is he up to self catering?"

"He's not so hot with a can opener, but he's pretty sharp at finding fresh mice he can prepare himself for supper. If you'll excuse me though, I've just thought of a possible way round this."

Holly disappeared into the ladies. She could either transport herself to the house, feed Barny, and bring herself back again, or she could try to feed him long distance. Both would be previously untried activities. Self-transportation was probably the riskier of the two, but she couldn't work out how to feed Barny from a distance when she wouldn't actually be able to see what she was doing. Neither seemed a really sensible thing to do. In her head, Partridge lectured her sternly against doing either. She, however, felt really bad because she had managed to do her hair and makeup, but had forgotten the needs of poor Barny. Guilt and the image of an upset, abandoned, and, most specifically, hungry Barny made her feel she had to do something. She decided to transport herself into her hallway at home, which she knew would be clear of clutter and furniture and Barny himself.

She arrived safely in the hall with a faint pop, similar to the sound that Partridge made when he arrived anywhere. A few seconds later, she thought she heard a second, fainter pop coming from upstairs, but put it down to her imagination.

She walked into the kitchen where Barny was sound asleep on one of the kitchen chairs, fed him, made a quick fuss of him, and then transported herself straight back to the restaurant ladies. The return journey required more concentration and effort on her part than the journey out, and she was feeling quite tired by the time she sat back down opposite Jake.

"Everything okay?"

"Er, fine thanks."

"Only you shot off quite suddenly and then were gone for some time. I began to wonder if you'd popped home to feed the cat."

Holly looked surprised, but Jake was grinning again as if he'd made a joke, not staggered across her secret cat-feeding activities in all seriousness.

"Er, no. All's fine. I, um, got a friend to sort Barny out. Called her. Mobile phone. She's got a spare key." Holly trailed off lamely. She was feeling far too tired to cover her tracks convincingly, but Jake didn't seem to notice.

The rest of the evening passed in a bit of a daze, as far as Holly was concerned. Jake kept the conversation flowing, which worked well for Holly; she was actually enjoying just listening to him talk, but on her next bona fide trip to the toilet Sarah followed her in to "motivate" her to make more of an effort with Jake. Holly did her best, but she was incredibly tired, and her head was full of thoughts not related to dinner. It was easier for her to sit back and listen encouragingly to Jake than contribute much in terms of small talk. Part of her regretfully assumed that, as a result, she wouldn't be seeing much more of Jake Wortham, and another part of her thought that would be a shame. There was little, however, she felt able to do to rectify the situation, and Sarah's steely glances in her direction weren't helping any. It was a pleasant surprise therefore, when, as they were all leaving the restaurant, Jake suggested they swap email addresses in order to stay in touch. Perhaps the evening had, in the end, been more successful than Holly had realised.

Chapter 6

It turned out to be another week before Holly could get the time off work to give Partridge the long weekend he had asked for. She didn't exactly know what the weekend would involve, because she hadn't really been talking to Partridge much. Yes, they had continued to meet up for the daily hour of practice, but they skirted round the incident at the library, and Holly had made sure she didn't mention the unpractised hair and transportation magics on the night she had first met Jake. She also kept quiet about the other extra-curricular magical experiments she had been conducting since then.

Jake and she, however, had been getting on like two mutually combusting residential properties. Emails had been exchanged, as had phone numbers, and subsequently texts, and a date, in both obvious senses of the word, had been arranged for the day after Holly was due to come back from her jaunt with Partridge. She had seriously toyed with the idea of meeting Jake sooner and before the long weekend, but was conscious of how distracted she'd been at the restaurant and didn't want to run the risk of repeating the same mistake. When they met up next, she wanted to be able to focus fully and only on Jake Wortham.

Partridge arrived as promptly as ever at 10.30 a.m. in Holly's kitchen. There was no sign of Grindlebones and no sign of any luggage.

"I thought we were going away?"

"We are."

"So why no luggage?"

"We're travelling light. We can summon up what we need along the way. The joy of magic, you know?"

"But I've packed."

"Fine. Leave your bag somewhere accessible, and you can transport it on over later. You'll need to practice transportation anyway. I've put it on the agenda for the weekend."

"Agenda? We have an agenda? That's news to me. So what and where is it? Show me."

"All in good time."

"Now is a good time for me."

Holly was aware it hadn't been that long ago since she had doubted Partridge's intentions. She had become remarkably more trusting in a short period of time, but not that much more. She didn't want any nasty surprises of whatever variety.

Partridge noticed the telltale look in Holly's eyes and decided it was easier to tell her his plans up front.

"Get ourselves set up, then a couple of days intense training and exploration of what you can do without me guiding you too closely. We'll practice some of the more difficult magic, transportation, glamours, and the like; and then maybe, but only maybe, if things go well, we could consider you going for an early DEC. That'll leave us a couple of days to speak to Sister Beldam and Brother Ashwell and follow up any leads we can get from them."

"And the where?"

"The Lake District, to begin with, out of the way of the tourist paths so we won't be disturbed, and then Oxford and Edinburgh when we go visiting."

"So, where exactly in the Lake District will we be staying?"

"You ask a lot of questions for a little woman."

"Well, at least you recognise that I'm not a 'girlie.' So where…?"

"In the hills above one of the smaller lakes. There's an old hill farm we can adapt to meet our needs. If you're ready and through asking questions, I can show you."

"I'm ready."

Partridge clapped his hands, and suddenly they were no longer in Holly's kitchen, but were standing on a grassy hillside overlooking the dilapidated shell of what had once been a building, but was now little more than a pile of rubble.

"I thought you said there was an old hill farm we could stay at, not the remains of a ruin we could practice being homeless in?"

"It's okay. We're going to adapt it. That's the joy of magic. A bit of rebuilding here and there, some internal decorating, and it will be fine for a few days."

Holly was totally disbelieving, but, for once, said nothing.

"Fine," said Partridge, "watch this." He stamped his pristine, well-heeled, hand-tooled cowboy boots, and fallen stones and mortar began to rearrange themselves back into an edifice. Wooden beams were resurrected, and broken slates painstakingly pieced themselves together again. The reconstruction went on for four or five minutes, by the end of which time the usually immaculate Partridge was looking sweaty, tired, and somewhat dishevelled. The reconstruction of a small, cottage-looking building was about fifty percent complete.

"Now, it's your turn," he said. "See how much you can manage by yourself while I take a bit of a breather. When you've had enough, and we're both rested, we can finish it off together."

Holly had rather guessed this was coming and had been thinking about how best to go about things and improve upon the rather meagre structure Partridge had left her with. She looked at Partridge, looked at the partially re-constructed building, pointed her left index finger at it, and willed. There was an extended flash of light and a thick cloud of lavender flecked dust. When the air cleared, a reasonably sized farmhouse stood in situ, its façade freshly painted and a red rambler rose in full bloom growing round the front door. Holly hadn't even broken a sweat. Partridge looked seriously troubled.

"How? What?" He almost ran down the slope they had been standing on to inspect the building at close quarters. After a solid five minutes examination of the externals, he couldn't find fault with it.

"I still don't fully understand how, but let's leave that aside for a moment. How do you feel? Exhausted?"

"Not really. A bit tired." Which was almost true. Holly was far from being worn out in the way that Partridge had seemed to be, but she was looking forward to a nice cup of tea sometime soon.

"Alright, Ms Know-It-All. If you can construct a house like this, you can decorate it inside as well. It's all yours. Make me proud."

Holly was not sure she liked the underlying tone of Partridge's voice, but it made her all the more determined to show him just what she could do given half a chance. This time it took her a full two minutes and by the end of it, she had to admit the need for a cup of tea was starting to become pressing. Nevertheless, the interior was complete and worthy of a feature in "Homes and Gardens," even if she said so herself.

She walked in via the front door, with Partridge following close behind her, straight into the large and well-stocked kitchen, its slate floor spotless and its polished brasswork gleaming. Holly made for the big oak table where two mugs of freshly brewed tea steamed invitingly. Partridge, showing signs of an advanced state of shock, sat down opposite her.

"Holly girl, I think you've been holding out on me." This time she didn't challenge him over his use of patronising and infantilising nomenclature. Instead, she smiled smugly, produced a plate of still-warm homemade cookies from mid-air, and handed them to him.

An hour or so and several mugs of restorative Earl Grey later, Partridge knew all there was to know about Holly's approach to rural re-constructive regeneration, state of the art interior design, subconscious hair and make-up make overs, untutored self-transportation, and the one or two other little experiments that Holly had been keeping to herself. Despite the impressive nature of Holly's suddenly revealed abilities, he seemed most amazed by the fact that Holly was not on her knees from sheer exhaustion, and that after the restorative tea, she seemed even brighter and sharper than ever.

"Are you sure you don't want to lie down for a bit?" he asked, yet again.

"I'm really fine, Partridge. That mug of tea was just what I needed, and I'm ready and raring to go on to the next exercise you invariably have lined up for me."

"Yes, well, we've actually completed the planned activities for today somewhat ahead of schedule. Plus, I'm beginning to doubt the value of any more of the basic exercises I've been making you do. I shall need to think about this for a little while longer. You're clearly packing more witchlight than I gave you credit for, that's for sure, and far more than I normally come across in a neophyte witch. Some serious assessment of your full abilities is called for before we do anything else. Hecate only knows why I didn't suss your power up front."

"Okay. So, how did you assess my level of witchlight in the first place? Was this while you were stalking me?"

"It wasn't stalking. It was official observation, following your referral by a person or persons unknown."

"Fine. So how did you rate my level of witchlight during your official observations of me? You know, the ones you conducted whilst standing furtively in the field behind my house wearing a dirty raincoat."

Partridge poured himself a stiff scotch from the bottle he had just now conjured up and settled down to tell Holly the story of her clandestine assessment by the Coven authorities, namely himself.

Malcolm Williams had visited him routinely one morning with the list of the month's observations and assessments. The list had included Holly's name as a potential witch requiring observation. There were no further details. Armed only with Holly's name and address and a willing stakeout partner in Grindlebones, Partridge had kept a discreet watch on her house and subsequently her workplace, for almost a week without the slightest flash of witchlight. Indeed, he had been on the point of throwing in the towel and declaring Holly strictly mundane when the overheard comment of one of Holly's clients made Partridge do a rethink.

The elderly lady in question, having come out of Holly's unit, soothed from her session, had just met a friend. The phrase "It's like she has hidden powers and knows just what I'm thinking, as well as what I'm saying" cut through the conversation direct to Partridge. It got him revisiting his previous opinions. He started eavesdropping on other client conversations. Holly had a surprising number of contented clients who put the almost instantaneous benefits of their counselling down to Holly's extraordinary powers of empathy.

It didn't require much effort and merely the discreet magical rearrangement of Holly's appointments diary, for Partridge to get himself in to see Holly as a temporary client needing support during the sick leave of another counsellor. Using a glamour to disguise his appearance, he came to Holly for a fifty-minute session and felt there was a glimmer of witchlight boosting Holly's mundane people skills as she used them to counsel people. Satisfied that Holly had at least some magical juice sluicing through her veins, Partridge returned to the Coven, issued the necessary DEA, and embarked on a more thorough, but still covert, observation of Holly.

By this stage in the story, Holly had already made repeated, loud protestations about breach of client confidentiality, unethical conduct and, of course, invasion of personal privacy and stalking, but Partridge poured himself another whiskey, plus one for Holly, and ploughed resolutely on with his tale.

Partridge had gone back to watching Holly's house in alternate shifts with Grindlebones. In the process, they had come across Barny. Cats are born with a set of paws in both the mundane and magical worlds. A gentle examination of Barny proved he had been exposed to a steady, if very low, level of witchlight since early kittenhood. Magic did not alarm him at all, and his connection to Holly seemed stronger than a standard mundane one. There was a level of cat/human understanding and communication beyond the routine feed me, stroke me, leave me alone, level of interchange.

Further observations (or stalking, as Holly still insisted on calling it) enabled Partridge to confirm that Holly had lived on her own for some considerable period following the tumultuous end to an equally tumultuous relationship, currently had no significant other in attendance, and didn't cut her grass as often as she really needed to. He also concluded that whilst witchlight flowed in her veins, she did not use magic beyond a basic, sub-conscious enhancement of her mundane talents and her bond with Barny. This suggested that her ability was slight and would require significant coaching.

"And there you have it. The time was right. I introduced myself and here we are."

"So, apart from the stalking, the deception, the breaching of my clients' confidentiality, and the possible psychological torture of Barny, no harm done. Why then are you knocking back a third scotch like you really need it?" said Holly over her second whiskey.

"Because I got things badly wrong. Look at you. Look at what you've done. Look at what you've been doing without me even knowing it. The sort of witchlight you are carrying doesn't develop overnight, or because of a bit of coaching. You have more power than I have and I'm ninety-six, for Hecate's sake. Witchlight accumulates, but it takes time. I've been around the block more than most, but you've just picked up the entire block and tossed it over your shoulder like it's a pebble. I didn't see this coming, not even after the incident in the library, and I should have; it's my role to see it. It's what I do and who I am, but this time I didn't manage to do it, and I don't know why."

Holly was too busy absorbing the truth about Partridge's real age and its head-on collision with his physical appearance, to see where Partridge's emotions were headed. By the time she had become conscious of the heavy pall of silence draped over them, Partridge was staring morosely into the bottom of the empty glass that had contained his fourth whiskey and muttering to himself. Holly thought he looked a little teary.

"I don't even know what you're really capable of and I'm your bloody mentor...supposedly."

Even though she still wanted to pay him back for all the deception and stalking, Holly didn't like to see Partridge so miserable and so unlike his normal, excessively jovial self. She felt positive activity would be better for him than further consumption of spirits accompanied by morbid introspection about his perceived magical failings.

"So, why don't you put me through my paces to find out? You've planned to do it this weekend anyway, and it clearly makes even more sense now. Seeing what I can do may help you work out how I can do it and why you didn't see things..." Holly hesitated briefly. "...as clearly as you would have liked up front."

Partridge looked as dubious as Holly normally felt but her powers of persuasion were good, and eventually the whiskey bottle disappeared, and they both went outside to see just what Holly was capable of, magically speaking.

They started with a glamour to disguise the renovated appearance of the farmhouse, then Partridge had Holly transporting inanimate objects, followed by self-transportation and after that, they worked their way up. Barny was brought up safely and happily from Basingfield Lane, along with Holly's overnight bag. Then Grindlebones was transported from wherever he'd been sleeping. It appeared that Holly did not need to know where a thing was in order to find and transport it, provided she could see the thing in her head in the first place.

Partridge designed harder and harder tasks, but provided Holly could mentally visualise what needed to be done in advance, she was capable of almost any challenge Partridge devised for her. True, there had been that little incident of the exploding rosebuds, but by then, even Holly was starting to get tired. Also, she hadn't been able to conjure up a witch's Pendula, but then she had no idea what it looked like, let alone what it was, even after Partridge had attempted to explain it to her. The other basic thing she was still struggling with was the nature and identification of witchlight itself. She couldn't see it or sense it and therefore couldn't understand how it could be detected, let alone measured. She pushed Partridge for more details, but the matter came too close to Partridge's initial failure to recognise the strength of Holly's witchlight, so Holly backed off and reluctantly accepted she was just going to have to remain ignorant for a little longer.

Apart from the aborted discussions about witchlight, the focussed and practical act of assessing Holly's abilities seemed to cheer Partridge up a little. At the end of the session, as Holly was coming to the conclusion that she really needed another cup of tea and was sufficiently tired to think that making it by hand, the old-fashioned way with a kettle, was a good idea, he suddenly produced a trumpet out of thin air, blew a swift and jaunty fanfare best suited to a children's birthday party, except that technically it was well played, and presented Holly with a rectangle of crisp, white card covered in bold, black handwriting. It was official confirmation she had been awarded her DEC.

"Passed with flying colours and at record speed, thus setting the record for the quickest achievement of a DEC by a mentored adult, and on my watch, too. That goes some way towards making up for my earlier failure to recognise your true potential."

Holly wasn't sure how that worked, as any failure had been Partridge's and the achievement was hers, but she charitably kept quiet. "You'll get the full signed certificate in a day or two, but in the meantime you can hang this with pride on the farmhouse wall. Unusually, you are also already at the technical standard required for a DEF, but given those exploding rosebuds, I think we'll give it another week or two before we put you in for that and allow you out to play without a chaperone."

Seeing as Holly had already been using magic without Partridge's guidance, she couldn't really see the point of maintaining the pretence of having a chaperone, but tactfully decided to say nothing on that matter too. Partridge's effusive, children's party performer jollity had returned, but Holly heard a brittleness to it that hadn't been there previously. She felt the need to treat Partridge gently, for the time being at least.

Chapter 7

Both Partridge and Holly had retreated to their respective beds early the night before. Even Holly had had to admit that the day's activities had been tiring and Partridge clearly still wasn't himself, despite the forced jollity of the evening meal, with Grindlebones and Barny being presented with their share of the dinner's meat served on silver plates placed on a reduced, cat-sized table created by Partridge to match the main kitchen one. If Holly was tempted to think Partridge was, once again, treating her like one of his "girlies," she had the sensitivity not to say so.

Partridge might have formally assessed Holly as DEC-worthy and almost DEF-ready, but there were no further discussions about her witchlight or where it had been hiding. Instead, Partridge had downed a good few more whiskies before turning in for the night. Grindlebones and Barny had exited together, presumably in search of a good night's hunting and the companionable torture of small rodents, and Holly was left by herself, until she retreated to her own perfectly designed room to text Jake and feel slightly less alone. She fell asleep with Jake's words imprinted on the undersides of her eyelids.

When Holly woke up the following morning, Barny had already crept back in and was curled up asleep at the foot of her bed. They went downstairs together, where they found Grindlebones patiently waiting by a well-licked, but now empty, saucer. There was no sign of Partridge. Holly fed both cats and then went outside in search of him. She found him a little way down the valley, sitting on an outcropping of rock and morosely juggling gaudily coloured gemstones without using his hands. He stopped when he heard her coming and put on his usual mask of effusiveness. Holly produced two steaming mugs of coffee from the morning sunshine-filled air, gave one to Partridge, and sat down companionably beside him.

"So what are we doing today, Fairy Godfather?"

Partridge managed a rather false-looking smile.

"We probably ought to try to see either Appledore Ashwell or Sister Beldam; you can be having a think about who you want to call on first. Before then, though, I want a decent breakfast with all the trimmings. And we'll need to spend a bit more time attempting to get you to understand the nature of witchlight, so that together we can try to work out why yours is so hot."

Despite the false grin and the jovial tone, or perhaps because of them, Partridge seemed tense when he mentioned Holly's witchlight. Holly decided to bide her time on the subject, at least until Partridge was as well fed as the cats.

After a large cooked breakfast involving copious quantities of dead pig, cured and prepared in a variety of ingenious traditional ways, as well as fried bread, tomatoes, mushrooms, and eggs, Partridge had Holly close all the doors and windows throughout the farmhouse and draw the curtains, so that the interior was filled with a gloom that felt almost solid, despite the morning sunshine outside.

"Witchlight is aptly named. It leaves a tracelight, ever so weak, but just about visible in the right conditions, if you know what you're looking for. You've noticed an echo of it when a glamour is cast, so I can't work out why you can't detect the real thing. However…"

Holly interrupted. "But I don't see a light, as such, when I see a glamour. I see…a dark. Mostly it's a faint shade of blue, but sometimes it's just a presence of something I can't actually see."

"That's not how most people claim to see it. It's not how I see it. You're sure it's not a blue light? Something shining? No? That's odd, but the point is you can detect it, so you should be able to see the full thing. I don't understand why you can't. Your own light may be surprisingly weak visually, but it shouldn't stop you from being able to see other people's. Are you really sure you can't see anything? Haven't you any idea why not?"

Partridge sounded peeved, but Holly couldn't work out if he was annoyed with her, or himself. She sensed it was aimed at her and couldn't help her reaction. "Well, why can't *you* work it out? You're supposed to be my ruddy fairy godfather!"

Partridge visibly flinched and ran his hands through his hair. Its habitually immaculate finish became somewhat less than perfect.

"I know. I know. You don't have to tell me. I'm supposed to know more than you, be the early warning system, and keep the Coven safe. But, I didn't see it until you used it and not even properly then, and I don't know why and I should. I trust you Holly. I don't think you are keeping things from me intentionally, but I need you to be safe. You are safe, aren't you?"

"What on earth do you mean? You're not making much sense, Partridge, and you're starting to worry me."

Partridge seemed surprised by his own outburst, and Holly's retort had brought him up short. He took a deep breath, "Mentors are supposed to guide and advise untrained witches. We are also supposed to identify the potential of newly identified witches so there are no nasty surprises. There was a time in the past—witches aren't as powerful as some were back then. Things got out of hand. Measures had to be taken and controls introduced, but there were still hiccups, at times bad ones. That was why the bureaucracy was created—to keep tabs on people. Mentors are part of the system. We're supposed to identify above-average power, keep an eye on it, control it before it gets out of hand. With you, I failed. I think you're too sensible to do anything stupid, but that's not the point. I failed. And I still don't know why."

Holly wasn't sure she wanted to be seen as sensible, even if it was obviously a good thing in Partridge's eyes. It sounded boring, unadventurous, tame. Still, if it made Partridge seem a tad happier, she could live with it for the time being. She didn't want to rock the boat; she just wanted to understand the powers that were suddenly hers and the unknown world that had unfurled, and was still unfurling, not always reassuringly, in front of her.

"Okay, so we're sitting in the dark, in more ways than one. Let's try whatever test or experiment you've had me preparing for and see if that sheds any more light on things."

Partridge hesitated.

"It's a series of tests, but they can get increasingly unpleasant. Are you ready for that?"

"How do I know without trying? How unpleasant is unpleasant? You're my mentor. If you think we need to do these tests, then I'll give them a try." Even as Holly said it, she wondered whether putting so much trust in Partridge was really such a good idea. She'd had doubts in the recent past, and she was finding out that there was more and more to Partridge Mayflower that she didn't really know. "We can always stop at any time if we need to, right?"

Partridge paused for longer than Holly really wanted him to before saying yes and then, without further hesitation, he waved his arms in a broad, circular motion. The gloom in the room suddenly became a whole lot gloomier. It was like a thick, dark grey wool blanket had been thrown over everything. Holly breathed in deeply and was both surprised and grateful she still could. In the resultant murk, Holly could barely make out Partridge's silhouette across the kitchen. She heard rather than saw him click his fingers, and she sensed a glamour had been created, but she couldn't make out to what effect.

"What do you see?" asked Partridge.

"Not a lot. I know you've made a glamour, but I can't tell what result it's had."

"How do you know I've made a glamour?"

"I can sense it. The darkness round you is somehow out of step with the rest of the murk."

"Now, what do you see?"

Partridge's arms were swinging wildly, but Holly couldn't make out why. It was possible he was juggling. It was possible he was just swatting flies.

"You're waving your arms about like a lunatic, but I still can't see what you're doing."

"Don't you see any lights? A lingering glow? Sort of like low-level sparklers."

"No."

Partridge stopped gesticulating. "Right. It's your turn. Do some magic. Something simple and repetitive like spinning a pencil or flying paper planes."

Holly produced a perfect paper replica of Concord and flew it round the room. Given the poor visibility, she couldn't always see the plane, but somewhere in the kitchen Barny gave a little mew of pleasure, and she could hear him scampering around the room after the paper craft, his claws tapping rapidly on the slate floor. At least Barny was happy. Partridge confirmed he couldn't see much of anything either, except, perhaps, a dull glow around Holly's outline that indicated the presence of low-level witchlight.

"Try a glamour. That will use more juice."

"What sort of glamour?"

"Whatever you fancy. Make yourself look like a famous film star. Grow a pair of bunny ears. Just perform a visual glamour of some sort on your appearance."

Holly obliged and made herself look like Angelina Jolie, a dearly held piece of wish fulfilment that failed to give her any pleasure because she couldn't actually see the effects of the fake transformation. Apparently Partridge couldn't either, but then all he was looking for were traces of witchlight.

"Your glamour gives off a slightly brighter glow than the paper plane, but it's still a very low level of light for what you are doing. Either you are using very little juice to do what you do, which would be odd, or you are cloaking your witchlight. Are you able to do that?"

"I don't know. What's cloaking?"

"Question answered."

"Not necessarily. I've produced magic subconsciously before— the hair and makeup on the night I met Jake, remember?"

"True. Just wait there a minute."

Partridge moved quickly. Holly saw his shadowy silhouette dart sideways and then crouch down. Furniture was shifted. Holly could hear scrabbling, and then there was a short, sharp, and plaintive meow. Holly thought it sounded like Barny.

In the dark space between her and Partridge, two darker shadows suddenly appeared. The lower of the two, which appeared to be resting heavily on the floor, was large and giving out considerable heat. Holly could hear bubbling. The object apparently hanging in mid-air above it was small and limp and worryingly cat shaped.

"I've suspended Barny over a pot of boiling water." Partridge no longer sounded jovial. "In a minute, I'm going to take away the magic that's holding him there, and he's going to fall straight into the scalding water unless you do something."

Before Holly could even shout out no, the small, limp object started falling towards the water. Instinctively Holly directed her will. Various things happened simultaneously: a flood of white light poured down onto Holly and streams of light zigzagged away from her in the form of forked lightening, the pot disappeared, the small shape stopped falling, vanished and then reappeared to lay lifeless in her arms. The combined effect was of an electric storm contained, just about, within the farmhouse, and it was blinding. Holly clung to the soft, limp form she was holding, tears running down her face, until she could see again. By then, the curtains had all been drawn back, and the morning sunlight was once more streaming into the house. She looked down to find herself clutching a furry, bright blue soft toy. Barny was sitting, looking as bemused as a cat can, next to Grindlebones, under the kitchen table. Partridge was standing by one of the windows mopping his eyes and smiling.

"Bloody hell, girlie, that was fearsome witchlight. I knew it was somewhere inside of you, but I didn't know it would be that bright."

Holly threw the soft toy at Partridge, strode towards the front door, scooped up a by-now-purring Barny, and stormed out of the farmhouse, slamming the door behind her with all the magical force she could muster.

Chapter 8

It was well into the afternoon before Holly returned to the farmhouse. She had taken Barny for a long walk in the hills. If this wasn't customary cat and human conduct, it didn't seem to occur to either of them. Afterwards, she had taken Barny home to Basingfield Lane, fed both him and herself, made a big fuss of him one more time, and then transported herself alone back to the hillside, just above the farmhouse.

Partridge was sitting in the sunshine at a wrought iron garden table to the front of the house, waiting for her. A bottle of scotch was on the table in front of him, but it vanished before Holly made it down the hill.

Partridge called up to her, "Hi Holly. How's it going? You've been gone a good while. I was beginning to wonder if I should come looking for you."

"Just as well you didn't."

"Want something to eat?"

"I've already had something, thank you. What I came back for is an apology and an explanation, and I want it upfront, straight, and without any prevarication."

"I guess you've earned that."

"I guess I have."

"I am sorry and I mean that, but I needed to see the truth of your witchlight, and I wanted you to see it too. I couldn't see it by normal means, even with all the additional preparation, so I had to get you to use a huge amount of witchlight all at once. Ideally, it needed to be instinctive and not thought-through in case you were subconsciously cloaking. I figured that an emotional and adrenaline-fuelled surge would bypass any subconscious blockages, and you proved me right. By Hecate, did you prove me right! I did warn you the tests could be tough. You know I never touched Barny, don't you? I just let you think I did."

"So you say. Fortunately, Barny seemed fine. It's just me that wasn't. Isn't."

"I'm sorry, but it was just an illusion."

There was a pause that neither felt willing to interrupt. Eventually, it was Holly who spoke.

"So, now you've seen my witchlight in all its glory, what did it tell you?"

"You were cloaking, presumably subconsciously. Why, I'm not sure; maybe it was instinctive. Maybe something caused you to do it—a past upset or threat, say. We'll probably never know, but you were cloaking, and that's why I could barely see your witchlight and mistakenly thought it was because you hardly had any. Damn me, but I was wrong. You're carrying so much, you can just draw down more from the ether when you want it. That was the downpouring of light into you. You were just pulling it in and pushing it out."

"Is that good?"

"For you? Sure. You've got access to a whole lot of power. You can do complicated magics and not get drained like the rest of us. The Coven will want to monitor you closely, though, once it's informed. We've not seen natural power like this in a long time. It means it's even more important we find out who your birth mother was. She passed on a helluva lot of juice, and I can't think of any witch alive today with that kind of kick. Your family line just became rather important."

"You can't think of anyone alive? You mean she's dead then, my birth mother?"

"It's got to be a very real possibility. Sorry."

"Fine. The sooner we start looking meaningfully, the sooner I'll know. I'm not in the mood for sitting with you and swapping pleasantries, anyway. Let's make contact with Appledore Ashwell and see where that gets us."

In practical terms, the answer was nowhere. Appledore Ashwell was not answering his phone or the etheric means of communication that Partridge showed Holly how to use. When Holly and Partridge materialised in front of his large and very expensive-looking Edinburgh townhouse, it turned out to be boarded up and deserted.

"Perhaps it would have been better to have contacted him first?" suggested Holly.

"We tried, didn't we? The only thing left was to turn up in person. It looks like Brother Appledore is either choosing not to respond, or is beyond any ability to do so."

"As in dead?"

"As in dead."

"So, had we better try Esme Beldam?"

"Tomorrow. After we've spent a few more hours using mundane methods to see what we can find out about Brother Appledore. Sometimes local gossip can dig up more than witchcraft alone can."

The rest of the day was spent talking to local people, trying to prise out more information about Appledore Ashwell, but other than he had lived there and then had gone away, they gained little more insight. The house was big, impressive, and well known in the neighbourhood, but its owner was only known for keeping himself to himself.

The next morning over a strained breakfast, and after Holly had transported herself home to feed a housebound and somewhat sulky Barny, Partridge confirmed that a trip in person to Esme Beldam was in order before any attempt, mundane or otherwise, was made to call her from a distance.

Esme Beldam's well-maintained and sizeable, black and white Oxfordshire cottage was fortuitously occupied by its owner, who came to the front door promptly when Holly and Partridge knocked. For a woman in her mid-sixties she looked remarkably youthful—immaculately made up, light brown hair in a smooth chignon, casual pastel-hued clothes hugging a slim figure and, over all, giving the impression of being the same age or younger than Holly. Holly, as ever, was taken aback by the conflict of known age and appearance, but it was of no matter to Partridge, who saw just such an anomaly every day in his own mirror.

"Sister Esme Beldam?"

"Yes? Can I help you?"

Partridge introduced himself and Holly as fellow witches trying to untangle a bureaucratic bungle, care of the Coven.

"Not another one?" Esme rolled her eyes sympathetically. "I thought all this mundane paperwork was supposed to make our lives easier as well as safer. Give me straightforward magic any day. You'd better come on in."

They walked along a short white-walled hallway and into a simple, but tastefully furnished living room. Holly noticed that for all its ostentatious simplicity, every piece of furniture was an antique—primarily eighteenth and nineteenth century, but with some wonderfully preserved older pieces. On the plain white walls there were paintings from the same periods and a surprisingly colourful and clearly painstakingly embroidered sampler that looked older. Holly sat down gingerly on an immaculate and rather unyielding nineteenth century sofa. It felt like being a child again: too scared to move in case you damaged anything valuable.

"Can I get you anything to drink? Tea, coffee, squash?"

Holly, feeling somewhat dry, almost asked for a thirst-quenching squash, but then had doubts about the image this would create. An inexperienced witch, yes, but she was still an adult, and she was becoming increasingly irked at being treated otherwise. She didn't want to give anyone else grounds to think she wasn't totally mature or to be taken seriously, and how stupid was that, anyhow? At her time of life, she had previously thought about knocking years off, not trying to acquire some extra age-related gravitas. Nevertheless, she asked for a cup of tea instead of the squash.

Partridge said no to all refreshments, making Holly feel awkward anyway and wishing she'd done the same. Holly was silently grateful when Esme Beldam produced two cups of tea, one for Holly and one for herself. At least Holly didn't feel quite so much the odd one out.

"So what, precisely, are you endeavouring to untangle?" Esme Beldam asked.

Holly was content to let Partridge do the talking. She had noticed he'd been circumspect in what he'd told Esme Beldam, and she didn't feel she knew enough about Coven ways to talk convincingly without giving away the true purpose of their search at a potentially inappropriate time. She also wasn't sure why Partridge was being cagey. Plus, he was a damn sight better at deception than she was.

"Sister Holly, here, only saw her witchlight in adulthood." Holly inwardly flinched at the still very raw memory of seeing her witchlight for the first time. "She recently achieved her DEC with flying colours." Here Partridge paused to allow the other witch to congratulate Holly and wish her various felicitations and bounties that, to Holly's ears, sounded horrendously false, but were clearly a given part of Witchery ritual and tradition in such circumstances. Holly briefly wondered why Partridge had not felt the need to offer her such traditional niceties, then decided she would have probably hit him had he done so. "When, as Sister Holly's appointed mentor, I came to complete the necessary paperwork, I found her original DEA had been incorrectly completed and the name of her first sponsor had been omitted. You know the Coven, sticklers for paperwork; so as Sister Holly's official mentor, I've been tasked with approaching the sponsor so the paperwork can be tidied up and completed appropriately and full records maintained and filed."

"So, how can I help?"

"Malcolm Williams' notes state you were the sponsor."

The atmosphere in the room appeared to change, not metaphorically, but in reality. Holly detected a distinct and tangible shift in the air; it had become lighter and, somehow, sharper. Somewhere in the house a dog barked.

"Then I'm afraid Brother Williams' notes are wrong. Have you spoken to him about this?"

"But, you did meet with Brother Williams at the apposite time."

"I did? So when was the 'apposite time,' exactly?"

"The end of last calendar year and the beginning of this; basically, the echo period around the Winter Solstice."

"Recently, then?"

"Indeed."

Holly felt she was watching a complex game of verbal chess without fully understanding the rules of engagement.

"I certainly visited a Coven official around that time, but Sister Holly's name never came up in conversation, as far as I can recall. What is your full name, by the way, dear?"

Holly felt like a pawn that had just been deposited on the board in the middle of play. She didn't feel comfortable with the sudden question, but couldn't think of a reason for not answering it.

"Er, Jepps, Holly Jepps."

"Oh? Never mind."

Partridge decided to make a move.

"So, why were you at the Coven at such an auspicious time, if I may enquire?"

Esme Beldam looked directly at Partridge, "As I'm sure Brother Williams has told you, I'm trying to find my mother, Ninanna Beldam. She hasn't been seen since 1970. I visited the Coven to remind them that I am still looking for her, in case they had forgotten they are supposed to be doing so, too."

The name "Ninanna" reminded Holly of the British Library records, and she felt a sudden irresistible itch to pursue the matter.

"I've seen a statement you signed concerning Ninanna Beldam, but it must have been made before she went missing because it was made in the nineteen sixties. It affirms she is your mother and your mentor. I was wondering why you made the statement?"

Holly realised her outburst sounded clumsy, nosey, and possibly rude, but she still didn't understand the rules of the game the two older witches were playing and, if she was honest, she didn't care to.

Esme Beldam did seem rather surprised by Holly's interjection, but had the grace and control to let it show for no more than a second or two.

"I vaguely recall making such an affidavit," she said. "The usual Coven red tape and interference where it is not required, whilst failing to engage with matters where it would be more profitable for all if they were to do so. At the time, I was almost fully illuminated, but they still wanted to verify that I had an appropriate mentor, even though I was too old for their ridiculous alphabet papers. Ninanna

Beldam was my mother and my mentor, a gifted and powerful witch. I wanted them to know that."

Another mental itch briefly tickled at the back of Holly's thought processes, where she couldn't quite get at it, but she had a go, anyway. "She was gifted and powerful enough to practice Old Magic, wasn't she?"

Holly sensed tension in Partridge, but Esme showed no signs of being ill at ease with the conversation.

"She certainly would have been able to, had she wished to do so. I think I made that clear at the time. She had a great deal of knowledge, as well as natural ability—a very impressive lady."

Holly wanted to know more about Old Magic and the knowledge necessary to practice it, but realised that now was not the right time, particularly with Partridge scowling at her.

"Thank you," was all she said.

"Is there anything else I can help you with today?" Esme Beldam had moved on and was politely, but pointedly, saying thank you and good day in her own style. Partridge and Holly took the obvious hint, said their own goodbyes and left.

They transported back to the farmhouse in silence. Once inside the kitchen, where Grindlebones was maintaining a now-solitary vigil, Partridge frowned at Holly.

"Well, that ground things nicely to a halt, I must say. Just why did you feel it necessary to raise the issue of the statement?"

Holly anticipated another dressing down and was not prepared to accept it.

"Because I'm an independent person and I could; because I am not prepared to be told what I can and cannot do by you like some small child, and because I had a mental itch I felt I needed to scratch. Okay?"

Partridge absorbed the tirade.

"Accepted. Maybe I deserved that, maybe not, but your mental itch is almost as interesting as the response you got to the scratching."

"Come again?"

"It was odd you felt the need to ask the question. It was an equally odd, almost naïve response from Sister Esme, given the year the statement was made."

"There's obviously something else I don't know about."

"Indeed there is." Partridge did not add, "and it's one of the reasons you still need a mentor," but Holly knew he was thinking it. "I've told you witches were once more powerful than we are now. Their enhanced level of power was linked to the frequent use of free or natural magic, Old Magic as we now call it, which was, is, a way of channelling power, drawing it from the elements around you and from the Earth herself. Words, the right ones, used in the right order and charged with witchlight, create resonances that can tap into and draw on levels of power that personal witchlight on its own can't encompass or control. Witches who regularly harnessed Old Magic could become exceedingly powerful. That power has not always been used well or wisely; we're only human after all.

"At various times in our past, use of Old Magic has got badly out of hand: the druidic theocracy just before the Roman invasions, the dark age Chaos, the Witch Wars of the sixteenth and seventeenth centuries and after the Second World War. On each occasion it took a long and co-ordinated approach by the remaining Brothers and Sisters to control and eventually overcome the wayward proponents of Old Magic. It's not surprising that so many witches favour cats as familiars; we are very like them in spirit: independent, wilful, and not entirely sociable. A co-ordinated approach comes as easily as herding cats, and when circumstances force it upon us, the results are not always pretty. Hundreds died in the Witch Wars. Mundane history won't tell you that the judges and executioners at places like Salem were witches themselves. Unfortunately, not all those we hanged or burnt alive were. These days it would be called collateral damage; a necessary evil for the greater good. The necessary evil never entirely eradicated the greater evil, though, just pruned it for a while until it grew back vigorously again."

Holly was starting to wonder where this unexpected history lesson was headed and what it had to do with Esme Beldam, but she let Partridge talk on; he seemed to need to.

"The global chaos after the Second World War was a perfect opportunity for Old Magic practitioners to re-establish a strong foothold. After a while, the signs of their activity became obvious.

Different covens dealt with the threat differently. Ours targeted individual practitioners and introduced a system of tracking and monitoring witch activity in order, in theory, to nip any Old Magic deviances in the bud."

"Coven bureaucracy?"

"Yes. The bureaucracy worked, for a while and up to a point. By the late fifties, there were unmistakable signs of Old Magic still being used for all the wrong reasons. The Coven instigated a witch hunt, in all meanings of the phrase. It wasn't a pleasant or a proud period of our history. I was an investigator as well as a mentor. Sometimes it was just taking statements from people of interest, sometimes… it wasn't.

"Given the timing and the phrasing of Esme Beldam's statement, she was either surreptitiously pointing the finger at her mother as a user of Old Magic, or she was being obliged to give a statement about her mother and her powers and was choosing to give as little away as possible. I doubt she was vouching for her mother's abilities as a mentor. That would have been the least of the Coven's worries around then."

"So, why would she fob us off with such a weak story?"

"Embarrassment? Shame? The late fifties and early sixties do not hold happy memories for many of us."

"Could it be contempt at the Coven for hounding her mother? She was pretty dismissive of its petty systems."

"Possibly." Partridge did not seem convinced, but Holly had sensed both anger and pride at the cottage, and they hadn't come from her or Partridge.

"So what happened?"

"To whom?"

"The witch hunts in general and Old Magic users in particular."

"Things seemed to fizzle out and die down. The old practices aren't illegal. There are positive benefits, provided the power is used properly. Old Magic was, and is, still used here and there, when circumstances require, but the large-scale corruption of it died down. I guess we did get the bad guys, after all. We certainly got the powerful ones."

"So is that why witches are less powerful now? The Coven killed off all the really powerful ones?"

Partridge did not appear shocked by this suggestion, or try to challenge it.

"Or they died out naturally. Either way, there are very few really old and powerful Old Magic practitioners left alive and those who are, we monitor very, very closely."

"You're pretty old."

"Thanks, but not as old as some could be. They had access to power that could extend life by three or four centuries, maybe even more. I'll be lucky if I make it to a hundred and fifty."

"You've never been tempted to tap into the Old Magic yourself?"

"You need a high level of witchlight in the first instance to properly control the power that comes with the old knowledge. I don't have it. Few of us do, now. The purges have been happening on and off for millennia, remember. A natural power like yours is pretty rare these days."

Holly shuddered, but she wasn't sure if it was at the thought of unknown past atrocities or at the suggestion she thought she heard in Partridge's voice.

"Where does that leave me?"

"Still looking for your birth mother, so we can track and understand the line of your witchlight properly. It's not the sixties any more. Like the Cold War, things have got better since then." Partridge grinned broadly, but Holly found the grin less than reassuring.

That night, she dreamed of pyres of flesh-scorching flames and mounds of thick, black ash being shovelled by willing hands into urns and pots, which were then sealed shut.

Chapter 9

The remainder of the time in the Lake District was taken up with uncomfortable introspection, as far as Holly was concerned. Partridge reverted to being annoyingly chipper and appeared keen to use the space and time left to try out further exercises and tests to explore Holly's powers. Holly went through the motions, but her thoughts were invariably elsewhere. Partridge also attempted to make up for any previous information vacuum and provided her with what he saw as relevant background to the world of Witchery, its customs, and its practices. Holly couldn't decide whether he was trying to channel a tour guide or the spirit of Henry Higgins, but in either event, there was way too much detail on most things and far too little in relation to what mattered. What Holly was fretting about was Old Magic: what, how, and the Coven's ambiguous approach to practitioners in the here and now. This, however, was a topic Partridge seemed unwilling to expand upon beyond a very superficial level. Instead, he offered up mainly the information he wanted Holly to know, but which served to worry her still further, as it became clearer and clearer to her that witchcraft was more pervasive and influential in the mundane world than she had previously imagined.

Over the remains of what was becoming a very long weekend, they also made further attempts to track down Appledore Ashwell, but all were without success. The man either wanted to stay hidden, or was dead, or had gone to the psychic equivalent of Suffolk. At least it gave Partridge the opportunity to show Holly a variety of eldritch methods for tracking down lost souls. Holly, unthinkingly, suggested she might practice some of the magical search methods to help track down Esme Beldam's absent mother, as the only other witch she knew of as missing, but Partridge ceased being chipper and administered a stern lecture on minding her own business (a key part of being a witch, apparently), keeping her nose out of affairs that did not concern her (another key aspect to being a witch), and curbing the arrogant presumption that she would fare better than older and more experienced witches who had, no doubt, already tried such devices in the past. Whilst Holly recognised he had a valid point about her presumption, she couldn't help feeling that the Coven had, in the past at least, not been as good at minding its own business as Partridge was insisting she be. Moreover, the combination of Esme Beldam's evasiveness and the lure of the old ways was creating another of those internal itches that Holly increasingly wanted to scratch. She resented Partridge for stopping her from doing so. This simply added to the pile of resentments and worries accumulating between them over the weekend.

The rapport between Holly and Partridge was steadily weakening, but both chose to play along with the rules of the game, if not the spirit. Things were convivial enough on the surface. It was, however, becoming a very thin surface. The cost of maintaining this veneer turned into downright avoidance of certain topics. The test of Holly's witchlight, which had taken cold-blooded advantage of her bond with Barny, was one such topic on Holly's side; the outcome of the test and all matters appertaining to Old Magic was absolutely the no-go area for Partridge; but it was the latter that continued to worm away at Holly's thoughts. Partridge's earlier description of Old Magic practitioners tapping into the power of the elements seemed very close, in practical terms, to his description of Holly drawing down power from the ether at the time of the test. Yet Holly knew next to nothing about the old ways, their practices, or the words presumably required to command Old Magic, so how could she have done what Partridge had said she had on that one occasion when they had both been prepared to talk about it. One thing was for sure; Partridge was not the witch to help her understand this.

Somehow they got to the end of the period together. Holly reluctantly unbuilt the farmhouse she had so painstakingly reconstructed only a few days before and returned thoughtfully to

Basingfield Lane and an ecstatic Barny, who was gratifyingly pleased to have her back.

Having catered to his most pressing needs, a bowl of biscuits and a saucer of cat food to stave off imminent starvation in the face of not having eaten for at least three whole hours, Holly decided she needed a cuddle. Barny initially made it clear by a noticeable lack of up-front purring that he could take it or leave it. Nevertheless, he didn't struggle when she picked him up and held him close. She still didn't know what to make of Partridge's talk of an enhanced bond between her and Barny, but the soft warmth of him in her arms and the vibration of his finally released purr in her ear made things, momentarily, seem better. Perhaps she was destined to become one of those eccentric old cat ladies who loved their cats more than people. Worryingly, she could see the attraction of that. She guessed such dotty old dears would have been mistaken for witches in the past. Holly now wondered how many of them had actually been witches. Barny stuck his cool, damp nose in her ear and purred even louder, distracting her from the beginnings of a morose reverie. It felt good to be back home properly. Perhaps being a spinster cat lady wouldn't be so bad. Plus, of course, she shouldn't forget Jake. So, perhaps not so much of a sad, old spinster, though mildly cat obsessed remained a distinct possibility.

She texted Jake just to be on the safe side and was pleased when he texted her back almost immediately, happy that she had returned from her 'business' trip and looking forward to meeting up with her the next day.

After basking in the glow of his text for a few minutes, Holly rang Sarah to catch up on her news and any important gossip. It also gave her an excuse to talk about her forthcoming date with Jake, a thing she was more than happy to do. Sarah, however, insisted on giving her the usual lecture about hanging onto this one, given her back catalogue of man-disasters. As ever, Holly thought this was a tad unfair, despite the fact that recent male interludes probably did merit the label of full-scale disasters. She had to admit there had been a good many of them. Things just didn't seem to work out. Ever. Before the recent run of non-fatal collisions, though, she and Richard had been for keeps, or at least that was the way they had initially intended things to be. Having said that, the end of her relationship with Richard certainly had been akin to the sinking of the Titanic, but without the benefit of cute romantic leads and emotionally uplifting music, and with added wrenching sub-structure and slow frozen death. The ten years of their life together, before they had finally conceded to their personal iceberg, had been alright though, mostly. Sometimes things just weren't meant to last.

This reminded Holly of Partridge's comments about making it to a hundred and fifty, and she suddenly had a vision of a long and lonely old age, albeit one surrounded by a plenitude of cats, having outlived a partner who could not stretch out his years by magic. Holly gave herself a mental shake and a good talking to. She and Jake hadn't even had a solo date yet, so it was somewhat premature to be thinking of living on alone mournfully after his death. Barny rubbed himself round her legs at this point and distracted her once more. She dutifully re-filled his bowl with biscuits; the work of a familiar's witch was never done.

Holly finally made a call to her parents in Croydon. They chatted happily enough, discussing Holly's comings and goings, or at least the edited version of them, and her parents' ongoing aches and pains. Her mother had been feeling a little under the weather recently, but had now got over it and wanted to know all of Holly's news.

The issue of coming out to them as a witch still hung over her head, assuming that, at their time of life, they could even come to terms with such a thing. She also felt a twinge of guilt at her search, without their knowledge, for her birth mother. She hadn't felt able to discuss that with Partridge, despite his earlier assurance that mentors helped with such things; it was too personal, and his apparent mistreatment of Barny, even once she knew it was fakery, had changed him in her eyes. His implied role in the darker side of Coven work simply alarmed her. Whatever the reasons, though, it came down to the basic fact that she didn't know him, had never really known him, and the fey, avuncular Partridge Mayflower he liked to come across as was as much a fake as the cat torturer had been. So, she struggled with the issue of her parents on her own, but made sure her phone call to them was upbeat and positive. She intended to pop down to London soon to visit them, and maybe she'd broach the subject of magical abilities then. Maybe.

The next day saw a return to the real world. Holly went back to work and was grateful for the perspective provided by her clients. It was refreshing focussing on others' emotional needs rather than her own. Yet even here, Partridge's comments about the role of her witchlight in her interaction with clients rubbed away at the back of her mind. She wondered what else her witchlight was influencing and how she had ever thought eldritch powers were an amusing, but separate, adjunct to day-to-day life. Slowly, but surely, witchlight was insinuating itself into everything she did, and she found its illumination often shone out more darkly than she would have liked.

That evening she was having dinner with Jake, and she was determined it was going to be an uncomplicated and mundane event.

She put on her favourite dark green dress and left herself plenty of time to get ready so she could do her hair and make-up the old fashioned way. She remembered to feed and make a fuss of Barny before she left the house, and she drove to the restaurant, leaving the house in good time, so there was no risk of being late. In fact, there was surprisingly very little traffic on the road, and all the traffic lights obligingly stayed green. It was therefore an unusually quick journey, and she arrived at the restaurant early. She was pleased to find Jake was early, too. They walked into the restaurant together. Holly always felt encouraged when her date appeared eager. It was a good sign, except "sign" was too much like "omen," and she didn't wish to be dealing with things like omens just now. All she wanted was for things to be simple, ordinary, and real.

Jake was a breath of fresh air after the events of the weekend: a charming, funny, ordinary, but rather good-looking, breath of fresh air. He said all the right things and laughed at all of her jokes. His favourite foods turned out to be her favourite foods, and the chemistry between them was fizzing and reacting in all the right places. Holly was finding it hard not to be bowled over, but she was determined to keep her feet on the ground, however well the evening was going.

The only touch of awkwardness came when Jake asked her how her business conference had gone.

"Oh, you know. So, so. Good bits and bad bits. As ever."

"So, what do counsellors do en-masse? Counsel one another?"

"Has been known, but we're pretty boring, really. We don't torture cats or anything." Now why had she gone and said that? "We're probably just like vets en-masse."

"What, you sit around discussing the best way to get your arm up a reluctant cow's backside?"

Holly giggled at that. "Probably not. Absolutely not, in fact, but there's professional chitchat, too. We have our own forms of magic." At which point there was a noticeable pause, which Jake, gallantly, did not notice. He attempted to fill the sudden silence that wasn't there by asking her which hotel she had stayed at, in case he'd once stayed there too. Holly was stymied for an answer. Fortunately, at that very moment, the waiter did exactly what Holly had hoped he would and came over to ask them if they wanted dessert. Holly wondered if her silent plea had had anything to do with this timely bailout.

Dessert ordered, the conversation turned back to less dangerous areas like favourite films, much-loved folk songs, and the best way to administer worming pills to a squirmingly reluctant cat. Holly was relieved to discover even experienced vets could still have problems with this one.

Jake knew his stuff, both as a vet and a dinner date. Just enough professional talk to be interesting, but not so much that it became shop talk and a bore. Everything just seemed right. Holly could feel herself sliding down the pleasantly slippery slope of heightened emotions and warm fuzzy feelings.

Holly was pretty sure Jake shared her sense of attraction and also, that the sense was throbbing more and more strongly between them as the evening progressed. All the signs were there. Their laughter sounded increasingly intimate, and the occasional physical contact, as wine was topped up or as dishes were shared, sent escalating messages to her nerve ends without a single word being said. Magic was not needed to help things along, although a temptation to enhance her appearance with a splash of witchlight, just to be on the safe side, never quite left Holly. Still, when she caught sight of her image in the restaurant mirror, she was pleased to note there was already a visible radiance there naturally.

Coffee came and went, and the evening progressed from very good to simply better. Liqueurs arrived, compliments of the restaurant, and it just so happened that Holly's was the Strega she had been fancying only a moment before.

Over the concluding drinks, Holly allowed her attraction to Jake to take over and lead her enthusiastically wherever it wanted. She followed in a happy, anticipatory daze and found herself pondering whether to invite Jake back to her house or sustain the moment and wait for their next date. Alternatively, Jake inviting her back to his place was not such a bad idea, either. Then she remembered the waiter and the arrival of the dessert menu. She wanted Jake, but she wanted him to want her because he wanted to, not because she wanted him to want to, because her wants seemed to be developing an almost magical reality of their own.

Holly could see where her thought processes were going, and she desperately wanted some form of *deus ex machina* to get her out of this emotional cul-de-sac. Then, Jake's mobile rang. It was his surgery and he was needed immediately because the evening's call-out vet couldn't handle the sudden crisis at the local animal park on his own. Jake apologised, but was already standing up to go. Then he stopped, bent back down, and kissed Holly soundly on the mouth.

"Next time, there'll be an on-duty back-up for the on-duty call-out and it won't be me. This is the last thing I wanted to happen. You know that, right? Next time I'll make it up to you. Properly. Assuming you'd like me to?" He grinned sheepishly at the last bit. Holly smiled back broadly.

"Yes, I'd like that. Very much."

Jake's grin broadened to match Holly's.

"That's so much what I wanted to hear. Gotta go, but I'll call you later. Don't know how much later, but I will call. Vet's promise." And he left Holly feeling warm and happy and excited and just a trifle anxious she may have created her own *deus ex machina*.

Holly drove home, still basking in a warm glow of pleasure and anticipation. She danced up the front path and was met by an ecstatically purring Barny and the remains of his self-catered post-dinner snack spread-eagled before the front door. Barny was always pleased to see her, but tonight her happiness seemed infectious; or perhaps it was his pride in his night-kill that was making him so affectionate. Pushing the bloody remains of the rabbit aside, Holly let both herself and Barny into the house to be confronted by a glowing, airborne message from Partridge, floating in three foot high twinkly turquoise lettering down the hallway towards her.

"Didn't want to disturb, but now you are back, please make contact. Now."

Holly groaned and went to pick up the phone; she still found the witchcraft alternatives to the mundane telecommunications network slightly off-putting. Apparently she was not the only witch to do so. On her telephone answering system were two new messages. One was from a softly spoken man introducing himself as Appledore Ashwell and inviting her to call him on the mobile phone number he carefully provided, rather than use any of the eldritch equivalents. The second message was delivered in the crisp tones of Esme Beldam,

"This is a message for Holly Jepps. Holly, dear, this is Sister Esme Beldam. I think it would be a good idea if we could talk. Just the two of us, by ourselves, without your chaperone. It's a delicate matter. I think I may be your mother."

Chapter 10

In the field behind number sixty-six Basingfield Lane, a large marmalade cat was keeping an eye on things whilst helping to keep the local rodent population under control and in respectful fear of all things feline. Its ears twitched at the muffled sound of a *pop* coming from inside the house. It sensed, rather than saw, the subtle implosion of faintly lavender coloured air that closely followed it, at the same time as a young and thoughtless mouse scampered into its line of sight. The cat badly wanted the mouse. All its natural instincts were urging it on to the chase-catch-kill response that millennia of ancestors had bred into its bones. The cat also had a task to perform, and this task would not accommodate the necessary but prolonged etiquette of rigorously pursuing supper before consuming it. The task was demanding the cat's attention. The mouse, although it wasn't aware of it and would have denied it emphatically if consulted, was demanding to be eaten. A decision was needed. The cat leapt. The mouse barely managed a final squeak before its squeaking days were over. Still swallowing the remains of its fast-food supper, the cat padded over to the darkest and most secluded part of the field and disappeared into the darkness. Two matters satisfactorily resolved. Etiquette be damned.

Holly stood in the road outside the Oxfordshire cottage of Esme Beldam. It had gone midnight, but Holly had felt drawn here as soon as she had heard the final message on her answer phone. Brothers Ashwell and Mayflower and their respective messages could both wait until the morning.

Now she was here, though, Holly was wondering whether it was really such a sensible time to be turning up unannounced. The house was in darkness, and it looked very much as if Esme Beldam had already gone to bed. To be fair, the message had requested an opportunity to talk to Holly alone, but it hadn't said immediately, or indeed when, at all. It was Holly who had felt the need to respond as soon as she could.

Holly stood expectantly in the road for a while longer, keeping an eye on the both the cottage and its front garden, but all was quiet, dark and unmoving. She had just made up her mind to return home to a cup of tea and Barny, when she heard footsteps coming along the road. Two sets: the steady *click click* of a pair of shoes and the more rapid tapping of four clawed paws. Holly peered into the gloom. She could just make out the shapes of a woman in a light-coloured trench coat and a large dog coming down the road. As they drew closer, Holly could see the dog was an Irish Wolfhound and the woman was Esme Beldam. In a few moments more, they would be level with her. Holly suddenly realised she had no idea what she was going to say. Her thoughts started to rush around in search of an appropriate phrase. "Hello Mummy" hardly seemed appropriate, and a more formal "Good evening, Sister Beldam" sounded unduly pompous and might well be biologically inaccurate. Holly had just decided upon "Hello, it's Holly Jepps. I got your message," when Esme Beldam took the problem away from her by hailing her with, "Hello, Holly. I'm glad you could make it. Come on in."

Inside, the cottage looked much the same as Holly remembered it from her daytime visit, except the hallway and the walk to the lounge seemed longer somehow and there seemed to be more doors. Holly, once again, perched herself somewhat uncomfortably on the immaculate antique sofa, whilst Esme Beldam proffered refreshments. The only significant difference from before was the absence of Partridge Mayflower. The room was no less empty, however, because the chair he would have occupied, had he been there and had they chosen to replicate the tableau of the previous visit, was filled by an extremely large wolfhound answering to the name of Regal.

Holly was not entirely comfortable with Regal. He was a fine-looking dog and clearly very well trained, but there was something very un-doglike in the way he was sitting and staring at her. In particular, it was the nature and depth of the stare that Holly found unnerving. She couldn't help but feel he was looking at her the way Barny would a mouse.

"Your coffee," said Esme Beldam, holding out a fine porcelain cup and saucer with an elegant, ring-encrusted hand. "Although, I'm not sure that drinking black coffee this late at night can really be good for you, or conducive to a good night's sleep. Would you care for a drop of brandy in it? I always find it incredibly warming and soothing as a pre-bedtime drink."

Holly gratefully accepted the brandy and sipped at her coffee, wondering what to say next.

"I don't really know what to say to you," was Esme Beldam's next remark, "or where to start, especially after my frostiness the last time we met, but I think there is a very real possibility that I am...that you...may be mine."

Holly waited for the emotional kick she had expected from such an admission: the joy, the relief, the end to uncertainty, the...anything. Any sort of emotional response would have been welcome, but there was nothing, just a dry, dusty emptiness where there should be... what? She didn't know, but she sensed there should be something very different from this.

Esme was still talking, having already moved on, and was telling her of the brief fling with a male witch her mother had considered unsuitable, the shock at discovering she was pregnant, the arguments with her mother, her decision to have the baby, and the final incendiary row with her mother when she had told her she was going to keep the child. Esme had left home, given birth, discovered that the father was not really prepared to help her, and then, when she had swallowed her pride and gone back to her mother, had found out, after the event, that her mother had gone away, leaving no contact details. This had proved to be the final straw, and Esme had gone to pieces. She couldn't cope with the baby, a little girl, and had decided to leave her, safely surrounded by low-level magics and a cardboard box, where someone would find her and take care of her.

"And there you have it, and here we are." Esme Beldam seemed as emotionally disengaged with her tale of abandoning her new-born baby daughter as Holly felt at hearing it, and it wasn't just her tone of voice that indicated this to Holly. There was no feeling of emotion in what she had said. Holly remembered the anger and pride she had sensed the last time she had been there. Now there was nothing. Holly strained to pick up signs of some kind of emotional response, but she found it more difficult to read the woman in front of her than she did Partridge.

"Are you alright, dear? Would you like another drop of brandy?"

"No, I'm fine, thanks. I was just thinking. Where did you leave the cardboard box? How do we know the baby you left in it was me?"

"I sense…something between us. Don't you?"

Holly shook her head doubtfully, not knowing how to respond to that one.

"Plus, there were the magics I wrapped around you. They cloaked your witchlight from prying eyes. I didn't trust the Coven. They were not…inclined…towards my mother or me. So I wrapped you up safe. You wouldn't feel or know your own witchlight, and others wouldn't be able to see it unless they were specifically looking, and even then, they'd only see a trace, a faint glimmer of your true potential. We come from a long line of powerful witches, mistresses of their power. Our witchlight is naturally strong—one of the few old blood lines that hasn't died out, despite the best intentions of petty meddlers."

Holly was finally sensing emotions, now. The pride and anger she had felt before were present again, leaking around whatever reinforced, steel-lined porcelain Esme normally encased her emotions in. She must have realised this, because her tone suddenly changed.

"I'm sorry. You don't want to hear about past family just now. You want to hear about you and rightly so. Word has already seeped out about your speedy ascent to Coven certification levels. Partridge Mayflower has been swift to crow about just how quickly you have learned to harness your powers under his guidance."

Holly knew he'd been proud, but she was surprised and slightly upset to think of him lording it over her success, but then should she be, given the harder side of the man she'd seen up at the Lakes?

There wasn't sufficient time to ponder this meaningfully. Esme was continuing with her new theme.

"To come into your power so quickly, after such a long time without even sensing it was there, can only be explained by a cloaking spell. Did Mayflower mention any of this to you?"

"He said I'd been cloaking."

"There, I knew it. Your witchlight was strong, wasn't it? Stronger than Mayflower knew what to do with?" Esme didn't wait for Holly to answer. "You see, I felt it, felt you, calling on the power that runs in both our veins. We are linked, Holly Jepps, and that can only mean one thing—you are mine." She emphasised the second of the last three words, making it sound as if she was laying claim to Holly against other competitors. Holly was confused.

"So, why didn't you tell me all this the other day when we came to visit you? Why did you deny all knowledge of me, reject me as if I was of no consequence, and let us go without even a hint?"

Esme appeared to let her control slip as she dropped her head onto her hands, displaying the multiplicity of rings on one hand and just one choice, ornate, moonstone setting on the other. Then her pale brown shoulder-length hair flopped across both her face and her hands, like the lowering of the curtain on a final dramatic scene.

"I'm sorry. It was wrong of me. I had sensed you before you came. It unsettled me. Stirred up emotions I thought I'd buried. I knew you were out there somewhere, but then to have you turn up in the flesh so unexpectedly, I didn't know how to react. And then there was that Coven representative with you, being here and observing. You wanted to know about Old Magic. It's not surprising, but I couldn't say anything, not in front of him. In the end, I couldn't say anything at all. Oh, my dear girl, I'm so sorry," And Esme Beldam unwrapped her elegant limbs and leant forward to hug Holly. Holly hugged her back, not knowing what else to do.

There was so much to talk about and none of it came naturally. Regardless of initial reservations, Holly wanted the reunion to be beautiful, but it didn't feel as if they had known one another all their lives, despite tales of this magically happening with other mother-child reunions. Esme was pleasant enough, charming even, but there was no organic rapport, and Holly sensed Esme was constantly guarded—holding back, rather than reaching out. Perhaps it was only natural. Perhaps Esme was feeling the same way about her, but Holly couldn't tell.

Holly wanted to know the identity of her father, but Esme was disconcertingly quick to reiterate the relationship had been a casual thing, little more than a one-night stand, really, and she barely knew the man. When Holly pushed to know his name, Esme curtly replied she had simply known him as Cox, no less and no more. Holly was disappointed by the lack of meaningful information and the ill grace with which it was offered, but it wasn't to be the only disappointment of the night.

It was dawn before Holly left the cottage. Cold, grey morning light was beginning to fill the sky, and Holly noted, somewhat melodramatically for her, that its blank chillness matched her own. She figured she should be happy, or overwhelmed, or something, but for all the hugging and talking of the last few hours, she felt as unemotional and divorced from it all as she still sensed Esme Beldam was, despite the tears and alleged heart searching. Not that she had sensed much from Esme Beldam at all. Perhaps that was the problem? Perhaps she had been hoping to find the expected comfort of a mother's love, but instead had run head first into a cold, ceramic wall. An aesthetically appealing wall—perfectly made up, despite the tears, not a hair out of place for long and not a day over thirty—and perhaps that was part of the problem, too? How were you supposed to feel towards the sudden revelation of a mother who looked younger than you? The woman she thought of as her mother, her real one if not her biological parent, was well into her seventies and looked every year of it. From her there was unconditional warmth and affection. The woman opposite her tonight, claiming blood ties and the pull of Old Magic could be a sister, her younger sister, but not a mother—not her mother, not anybody's mother.

A ripple of lavender light blended with the early morning chill as Holly disappeared from the Oxfordshire lane and re-materialised in the kitchen at Basingfield Lane. She grabbed a dozing Barny from his post-hunting slumbers, held him close, and burst into tears.

Chapter 11

Another morning. The sun was doing its best to creep in around the closed bedroom curtains. Holly stretched in a self-satisfied way and rolled over into the empty bed-space beside her. Probably time to get up. She swung her legs over the edge of the bed, reached for her dressing gown, pulled it on, and ambled dreamily downstairs.

In the kitchen, Jake was sitting at the table, already showered and dressed, with Barny perched on his lap. Both man and cat looked up as Holly walked in. She thought they looked slightly guilty.

"What are you two boys up to?"

"Nothing much." Jake didn't sound totally convincing, "I was eating a bacon sandwich, and Barny here was helping me eat a few scrappy bits of bacon that had come loose from the bread." Barny accompanied this explanation with loud, reverberating purrs.

Holly did not look impressed. "You're a vet. You know he's not supposed to eat bacon, and anyway, how come he gets some bacon and I don't?"

"Your freshly made sandwich awaits you, Madame, and a cup of coffee to go with it." Jake gently put Barny down on the floor, stood up, and walked over to the microwave, which he opened and from which he extracted a sandwich and a cup of coffee. He brought them over and put them on the table. "I was just keeping temptation well away from Barny. It's all yours. Come and get it, lover."

Holly sauntered over to the table, wrapped herself around Jake, kissed him deeply, and then reached over and picked up the bacon sandwich.

"Nice?"

"Mmmm," Holly answered as best she could with a mouth full of hot, greasy bacon. Barny wiped himself around her legs and purred loudly. It was a good way to start a day.

There had been an increasingly wonderful number of such days in the last couple of months. They more than compensated for the days when life got complicated.

"I've got to go to work now, Prickles, and I'm on call this evening, so I'll see you tomorrow night? Are you coming round to me?"

"Yes. You're cooking, remember?"

"As if you'd let me forget. Anyway, gotta go. When are you off?"

"Soon. I've got a couple of things to do first."

Jake hugged Holly and kissed her as vigorously as she had recently kissed him. He bent down and scratched Barny's ears, straightened up and kissed Holly again, picked up his jacket, and walked out the front door with a broad grin on his face.

As soon as Holly heard the front door shut, she waved her left hand vaguely over her head and was immediately washed, dressed, hair brushed, and ready for the day. It was several hours before she needed to go into work, but before then she had a meeting with Partridge.

Partridge often seemed to make days complicated. It was probably just as well, therefore, that she and Partridge didn't tend to meet up that frequently any more.

Holly checked that Barny's bowls were full, not that he needed much more food after his breakfast of freshly cooked bacon, and checked herself in the mirror before transporting herself to the ladies toilets on the shopping concourse at St. Pancras.

As she stepped out onto the busy concourse, she scanned the tables outside the café opposite for signs of Partridge. She found him sitting at what, at first glance, seemed to be a crowded table, but Holly looked through the glamour and saw that, in reality, he was sitting on his own as expected. Holly walked over and sat down opposite him.

"Ah, Sister Beldam, nice of you to join me."

"Hi, been waiting long?"

"Not that long, really. About two minutes at most. I've only just got myself a coffee. Want one?"

"No thanks. I had one before I came out."

The pleasantries over, there was a noticeable silence. Partridge eventually broke it.

"Thought any more about taking your DEF?"

"I'm still not sure. It's a lot of faff for a piece of paper. Esme doesn't put much store by it."

"No, she wouldn't, would she? How are you and she getting on?"

"Well, I think. She's not exactly an emotionally expressive person, but she knows a fair bit, and she is willing to share her knowledge with me. I'm learning about things that interest me, but she's never going to tuck me in at night and read me a good-night story. At my age though, I guess, that's hardly an issue."

"So, is she mentoring you now, if she's sharing what she knows with you?"

"You're my mentor."

"I know I am, but what about her?"

"She's my birth mother. She has a right to be interested in what I do and anyway, we're looking at things that you and I didn't— don't—cover."

"We could cover more if we met more frequently."

"I've been busy recently, and then there's Jake. Daily sessions are hardly practical."

"It doesn't have to be daily."

"You know what I mean." Holly wished she'd had a coffee; at least she'd have had something to fiddle with while not making eye contact with Partridge. She toyed with the idea of producing one, but thought it would look too obviously like distraction activity. Instead, she appeared to admire the glass and steel structure that gave the old station its modern, shiny façade, while searching for suitable topics of conversation. "Have you heard any more from Appledore Ashwell?"

"Brother Ashwell still hasn't made any further contact since he left those messages for both of us, and I briefly managed to speak to him." Holly wondered if she was right to sense an increased frostiness in the space between them, but these days it was difficult to detect frost amongst all the deep-freeze icicles. The issue over the messages certainly hadn't improved her already fraying relationship with Partridge at the time, but it surprised her that it was still adding layers to the permafrost this long after the event.

She'd come back from her meeting with Esme that night in no fit state to contact Partridge, even if she'd thought to, which she hadn't. She'd eventually got to bed about half past five in the morning and then had slept through to ten, by which time Partridge had arrived in her kitchen worried she hadn't responded to his urgent message of the night before and also slightly piqued that she hadn't.

Holly had picked up on the irritation, rather than the concern, and had bitten back, reading him the riot act about personal privacy and turning up unannounced whilst she was still in bed. When, in the midst of their spat, Partridge had flung at her that her lie-in may have cost them the opportunity to talk with Appledore Ashwell and the chance to find out what he had wanted to divulge to them about Esme Beldam, she had retorted with an offhand, "Presumably the somewhat-belated news that she is my birth mother. So there's no problem, because I already know."

Partridge was stung by Holly's tone and the discovery she had beaten him to the news he had been fretting over all night. Although Partridge had responded promptly to the message he had received from Ashwell, Ashwell had declined to tell him what he knew of Esme Beldam without Holly being present. He'd also warned Partridge he wouldn't be available on the mobile number he had provided for more than a few more hours. Those hours had long since gone. Partridge had worried them away for Holly's sake, only to find there had been no need and the object of his concerns was not at all grateful. When he had subsequently discovered she'd visited Esme Beldam on her own, without even telling him, several more rows of their frayed relationship had come unravelled. Further unravelling now seemed a routine occurrence whenever mention was made, even indirectly, of that night and its next morning. Depending on how you itemised the issues, it was beginning to require all the fingers on both hands to count up the subjects Holly and Partridge were no longer prepared to talk to one another about.

"So, what are we going to do today?" This from Holly.

"Drink my coffee, ask you if there's anything you need to talk to me about as your mentor, and try to persuade you to take your DEF; it never hurts to keep in with the Coven, you know. Much better to approach them, rather than wait for them to come calling on you. Particularly given your revealed aptitudes."

"I keep in with you, don't I? But I'll think about it—the DEF, I mean. I will. It would help me to make up my mind if I knew how much time the preparation is likely to take."

"How long's a piece of untwisted string? I can't say until I can see you in action and evaluate where you've got to, these days. We can hardly do that in the middle of St. Pancras. You need to set some time aside so I can appraise your current levels."

"Yeah, right, coz that worked so well the last time."

Silence.

"So have you told your mundane mother about Mother Beldam?"

"No." A pause. "Is it worth trying a further search for Appledore Ashwell?"

"No." A pause. "You know he wouldn't tell me where he was or how to contact him. Beyond giving me that temporary mobile phone number, of course. He was only prepared to talk to you, and you had made yourself unavailable."

Silence.

"I really ought to be getting off to work now."

"Fine."

"Shall I send Barny to arrange our next meet via Grindlebones?"

No response, just thick, chewy silence.

Feeling guilty, but without fully understanding why, Holly stood up and walked back to the toilets. She didn't notice if Partridge acknowledged her departure or not.

Diving into a cubicle in the ladies, she flushed the toilet to cover up the noise of her departure, and transported herself back home.

There was just enough time to go to the loo for real and say a passing hello to Barny before transporting herself to Oxfordshire and her hour's scheduled slot with Esme. Perhaps she should ask Esme about the time-bending spell she had mentioned the other day. But then again, perhaps not—at least not just now. Despite its perfect beginning, today risked turning into one of those complicated days.

Holly was still trying to find her way in her relationship with Esme Beldam. She liked to think that Esme was trying too, but she knew instinctively, or maybe within the deeper flow of her witchlight, or perhaps both, that she wasn't really trying that much. Esme was as Esme was, and the advent of a long-lost, possibly cast-aside, grown-up daughter was not going to change that.

Having said that, in her own highly polished and water-resistant way, Esme was attempting to accommodate Holly, slightly, maybe a little, sort of. They met two or three times a week, and Esme was sharing with Holly many practical things about witchcraft and, importantly to Holly, the old ways of natural magic. She was also giving her an insight, albeit an obviously biased one, into the convoluted workings of the Coven. In other words, she was prepared to discuss all the subjects that Partridge had silently declared no-go and declined to visit. Also, ironically, there were less emotional complications with Esme than with Partridge. At times, Holly thought there were no emotions to be complicated, but then she felt she was being hard hearted. Yes, there were emotions; it was just that Esme kept them hidden and firmly under control, which was hardly surprising given the little she'd let slip about her relationship with her own, long-disappeared mother. Perhaps it was inevitable the scars of the past would mark the present.

Even without the issues of Esme's past, theirs was bound to be a strange relationship; thirty-eight years apart and they'd only known one another for a little over two months. There were some signs of family similarity, though. In addition to a number of demonstrably shared character traits, both had agreed almost immediately that it would be wrong for Holly to tell her parents about Esme just at this moment and that the emotional bonds of the mother-child relationship, formed by bringing up a child to adulthood, had to be protected at the expense of blood ties. Holly felt guilty about this, not in relation to Esme, but in relation to her mother. She recognised, however, that the emergence of both a birth mother and witchery skills would be a lot to come to terms with, and Holly didn't want to upset her parents. At the moment, they were getting to know Jake, and although that seemed a pleasant enough task for all concerned, it meant change and adjustment, and Holly did not see the need to introduce any more complications into the equation for the time being. She silently absorbed the guilt and got on with life.

On the mundane side of her life, Holly chose to remain as Holly was. She had made no obvious public changes to her name or circumstances, except for the alarmingly wonderful presence of Jake within them. Within the records of the Coven, however, Holly Jepps had given way to Holly Beldam. Both Esme and Partridge had been in surprising agreement that the flow of her witchlight had to be properly and formally acknowledged. Partridge's insistence was to be expected: adherence to Coven protocols and the maintenance of accurate records were what he seemed to be about. Holly was surprised Esme could see any advantage to playing within Coven rules, but Esme was exceedingly proud of the family heritage and wasted no time in making sure that all the words were in the right place to recognise this. Esme was very precise about words. Indeed, Esme was very precise.

Today, as per every visit, Holly materialised in the garden of the cottage under the trees at the back of the property where the garden gave way to the small apple orchard behind it and where several elders, an old lilac, and a crab apple tree were all fighting for their space in the sun. Here was the part of the garden where things were always darkest. Esme was a stickler for etiquette and was adamant that it was unspeakably impolite to materialise directly in someone's house, even a relative's. Holly recalled her own response to Partridge's arrival in her kitchen the day after she had first visited Esme on her own and let it go.

Holly hesitated before she knocked on the back door. Esme was not always an easy person to get along with. She needed a moment to ready herself and make sure she looked presentable to Esme's eyes. She took a deep breath and raised her hand to knock, when inside a dog barked. Regal already knew she was here.

The door opened. Holly stepped through and into the empty kitchen. She walked across the pristine flagstones and through the internal door into the hall, along the hall, and into the sitting room. She could swear that some days the hall seemed longer than others. It had a lot to do with how she was feeling at the time.

Esme was, as usual, in the sitting room, or the parlour, as she preferred to call it. She was seated beside a delicate occasional table, pouring two cups of freshly brewed tea from an equally delicate china teapot.

"Good morning, dear. How are you today?"

"Fine, Mother. Thank you for asking." Holly felt awkward calling Esme mother. She didn't really think of her that way, but Esme had requested proper titles be observed, and Holly hadn't felt able to decline.

"Have you seen Brother Mayflower this morning? What did he have to say for himself?"

Holly sipped her tea. She couldn't remember telling Esme about her planned meeting with Partridge, but she must have done. "Yes, we met up. He's still trying to persuade me to take the DEF." Holly glanced at Esme. "I wondered whether it might be easier in the long run to do it?"

Esme snorted. "I still see it as an affront to the family lineage; when did power ever have to be allocated a flimsy piece of paper for it to be real? But, it's your decision, dear. Such a waste of time, though. You're already well beyond their pathetic standard and have been for some time."

Holly wondered if Esme would feel the same way if she knew about the exploding rosebuds, but out of embarrassment she had never mentioned them to her, and fortunately there hadn't been a repeat of the incident.

"If you really want to waste your time sucking up to the Coven, I'm sure Brother Mayflower will be very keen to help you; I can't be bothered with such anus-licking pettiness." Holly swallowed a mouthful of hot tea and said nothing. "Just make sure it doesn't detract from our time together. You still have much to learn about the old ways. So much catching up to do, I'm afraid." Holly once more found herself forgetting that she wasn't far off forty, and felt like a teenager again after an absence from school. It wasn't a feeling she enjoyed.

"Are you still seeing that young man of yours?" Holly inwardly frowned at the somewhat patronising reference to Jake, who couldn't be much more than twenty years Esme's junior and the tacit suggestion he was another waste of time that detracted from Holly's studies. "It would be so nice if you could find a mature man with witchlight to service you."

"Esm… Mother!"

"I'm just saying. If you feel the need to satisfy your animal imperatives, you could at least try to find one of our own to be bestial with."

Holly had heard similar before, although never quite as directly put. She swallowed her outrage and had another sip of tea. On a number of occasions during the last two months she had asked herself why she was prepared to put up with some of Esme's opinions, when she wouldn't be prepared to accept them from any other human being. The answer was inevitably blood-ties, birth mother, and Old Magic.

On the latter topic, Esme had reassured her Old Magic was a natural and important part of her birthright and not something to be feared. Covens in more forward-thinking parts of the world saw its existence as a strength and a valuable, rare commodity. The few remaining practitioners were nurtured and rewarded. It was only the petty-minded bureaucrats of the British and Etheric Isles who worried, trying ineffectually to neuter and muzzle it. Esme was swift to praise her mother and Holly's grandmother (a concept of ancestry and family that made Holly pause for a moment) as someone who had been one of the strongest practitioners of natural magic in the Isles. She blamed Ninanna's disappearance on the Coven's petty-minded ways.

"I know she'd be here, living openly in what was her cottage, if not for them."

When Holly had described to her in detail the revelation of her true witchlight in the farmhouse in the Lakes, Esme had come the closest to being freely emotional Holly had seen and had applauded her as a true Beldam. She offered her the reassurance Partridge hadn't, clarifying Holly's ability to draw upon external power and explaining that Old Magic was just another term for the feral power with which the Beldam bloodline were naturally gifted.

Esme had begun to tutor Holly in the old practices. She insisted on Holly learning things by rote because of a need to use specific words in specific patterns to achieve specific outcomes. Holly, therefore, found herself sucked back into the routine of repetitive exercises, but at least this time she thought she could see the benefit of it all.

After their morning cup of tea, Esme made sure Regal was safely shut in one of the back rooms, while she had Holly run through her current set of exercises. Whilst Esme acknowledged Regal as her familiar, she was less insistent than Partridge on the value of a familiar's involvement in every aspect of practical magic. She saw it as a witchlight boost for little people who needed it. Barny's presence was not required, therefore, and he remained free to wander the fields and gardens of his personal territory, safely well away from the disconcertingly ravenous gaze of Regal.

Holly's current exercises were focussed on the drawing down and passing on of power. Esme had explained it was possible to share power to enhance activity, and she therefore had Holly passing glowing balls of witchlight to her before she sent them back with added kick. If nothing else, the activity was quite colourful. Holly's globes of light tended to be mauve or lavender in hue. They flowed to Esme leaving visible and shining comet tails of silver, red, and blue. Esme returned them in shades of cool, pale blue with trails of silver, blue, and white. Another regular exercise involved the transference of thought, including the art of borrowing another living creature. Eventually, practice of this skill might require the participation of Regal or Barny, but in the meantime, Holly had the less exciting task of trying to influence the behaviour of a recalcitrant blue bottle. Holly was looking forward to upgrading to a slightly larger creature in the near future.

Esme was also keen for Holly to put in some time to improving her physical appearance, in particular, shedding a few visible years.

She seemed to view it as something of a personal affront that her biological daughter looked older than she did. When Holly had queried why Old Magic was necessary to shave off a few years, when a witchlight facelift could be just as easy, if not simpler, using only a basic magic glamour, she was greeted with such a look she thought it better not to ask again. Holly always made sure, however, that her appearance returned to mundane normal after she left the cottage. She wasn't yet ready for Jake, Sarah, or her parents to start asking inconvenient questions about her sudden rejuvenation.

The hour of practice and repetition passed quickly. The morning's exercises had gone well, as far as Holly could see. At least Esme hadn't made any sarcastic comments about breaches of etiquette, mispronunciation, or sloppy wordcraft, all of which Holly regarded as positive signs. When Holly made the mistake of surreptitiously glancing at her watch to make sure she wasn't going to be late for work, Esme even offered to spend some time during her next visit showing her the basics of time bending. Holly left the cottage on light feet and in a positive frame of mind.

Looking as she normally did, she arrived at work in good time, despite her already busy morning. The day's client sessions all went very positively. In response to Sarah's recent gripes that they'd seen very little of one another in the last month or so, she managed to meet up with her for a very pleasant, if slightly rushed, lunch in a local café they both liked. On top of all that, she'd still found time to text Jake lengthily and at regular intervals. Who needed time-bending spells?

All in all, the day had transformed itself into a productive and remarkably uncomplicated one, despite earlier premonitions. The only negative still to be tackled, as far as Holly was concerned, was the fact she wouldn't be seeing Jake until the following evening, but she found texting was helping to keep the pangs at bay, at least partially.

Given the overall positive feel to the day, therefore, Holly was totally unprepared for the phone call she received just after she got in from work that evening and as she was feeding Barny his branded cat food of choice. In the matter of food, Barny was more than willing to be one of a herd; if seven out of ten other cats liked it, then it was more than good enough for him too. His pleasure was rumbling happily around in her head as she picked up the phone, only to hear her father, almost in tears, say,

"Holly, love, it's your mother. She's been admitted to the Mayday Hospital."

Chapter 12

Holly put the phone down very slowly. It was a two-hour fast drive from her house to the Mayday. Minimum. She could transport herself there instantly, but how would she explain her sudden presence to her father, when he had only just now put the phone down on their tear-tinged conversation? That wasn't something she was up to doing right now, and it was almost certainly something he was not ready to hear—not with her mother comatose in Intensive Care with a suspected stroke. How she could bring herself to wait for another two hours, when she knew she could be at her mother's bedside in under a second, was another issue. In the end, she decided to wait an hour and then transport herself to South London. Hopefully, her father would be so distracted he wouldn't pay much attention to the apparent foreshortening of time. If he did, she could always claim her landline had been on divert to her mobile and she had actually been in Central London when he first called.

She sat out the hour. Even with the small comfort of talking to both Jake and Sarah on the phone, it was one of the longest hours of her life.

She passed the eternity of minutes she wasn't on the phone constructing a large bunch of her mother's favourite flowers. The fact her mother favoured plants that bloomed in spring and early summer was not a problem these days, and she soon had a huge bouquet of freesias, Lily of the Valley, Gyp, Lilac, Sweet Peas, Sweet William, and pink roses. She just hoped no one asked her the name of the florist who was able to produce such an enormous display out of season and at such short notice.

Exactly an hour after her father's phone call, she was standing beside her father at her mother's bedside, the bouquet held closely in her arms. A passing nurse extracted the flowers, commenting on the size and freshness of the blooms, as well as the hospital's no flowers in Intensive Care rule. Nobody around the bed was paying much attention, though.

At midnight, Holly made her father call a taxi so he could go home to get some sleep. Holly used the dark hours of her solitary vigil to contact first Partridge and then Esme to see what could be done to intervene in the inevitable slide of human mortality. Partridge was clear there was nothing ordinary magic could do at this late stage, but suggested, the words clearly clogging in his mouth, that she speak to Esme about the possibilities of Old Magic. Esme was sympathetic, or as sympathetic as she knew how to be, but said it was even too late to resort to the old ways.

At six-thirty in the morning, her father returned to the hospital and insisted it was Holly's turn to get some sleep. Holly went out into the still-dark hospital grounds, located a gloomy corner, and transported herself back to Basingfield Lane. She checked on Barny and fed him, made sure the house was secure, left messages for work, Jake, and Sarah, and went to her parents' house, where her father would expect her to be, to sleep. She was there when her father rang at eleven that morning, asking her to come back to the hospital as soon as she could. Once again, she had to resist the impulse to transport herself to the hospital immediately, but pragmatically used up some time to shower and put on fresh clothes the old-fashioned, mundane way before appearing at the hospital.

Her mother had been moved to a side room. The flowers Holly had brought with her the previous evening were now displayed in a large hospital jug on the cabinet beside her mother's bed, but other than that, little had changed. Her father was still sitting beside her mother, holding her hand. It didn't even look as if he had shifted position in the last five hours, but had been transported there, otherwise unmoved, when they had swapped rooms. Despite the fear in his eyes, his voice was very calm.

"Holly, love, the doctor says we have to expect the worst and likely, it will be anytime soon. She says it would be better for your Mum if she doesn't wake up, but just drifts off." There was a catch in his voice at the end of the last sentence, but he kept things together.

Holly, therefore, felt obliged to do the same. She focussed on the flowers that her mother couldn't see. One or two buds opened suddenly, and the room was filled with their sweet, fresh scent, but no one in the room noticed. Eventually, she felt able to say, with some stability to her voice, "It's alright, Dad. We'll both be here beside her; she's not going to have to go alone."

Holly sat down beside her mother's bed, opposite her father. Each held one of her mother's hands. The scent of flowers filled the space between them. At two-thirty in the afternoon, Holly's mother died. She had never got to see the flowers her daughter had put together for her.

The next week or so passed in a daze for Holly. Funeral arrangements had to be made, her father needed looking after, and somehow she was expected to hold all of it, as well as herself, together.

Her father was of the old school and maintained a stiff upper lip, but he was in his eighties, and his wife's death had hit him hard. Holly was very grateful for her witchlight as she balanced looking after him and his needs against dealing with her own grief, making the necessary arrangements, maintaining her own home, her work commitments, and continuing her visits to Esme. Despite its undoubted convenience, however, Holly couldn't shake the feeling of disappointment brought about by the realisation that her power hadn't been up to doing what she had wanted it to.

With everything going on, Holly's workplace had advised her to take compassionate leave, but Holly craved the distraction of work and so carried on going in. Esme had attempted sympathy, as far as she was able, but tacitly indicated she could see no reason why a mundane bereavement should get in the way of their meetings and, in a daze, Holly had complied with her expectations without reflecting upon their reasonableness. Partridge had been more understanding and movingly sympathetic, and they stopped meeting up for a while. In the face of Partridge's sympathy, Holly felt guilty she didn't miss their meetings and found the hiatus something of a relief. The number of nights she was able to spend with Jake also declined for a while, and this she did miss. Significantly.

She hoped things would start to return to normal after the funeral, but her father obviously needed ongoing support, for a while longer at least. Unfortunately, the time she was spending with him only made him worry the more. He was starting to fret about the hours he assumed she was taking up driving around the country to be with him and meet her work commitments. Now was hardly the right time to come out to her father as a witch, so Holly addressed the problem by having her father over to Basingfield Lane to stay, at least until Christmas and New Year were safely out of the way. Jake and her father got on well, and she reckoned her father's presence shouldn't interfere with her relationship with Jake, but somehow it did. She couldn't work out what it was, but she found she and Jake were becoming less and less certain with one another, whilst their communication was becoming increasingly limited. Her father's presence at their previously planned Christmas Eve dinner à deux proved both a help and a hindrance. On Christmas Day, fate and veterinary practice combined to complicate matters still further, when Holly unexpectedly found herself having to keep Jake's Christmas dinner warm in the oven for several hours because, unbeknownst to her, he had agreed to cover the Christmas call-out duty of his practice partner who was married and had children. Needless to say there was an emergency call just as Holly, her father, and Jake were about to sit down to dinner. Jake finally ate his somewhat dried-out turkey on his own several hours later, while Holly sat with her father and Barny in another room.

And so it went on throughout the Christmas break. By New Year's Eve, even her father could tell that something was wrong between the pair of them. He insisted they should go out for the evening as a couple without him in tow. He demanded his right to an old man's night in with Barny and a decent single malt, an arrangement much enjoyed by both human and feline, whilst Holly was obliged to procure a pair of last minute dinner/dance tickets by non-mundane and less than honest means. The fact she had got hold of tickets to a do that Sarah and Mark were already going to delighted Sarah, who was still complaining she hadn't seen as much of Holly as she would have liked recently and who thought the idea of re-creating their original dinner quartet was wonderfully amusing. It left Jake, however, looking less than amused. He had wanted Holly to himself for the night. Holly had failed to notice his mood until it was too late, and the evening, whilst reasonably pleasant superficially, was less than both Holly and Jake had hoped it would be. It was a sign of the times that neither chose to discuss this with the other.

There were other tensions crackling through the air that holiday period. Esme had expected Holly to visit her intensively over the Winter Solstice, given its significance to witchery in general and Old Magic in particular and was less than pleased when she realised Holly had made plans to spend it differently. She was even unhappier when she discovered that "differently" involved Jake as well as Holly's father. At the same time, Partridge, who was less demanding and more patient than Esme, was also starting to ask when Holly might get around to finding some time to spend with him.

Whilst begrudging her own situation, Esme had no time for Partridge's concerns, "If he feels like that, it would be simpler if he just stopped being your mentor. You have me, now. Why bother with him?"

Holly hadn't felt she needed a mentor for some time, but she was reluctant to break all ties with Partridge. Somewhere at the back of her consciousness, a squirming feeling that it would not be a good idea to be totally reliant on Esme was starting to wriggle to the surface. She wasn't yet certain how she felt about that. She therefore kept her feelings to herself on this matter and said nothing to anyone until the second week of January, when the world had recovered from its outbreak of Christmasitus, and she decided she could no longer go on putting things off.

Holly was being kept very busy following her return to work. On the home front, her father was wondering whether to return to Croydon, move in with his younger sister in Canada, or simply go to visit her for a while. In the meantime, he was staying put at

Holly's without an identifiable date for departure. Barny was in need of attention and ongoing medication, as he was on a course of antibiotics for an infected scratch (another cat, or possibly a dog, the vet wasn't really sure) and was out of sorts. Jake was becoming progressively distant. Holly was not, therefore, necessarily in the right frame of mind to deal with Partridge's growing impatience with her failure to take the DEF or, indeed, with his habitual sense of humour.

They were back in the echoing galleries of the refurbished and rejuvenated St. Pancras, as Mister Jepp's continued presence at Basingfield Lane prevented them from meeting at Holly's. Partridge was again seated at a café table to await Holly's arrival, but this time Holly was significantly late. Barny had repeatedly spat out the hated antibiotic pill, even when administered magically. Somehow, he always knew, and it always came back up like an unwanted furball. By the time Holly finally had persuaded him to take the pill and keep it down, she was already late and, as she still hadn't managed to bend time safely without Esme's guidance, there was little she could do about it. Partridge was pointedly peering at his watch as she hurried over to him.

"Hello, Holly girl. Cutting it a bit fine are we, or did you just find something more important to do? I thought Mummy Beldam was going to help you with your time maintenance issues?"

"Yes, Esme and I are working on the time thing, but, ironically, it takes time, which is what I am constantly a bit short of these days. I am sorry I'm late, but Barny wouldn't take his medicine."

"Blaming it on the boy is a bit uncharitable. He's a good lad and deserves some respect. He's a cat, not a scapegoat."

"That's a bit rich coming from you. You know he's got my respect and my love, but he's also got a badly infected scratch, a pressing need for antibiotics, and a cat's innate ability to avoid taking medication, howsoever it is presented to him—not a happy combination, let me tell you. He can also be an awkward little cuss."

"Takes after his witch, then?" Partridge was grinning as he said this, but Holly sensed the underlying acid in his voice. She grimaced back and said nothing.

"Cat got *your* tongue, for once then? Now that would be a bitter and bloody awkward thing to swallow."

Holly's grin became broader and more forced. Her stare was pointedly fixed on Partridge.

"Are we going to sit here and swap pleasantries all afternoon, Brother Mayflower, or are there, maybe, some other and more worthwhile things you would like to talk about?"

"Well now, we have finally managed to meet up alone, I'll give you that, but not anywhere where we can realistically do more than just talk, so I guess talking it is. I can't really do much more than ask you for an update on your progress with Mummy Dearest and try to persuade you, yet again, to reconsider taking your DEF. How is Mummy Dearest, by the way?"

"Could you stop calling her that? I call her Esme. Why can't you?"

"I bet you don't call her Esme to her face. I can't imagine Mum tolerating that."

Holly bit, "She's not my mum. Mum's dead. Don't you dare belittle her, too."

"Lucky to have had two of them, then. Most people only get to have one."

The table between Holly and Partridge started to rattle ominously, and Partridge's coffee began to vibrate and then rock until it spilled over into his lap. Fortunately, because of Holly's lateness, it was, by now, only lukewarm. Partridge mopped at his trousers and discreetly cleaned himself up by magical means, while Holly tried to regain control of her emotions.

Partridge proved the more successful in sorting himself out.

"I'm sorry. That was uncalled for on my part," he said. Holly said nothing. "Look, I didn't mean to be so snippy, but you've got to understand I'm under a lot of pressure here. The Coven wants you to show acceptance of them by taking your DEF. They'd feel happier if a witch of your talents was seen to accept and actively participate in their systems. They don't want people starting to think they are only an optional extra. They are expecting me to deliver. So what about it, Holly, eh? You'll sail through the DEF, no effort at all. You know you will. You'll make the Coven happy. You'll make me happy, and you'll have done yourself a favour by at least appearing to acknowledge the Coven. Plus, of course, you'll officially be mentor-free and won't have to put up with seeing me so often. What do you think?"

Holly glared at Partridge. Where once she had reminded him of a hungry, disgruntled owl, he now saw something bigger, sleeker, and angrier, and this time it was seriously pissed off. The creature blinked.

"Okay. I'll agree to take the bleeding DEF. This week. As soon as possible, so it's over and done with, but it's on the understanding that afterwards I'm not just shot of a mentor, I'm shot of you. For good. Period."

Chapter 13

It was a cold, sun-starved, late January day. Holly heard her father walking slowly along the landing on one of his many early morning trips to the bathroom. He had made his mind up to go and stay with his sister in Canada for a few months before coming back to live in the house in Croydon, and it would be one of the last few dawn time disturbances Holly was likely to be subject to for some time.

Jake snored gently and quietly beside Holly. Unfortunately, it would also be the last time that Jake would be here for a while. He'd had a last-minute opportunity to go to a prestigious conference in the States, several hundred kilometres south of where her father would soon be staying, and he'd jumped at the chance, somewhat enthusiastically, Holly noted. It would be good for his reputation and career and, he had almost tactfully suggested to Holly, it might be good for the pair of them. The effect of absence on the heart, if they were apart for a while, might be beneficial. Holly had been taken aback by the suggestion, whilst secretly recognising the underlying truth of it. Then she had discovered Jake would be away for three weeks to allow for pre- and post-conference meetings, and she decided truth was a painful business.

Today wasn't a happy day because Jake was flying off from Heathrow to the States, and Holly was finally going to have to break it to Esme that she was committed to taking the highly unpopular DEF, as Esme would have it, the very next day. There had been some delay since she had told Partridge she would take it. First the Coven had dragged its heels, presumably to signal their pique it had taken her so long to agree to undergo it, and then Holly had delayed because of Jake's imminent departure. In the meantime, she hadn't mentioned her decision to take the DEF to Esme on the grounds that sleeping cats were happy cats. Or perhaps, in acknowledgement of Regal, it should be the old, well-toasted chestnut of letting sleeping dogs lie. Now, however, she couldn't put off the evil moment any longer. On the plus side, as far as Esme was likely to be concerned, it would allow her to dispense with her official Coven mentor. Even Holly saw that as a positive, especially as there had been further friction between her and Partridge whilst arrangements dragged on. First, however, she had to tell Esme about taking the DEF and before that, she had to say goodbye to Jake.

When it came to seeing him out of the door, Holly didn't know what to say. "Bye, take care" seemed inadequate. "Come back soon" was not going to happen, and "Perhaps I could pop over to see you for an hour or so every other day" sounded demented. The inability to use the power bubbling up inside her to do what she really wanted to do—again—cut deep. The sooner she came out, the better, but it never seemed to be the right time. Perhaps when Jake came back and things were a bit more settled. That would be good, but in the meantime, all she could manage to say was, "Have a good time over there, but do try to think of me from time to time. I'll miss you." She thought the last bit was true; she hoped it was.

Jake kissed her on the forehead. " I will. On both counts. We'll talk properly when I get back. Vet's promise." And he left without looking back. Holly discreetly dried her eyes and went into the kitchen to make breakfast for her father.

An hour or several later, and she was standing in the back garden to Esme's cottage. Even before she had moved forward to knock on the back door, Regal was barking from inside the house. The dog's sensitivity to her presence was uncanny.

The door opened by itself, and Holly walked on through into the kitchen where she found Esme sitting with two large cups of coffee and a plate of homemade biscuits.

"Good morning, dear. How are you today?"

"Fairly good, thank you, Mother."

"I've made some coffee and biscuits."

"Thank you. The cookies look delicious."

Holly always felt their greeting ritual sounded more like pages from an out-of-date teach yourself English book than a natural mother and daughter conversation: Holly and Esme are in the kitchen; Esme has made some cookies for Holly. "Thank you, Mother," says Holly. "It is no problem dear. I saved up my ration cards especially," says Esme. Still, it seemed to make Esme happy, or, to be more precise, it avoided making her unhappy.

"Jake is flying off to the States today, and Dad will be off to Canada by the end of the week, so things are going to be a good bit quieter for a while."

Esme nodded absentmindedly, which seemed somewhat out of character. Whatever else Esme was, she wasn't absentminded.

"It's a bit of a clean sweep, if you like. So, while I'm at it, I thought I'd get the DEF over and done with, and then I can say goodbye to Partridge as my official mentor."

"Very good, dear. As you wish."

Holy was expecting more of a protest, or at least a trace burn of the acidic sarcasm that Esme was so good at. Esme's non-committal comment had come as something of an anti-climax. Holly risked being a little more precise.

"I'm taking the afternoon off work tomorrow, actually, and we're going to pop up to the Lakes to do the practical testing, but I'll be home in time to fix Dad's tea."

"Very good, dear. You'll pass with flying colours, of course. It's almost a waste of your time taking it, but as you are going to, there's no doubt about the outcome. Once your father has gone, you ought to do something to celebrate your success, along with casting off the unnecessary irritation of the Coven. A dinner in a top-notch restaurant would be just the thing, and I know someone who'd love to take you."

"Oh you don't need…"

"No, I don't mean me, dear. His name is Merton Holmfirth—comes from a good line of witchlight, not yet thirty. He could be your, what's the modern phrase, 'toy boy,' if you wanted."

"I'm with Jake, remember, Mother."

"Yes, dear, but Jake's not around, and it's only right you celebrate your DEF properly. Brother Holmfirth will squire you most appropriately. I'll contact him to arrange your date."

"I don't want a date. I've got Jake."

"I'm tempted to ask for how much longer, but I shall be good. It won't be a date if you don't want it to be, but a celebratory meal is called for, and while the mouse is away and all that. It would be such a shame not to celebrate the occasion. I had little enough opportunity to have fun when I was young. Don't waste the chance when you're given it."

"Well…"

"Good. I'd like to arrange this little something for you. I realise I've been far too negative about that damned certificate. Perhaps unfairly so. It does, after all, mark a coming into your full power and, as one of your witchlight line, I welcome that. It's only right that you celebrate properly, and I'd like to arrange that for you. As a gift. Please."

Holly felt that, given what Esme had just said, it would now be ungrateful to say no, but she still had her doubts.

"It's a lovely thought, b…"

"Good. That's settled then. I'll contact the Holmfirths and let young Merton know. He's a lovely boy—makes lots of money in the City. You'll like him."

"But, please remember it's not a date."

"Oh, absolutely."

"Anyway, if he's a witch, how come he's got a mundane job?"

"You'd be surprised at the number of witches with City jobs. It's a good place to use magic without anyone noticing. No one really understands the markets, so a little magical manipulation goes unnoticed, and vast gains are not considered surprising. You try working as a teacher or an NHS counsellor, say, and living the sort of lifestyle that most witches choose, without anyone getting suspicious. You'd have to spend your life under a constant glamour. In the City, no one notices a few million here or there, and one or two amazingly successful deals can always be created to explain things, as of course, can a crash. You should think about it, rather than living as a pauper."

"I'm happy with what I do."

"Yes, dear, but you're living on the poverty line as far as witches are concerned, and you are actually working for a wage, at others' beck and call. Neither can be good for you."

"I'm not a pauper. I've a very nice house in South Cambridgeshire and I like my job."

"Fine, dear. I'm just saying. It's rare to meet a witch, let alone a powerful one, who chooses to live as you do once they come into their power."

"But, you've chosen to live in a cottage rather than a mansion."

"Yes, but it's Ninanna's and it's larger than it looks." Esme smiled. "More coffee?"

And with that, the particular thread of conversation was over, and they moved on to Holly's Old Magic studies.

When Holly left the cottage an hour or so earlier, having improved her ability to bend time considerably, she was still worrying that somehow Esme had talked her into going out to dinner with a man who wasn't Jake and who Esme clearly preferred to Jake. Holly missed Jake, even if, technically speaking, he hadn't even flown out of the country yet—again—time bending obviously brought with it its own complications, as if life wasn't complicated enough. Still, looking at the positives from this morning's session with Esme, her control of her own witchlight was improving, and Esme had taken the news of tomorrow's DEF amazingly calmly—no upset, no fireworks, no drama.

There was no drama for Holly's actual DEF, either, although there were fireworks, care of the final exercise that was, apparently, always given to candidates who were about to pass their DEF with colours proudly flying. Holly made sure her fireworks were brighter and better than any she had produced before and astoundingly visible against the pale day blue sky. Indeed, her daytime fireworks shone out better than more traditional nighttime ones. Holly was steadily becoming a believer in the maxim of anything is possible if you throw enough witchlight into it.

Partridge was pleased with her performance and, it seemed, genuinely pleased for her. Holly was pleased with herself, but there was no getting around the underlying sense of anti-climax when Partridge handed her a pre-completed DEF certificate and wished her strong light and good flow in the time-honoured tradition.

"I guess we won't be seeing so much of one another, Holly girl, now you're fully fledged, as it were. I know we've had our moments, but it has been memorable. Who'd have known, eh? Who'd have known?" Partridge was slowly and thoughtfully shaking his head as he started to fade into invisibility. Holly was feeling almost sorry for the man and wishing that, in recent weeks, they'd managed to be more amicable with one another when, with a turquoise twinkle of his former self, Partridge stopped fading and looked Holly straight in the eye.

"Don't you worry, girlie. I'm still going to be watching over you. You don't get rid of me that easily. That's a promise from your fairy godfather, and a heads up. The Coven doesn't want to lose all track of power like yours." With a slight puff of turquoise light, he vanished, leaving Holly to wonder if she'd just been reassured or threatened.

Chapter 14

Holly was not in a hurry to get ready for dinner, but there was no putting off the event this close to curtain up. She had managed to postpone arrangements long enough to see her father safely on his plane to Canada, but once that excuse had gone, Esme had stubbornly been true to her word and had arranged an evening to remember: a suite for Holly in one of the most expensive Central London hotels, an unnecessary, but ostentatious, chauffeur-driven limousine to the restaurant, which was heavily Michelin starred and had a waiting list of many months (not that that had caused Esme any problems with the booking), and a range of designer dresses for Holly to select from. All Holly had to do was make her choice, and the dress would adjust to fit her perfectly (or she would adjust to fit it; Esme had been a bit vague on the actual fitting arrangements). The same with the selection of high-heeled designer shoes laid out across the floor of Holly's hotel bedroom; then there were the bags and wraps. Esme had trusted her to do her own hair and makeup, but she was under strict instructions to make herself look as good as magically possible and shed at least ten years in the process—actually and not by a detectable glamour. Esme expected her to look as youthful as her dining companion. As much as Holly had emphasised this was not a date, it was quite apparent Esme had a different opinion of things, and Esme was clearly used to getting her own way. Still, she wasn't there this evening, so it would be down to Holly and Merton Holmfirth to decide how the evening would actually go.

Holly made her selections and checked her appearance in the bedroom's full-length mirror. Her brown hair was sleek and glossy, and the midnight blue cocktail dress really did suit her. She hadn't looked this good for over ten years and probably not then; witchlight added a glow which youth alone couldn't match. Holly automatically turned to seek Barny's usual affirmative meow and then stopped herself. No Barny tonight. Barny was curled up around a warm radiator at home—a necessary knock-on from Holly's night in hotel luxury, although she could always surreptitiously transport him in later. So, no Barny and, of course, no Jake to admire her transformation—but then again he had chosen to be somewhere else, had decided to go away. Barny just went with the choices made for him. Mostly.

At seven o'clock she made her way down to the hotel's reception area where a stunningly beautiful dark-haired man in his late twenties glided over to her and introduced himself as Merton Holmfirth. There was a telling twinkle in his bright blue eyes, and Holly instantly found herself warming to him. Instinctively, these days, she checked for a telltale glamour, but found no trace of one. So, either Merton Holmfirth was as young as Esme had said and as beautiful as he looked, or like Esme, Partridge, and now Holly herself, he had actually and physically knocked the years away from his appearance. Holly didn't know of a way to evidence that. Then again, did she need to? However it was achieved, it was actual.

The introductions and how do you dos over, Merton escorted Holly to the limousine, which was waiting directly outside the front doors of the hotel. So far, so wonderful. Holly was finding it difficult to fault Merton, although perhaps, if she was being picky, he came across as ever so slightly old fashioned. Timeless, might have been a nicer way to phrase it. He could have been a gentleman escort from any period since the 1870s up to the early 1970s, or possibly a wee bit later. It was just in the twenty-first century he seemed a tad anachronistic.

Once in the back of the limousine, Merton produced two glasses of chilled champagne and together they toasted Holly's recent success.

"Oh goodness. It was only a DEF. You must have taken yours… less than ten years ago?"

"Something like that, but I never passed with such style, elegance, or sheer, blinding ability. All the Coven is talking about it. Plus, of course, I haven't had your disadvantages."

"Disadvantages?"

"Growing up in the mortal world, unaware of your witchlight or even the existence of magic and not coming into your witchlight until such an old age."

Holly winced inwardly at Merton's use of the term "old age." He had instantly lost points in the gallantry charts with that particular reference, although finding a witch who acknowledged her maturity was actually surprisingly refreshing.

"I don't actually see it as a disadvantage. I simply had a normal childhood. And adulthood, seeing as you mentioned it. I guess what's come after just seems all that more special by contrast."

"While for me, it is all a matter of boring normality." There was a note of ennui in Merton's voice that didn't sit right with a young man still in his twenties, but Holly didn't have long to ponder that as the limousine was already drawing up outside the restaurant.

Merton got out of the car first, walked round to Holly's door, and opened it for her. Offering her his arm, he escorted Holly across the pavement and in through the crystal-clear plate glass doors of the restaurant. Holly felt looked after and rather liked it.

Once inside and seated, Merton ordered two more glasses of champagne whilst they perused the menu.

"We shall drink nothing but vintage champagne, if you want, but with a wine list as good as theirs, I would caution it might be a bit of a waste." Merton grinned and his blue eyes twinkled encouragingly.

"You've been here before, then?"

"Fairly frequently, in fact. One of the benefits of a witchlight-fuelled City lifestyle." Merton grinned broadly, although this time Holly couldn't help feeling that it came across as more of a smirk.

Holly focussed on the menu. It was amazing. As if by magic, and probably actually by magic, all her favourite dishes were listed in some guise or other, and the dishes she didn't recognise contained ingredients she did and salivated over. Merton also claimed to be impressed with this evening's menu. Either his tastes matched hers or he was making every effort to ensure that the evening revolved around her. Both won him some brownie points.

Their first two courses finally ordered and more champagne consumed, as well as a bottle of wine selected from the restaurant's impressive cellars, they were free to talk about more than Holly's DEF success and the delights of the menu. Holly fleetingly wondered what they would have to chat about, given their obviously very different backgrounds, but she needn't have worried. It seemed they had more in common than she had given Merton credit for, and he proved to be both attentive and entertaining.

The conversation ranged across the benefits of working in the City with added "illumination," as Merton termed it, through current West End theatrical hits, favourite films versus recent releases, cat maintenance, and the oeuvre of lesser known folk musicians. All subjects dear to Holly's heart and, it appeared, Merton's. The conversation only stopped to allow for the consumption of the food, once it was brought to them, and, of course, the wine. Although that could be sampled steadily when the other was talking. Holly found herself warming considerably to Merton, despite her best intentions. He really was an incredibly good-looking man and, it wasn't just his eye-pleasing looks. He even laughed at her jokes. The only other people to do that were Jake and her mother. Had been her mother.

Merton noticed Holly's sudden drop in mood.

"Is everything alright? I haven't been boring you, have I? Only, suddenly you seem a little down."

"Yes, I'm fine and no, you haven't been boring—far from it. Sorry. Slightly mournful thoughts, that's all. I lost my mother, my adoptive mother, relatively recently. From time to time it catches up on me."

"No. I'm the one who should be sorry." Merton took her hand and squeezed it sympathetically. "Sister Beldam did mention your loss to me, and I should have been more thoughtful."

"Please, no. It wasn't your fault or anything you said; it's just me. Let's change the subject." Holly breathed in and steadied herself. "So, how do you happen to know Sister Beldam, my birth mother?"

"The illuminated world is a small one, and it helps there is a distant family connection."

"A family connection? Does that mean we're related?"

"I believe so, but very distantly—a connection on Ninanna Beldam's side of the line by marriage, not witchlight or even mere blood, regrettably."

"Oh, Esme's never mentioned that. She seems to think so highly of her mother and everything connected to her I'm surprised she hasn't. She crops up in our conversations with an amazing regularity."

"Everyone holds Sister Ninanna Beldam in high regard, or at least everyone who values the power of pure witchlight and the potential of the Old Magic. She was a most impressive lady."

"Did you ever meet her?" Holly asked without thinking and before it dawned on her that Merton couldn't have been born by the time Ninanna had disappeared. When it did, she kicked herself for her stupidity, so his answer surprised her.

"Not properly. I saw her from a distance on a couple of occasions and there was one, ah…moment, but Ninanna Beldam was the sort of person you had pointed out to you in hushed whispers, rather than being introduced to. A very impressive lady, but one who preferred to keep herself to herself."

"Oh?" Holly's impression of Merton shifted slightly. Clearly here was someone else for whom age was a variable rather than a fact and who wasn't prepared to be up front about it. "So, what else can you tell me about my grandmother?"

Merton poured Holly yet another glass of wine, whilst apologising that he could not enlighten her with much more about Ninanna Beldam. Her whispered reputation as a powerful practitioner of the Old Magics preceded her and blotted out almost everything else. Holly noted that her glass was being kept constantly full of wine and discreetly adjusted her body chemistry to make sure she stayed sober.

"But weren't the Coven aware of this? Her reputation with the Old Magics, that is? I didn't think they were in favour of free magic being practised and at times actively pursued, if not actually persecuted, those who did? I read something that made me think they remained uncertain about Ninanna's actual involvement in the old ways."

"I am sure the Coven knew the rumours, but at the end of the day, that's all they ever really were. Even in family circles. Ninanna kept herself to herself. Nothing was ever definite, and if you followed a story it tended to dissipate like witchlight in a full moon. Sister Beldam, your mother, must have already told you far more about her than I can, though family gossip does suggest there was something of a rift the size of the Grand Canyon between the two of them about the time they both disappeared."

"Ninanna and Esme? Long term disappeared? Both of them?"

"Well, obviously with hindsight, only one, but both Ninanna and Esme Beldam dropped well below the magic radar for quite some time and at the same time. Still, that's not uncommon amongst the illuminated. We have a tendency to wander off like cats. We all have our little plots and projects, eh?"

Holly wasn't aware she had any plots or projects on the go at that moment, but decided that finding out a bit more about her birth family should probably become one. It looked like Esme hadn't been as forthcoming about her relationship with her mother as she had implied. Pumping Merton for more information didn't further Holly's new project any, and Holly reluctantly let the conversation drift on to lighter topics. Merton was exceedingly entertaining and very pleasing to look at, so it was far from a hardship.

The rest of the dinner passed very pleasantly. Merton continued to be good company and very generous with the wine, although as Esme was paying he could afford to be. Holly relaxed back into the evening, whilst remembering to keep close control over her metabolism to ensure the wine did not gain the upper hand. Memories of Jake waxed and waned on the edges of her thoughts, but not so much as to prevent her from enjoying herself, or the proximity of Merton. Any twinges of guilt were largely minimal and assuaged by the resolution that she was only window shopping.

Merton himself clearly found Holly attractive. At least, he gave all the upfront signs that he did, but remained a perfect old-fashioned gentleman throughout the evening, even when they took a stroll together down by the river to get some fresh air before calling up the limousine for the return journey. He was perfectly attentive, but not overly familiar. This restraint served to heighten Holly's feeling that there was a warming, positive tension between them and helped to make Merton all the more attractive in her eyes.

It was only once in the limousine, and halfway through the short journey back to Holly's hotel, that Merton suddenly became very flushed and without any warning or finesse launched himself at Holly, pinning her down uncomfortably onto the back seat. He managed a good stab at sticking his tongue down her throat and his hand a long way up her skirt and into her underwear. Holly wriggled and pushed, but Merton was clumsily persistent. She was just beginning to get worried when she achieved an undignified slide on to the limousine floor, but was at least beyond reach of Merton's fumbling. The chauffeur drove on, face forward, as if nothing was happening.

"What on earth was that all about?" snapped Holly, as she wiped the back of her hand across her mouth.

Now his attempt at passion was over, Merton looked almost as stunned as she was. "Err, I want you." It sounded more like a question than a passionate statement.

"Don't you know?"

"Yes. Yes, of course I do. I wanted you." That sounded more definite, but no more convincing. "Sister Beldam said you were looking for a man and we would make a good match, what with your power and the family connection. She said you liked decisiveness. She says." Merton paused to shake his head rather like a farm animal trying to shoo away flies. "Said. She said, you'd be responsive."

"Did she now?"

Merton's sudden flush of alleged animal passion had now become the vivid strawberry mark of embarrassment. He reverted to an old style and obviously rehearsed apology.

"Clearly, I have misunderstood the situation. I can only apologise for any discourtesy on my part."

"I'd like to say accepted, but then I would be doing you the discourtesy of lying. I'm really not sure what sort of game you think you're playing, Merton, but conveniently we appear to have been saved further embarrassment by the limousine's arrival at my hotel. Goodnight and goodbye, Brother Holmfirth."

Holly let herself out of the limousine, swung the door shut as emphatically as she could, and strode into the hotel. What had he been thinking of? She hadn't had to struggle her way out of that sort of unwelcome rugby scrum since her teenage years. If he was going to make a move, the least he could have done was to do it properly and with some real passion. Holly wasn't sure whether she should despise or pity him and if, as he had implied, Esme had somehow put him up to it, Holly had no idea how she should feel about that.

Back in the relative security of her hotel suite, Holly tried to ring Jake, but he wasn't answering his mobile—a fairly common occurrence since he'd gone to the States. He would eventually ring her back, but Holly wanted to talk now, and what she really wanted was to be held by someone who truly cared for her and whom she cared for right back. The hotel suite, as grand as it was, felt empty and lonely. There was too much room for her thoughts.

Though she considered Merton was to blame for the evening ending badly, Holly was feeling twinges of guilt she might have led him on. If Jake had been there it would never have happened, but Jake wasn't there and even now he still wasn't available. The question was why? She needed him to call her back now, but her mobile remained silent and inert. She willed him to call, but for once, frustratingly, her wants were not immediately satisfied.

She wanted the reassurance of Jake, but at least she had other alternatives. Stretching out her witchlight, Holly transported over a very dozy Barny who, with laudable and un-catlike patience, accepted being held and cuddled long into the night before Holly managed to fall asleep. His warm, furry presence was a distinct comfort, but she would much rather have been holding Jake. She was worried that, given the recent distance between them, the trouble was going to be getting Jake to understand that, too.

Chapter 15

Having left a slightly desperate message on Jake's mobile the night before, Holly was expecting a call first thing the following morning, but it didn't come. She returned Barny safely to Basingfield Lane, checked out of the hotel, and then discreetly transported herself and her luggage home. There was still no phone call.

Holly gave up on being patient and called Jake's mobile again, but judging by the way it switched straight onto voicemail, it was almost certainly turned off. She tried again and again, but each time was the same. Finally, early afternoon, her phone rang, displaying Jake's mobile number. She snatched at the phone, clicked answer, and almost yelled into the mouthpiece.

The voice that said, "Hi. Who am I speaking to?" was not, however, Jake's. It was American and it was female.

"I'm Holly. Who are *you*?"

"Hi Holly, my name is Amy Pinkett, and I work at Scarlet Falls Memorial Hospital. Do you know a Mister Jake Wortham?"

Holly's voice when she said, "I do" sounded calm, but inside she had already been reduced to a jangling rattle bag of rusty nuts and bolts.

"No need to panic," the advice had come a lifetime of heartbeats too late. "Mister Wortham has asked me to phone you because he's not in a position to do so himself right now."

"Why? What's happened? Is he alright?" Telling Holly not to panic was never a good idea. It tended to have the opposite effect. Plus, of course, her memories of the last time she had had contact with a hospital were not reassuring. The panic had obviously found its way to her voice.

"There really is no need to panic, ma'am. Mister Wortham is basically well, but he had to go get his treatment, and they don't allow cell phones in there. He knew you'd be expecting a call, so he asked me to make the call for him on his cell. I'm sure he'll be calling you himself in an hour or so."

"Fine. Great. So please just tell me what's happened."

"A minor car accident I believe, ma'am. Nothing serious and nothing you really need to worry about. He has a minor fracture to his arm, but it's a simple break and will mend quickly, you'll see. Otherwise he seems fine. You have my word on that. He'll be calling you himself in no time at all. In the meantime, he just wanted you to know he's fine and is thinking of you."

"Erm, thanks. Thank you for calling me. It was good of you to do it. I was starting to worry."

"No problem, ma'am. Is there anything else I can do for you guys today?"

"Um. Just ask him to ring me, please. As soon as he can. And tell him I'm thinking of him, too. That's all, but please do get him to ring me."

"Sure thing. As soon as he comes to collect this phone, I'll be sure to let him know what you said."

"Thank you. Thank you very much."

"No problem. If that's all, I'm going to turn the cell off now. You take care now, ma'am, and have a nice day."

"Err, you too."

Holly heard the connection click and cross-Atlantic silence settle on the phone. She waited. She knew she shouldn't fret. She had been specifically told there was no need, but now she knew Jake had been involved in an accident, she couldn't help herself. She had to wait for nearly the full hour. It turned out to be an hour with self-lengthening tendencies.

The phone rang again. This time it was Jake himself.

"Hi Holly, it's me."

"Jake, how are you? What happened? Are you alright?"

"Whoa. One question at a time. I'm fine, but now I know what that Labrador with the busted leg felt like after I treated him the other week. I'm all over the shop with the painkillers they've given me and, if I'm honest, I'm probably still in a bit of shock from the accident itself. So be gentle with me, yeah, Prickles?"

"Sorry, I'll try to be gentle, but I took the phone call from the hospital, and I've been worried thoughtless ever since."

"No need, honest. They told you I was okay, didn't they? It's a relatively minor fracture. They've put me in plaster for safety's sake. After the accident itself, it's all a bit of an anti-climax."

"So what happened? The woman on the phone said it was a car accident."

Jake hesitated.

"Yes it was. The car was in an accident, but the thing that caused it was really weird. A mini tornado, you know, a cone of wind like they have in films, all Wizard of Oz kind of thing, suddenly appeared in front of the car I was in. It hit us head on, upended us, and spun us across the road. I couldn't believe it was happening, except it was and we were in the middle of it. Fortunately we ended right side up. I was so lucky. It really is a minor fracture. The guy I was travelling with broke both ankles, an arm, and his collarbone, and the traffic cops said it could easily have been a lot worse. They'd never seen anything like it. The state doesn't normally get those type of winds. We'll probably be on local TV."

"Oh Jake. Are you sure you're okay? Were many other cars involved?"

"No. That was another part of the strangeness. This thing appeared in front of us, shook us around, and then whirled off, fizzling out as it went. Can you imagine it?"

The trouble was Holly could. She'd made mini twisters just like that and broken them up just as quickly.

"No," she said firmly to Jake, "I can't imagine that and I don't want to. It scares me just thinking about it. All I want to imagine is you coming back home. I miss you. You do know that, right?"

Jake was momentarily silent. Holly took a deep breath and launched, "Look, I don't understand what's been going on between us recently. I don't like it. If it's all down to me then I'm sorry. I know I've been busy and rather distracted of late, but I didn't mean it to get in the way of us. I just want there to be an us, as we were, before things got strained and strange. I don't like strange, whether it's twisters or relationships. I just want us happy and normal as we were. I just want you. I want to be with you. When are you coming home?"

There was continued silence at the other end of the phone, and for an awful moment Holly thought she'd said too much of the wrong thing, but then she heard Jake sigh.

"You don't know how much I've been wanting to hear you say something like that, Prickles. Maybe it's the shock of the accident, though I don't think so, but I'm trying not to cry here. I thought you were bored with me and were choosing to occupy yourself elsewhere. I know it's been difficult with your mum and all, but...Look, I'll be on my way back as soon as I can get my flight changed. Is that alright with you?"

"Oh, yes." Now it was Holly's turn to cry.

The rest of their conversation passed in a warm blur of happy tears and heartfelt affirmations.

Once Jake had hung up, Holly waltzed an unprotesting Barny around the kitchen to a jauntily hummed Bellowhead tune, but for all her euphoria, Jake's description of the strange whirlwind had got her thinking. It could have been a natural phenomenon, but it could equally have been witch-made. She'd done subconscious magic before. Could she have inadvertently caused it because she was upset with him for not phoning? But she hadn't been that upset, surely, and anyway, any upset was because she loved him. She didn't want to harm him. She would need to find out the precise time the wind had appeared. That might give her a clue. When Jake phoned again, she'd ask him.

Almost immediately, Holly's phone rang, but this time it was the landline rather than her mobile. Holly picked up the phone more than half expecting it to be Jake, but she was disappointed. An unknown man's voice she didn't recognise said,

"Is that Holly Jepps?"

"Yes."

"Are you also known as Holly Beldam?"

Holly hesitated.

"To certain people, yes. Why are you asking?"

"Do I gather from the name change you think Esme Beldam is your mother?"

"That's an awful lot of questions from someone who hasn't introduced himself or explained why he's asking."

"Fair comment. I'm Appledore Ashwell. I tried to contact you a while back, but I had to move on quickly and am only just now in a position to phone you again. As for the questions, the reason I'm asking them is because if Esme Beldam's your mother, there's a fair chance I'm your father. I'd like to meet you to see if that's so."

"Oh." Holly didn't really know what else to say, but settled on, "Were you ever known as 'Cox'?"

"No. Why are you asking?"

"Because I've been told that's the name of my biological father."

"Well it's not a name I've ever used, but if Esme is your mother, I still think there's a real chance that I'm your father. Shouldn't we at least meet up to talk about it?"

"I guess so."

There was hesitation in Holly's voice.

"You can bring Partridge Mayflower along, if you'd feel happier."

That decided Holly.

"No, there's no need. I'm a grown woman. I can meet you without him."

"Fine. The sooner we can meet, the happier I'll feel. I don't suppose you could manage today?"

"I can, actually. I've got the day off work."

"Great. How about London? Do you know the pagoda in Kew Gardens?"

"Yes, I used to go there as a kid with my mum—my adopted mum, that is."

"Ace. See you there in ten to fifteen minutes?"

"I'll be there in ten. See you then."

The pagoda rose tall, dark, and red from amongst the black winter trees that surrounded it. Holly was early and sensed, rather than saw,

Appledore Ashwell's arrival up until the point when a short, brown-haired man emerged from a secluded area and marched across the grass towards her. He seemed to be in his early fifties, but Holly had given up trying to work out the age of anyone in the witching community from their physical appearance.

"Holly Beldam?"

"Yes, Mister, er, Brother Ashwell?"

"Yes, but call me Apple—most people do." He smiled. "Can we walk? I don't like stopping in any one place for too long. It doesn't seem to be good for my health." Holly must have looked quizzical because he then said, "I'll explain, but let's get walking first."

They struck away from the Pagoda across the grass.

"I'm sure you must have hundreds of questions; so have I. Though now I've seen you and can see how much you look like Esme, my questions have all become much simpler. Bear with me for a little while longer and let me talk at you for a bit."

Holly resigned herself to being unnaturally patient, while reflecting on what he had already said, specifically about her physical similarity to Esme. She couldn't see it. Ironically, she could see potential connections with Apple: the lack of height, both with medium brown hair and hazel eyes. Apple Ashwell had chosen to age more than Esme. Perhaps Esme had made more adjustments than just rolling back time?

Apple was still talking, so Holly tried to concentrate on what he was telling her.

"Esme and I used to meet here when we were together. I remember Kew fondly plus, of course, it combines public space and people with open space and privacy. That's a good combination for me. Perhaps I'd better explain that bit, first. It may help you to understand why I'm such a difficult fellow to get hold of."

Holly nodded encouragement.

"I guess Esme and I started it, in some ways. We had to be secretive because of her mother. The old crone, though I admit you wouldn't have known it to look at her, hated Esme forming any kind of attachment, let alone one with the opposite sex. We learned to be very discreet about things, but I'll save all that for later. I thought we were very much in love, you see. When she disappeared, I didn't know what to think. I guess I had lots of wild thoughts, none of which I could prove and I stayed on my guard against, I don't really know what, for quite some time. When I finally let down my guard I overcompensated, got reckless, and got into bad habits and even worse company. Eventually I settled down, got over Esme, sort of, but I guess some damage had been done. It just took a while to catch up with me. A year or so ago I found myself a sitting target for somebody or bodies. I still don't really know who. There are a number of potential candidates from my past. Let's just say that after losing Esme I was careless about what I did and with whom. Life didn't seem to be so important then. These days it does." He smiled.

"Anyway, I wasn't prepared to sit still and wait for the end to come to me. I took to the hills, literally for a while, and then I made sure I kept moving—stayed below the witchcraft radar. That's why I only communicate by mundane means. I don't mean to sound overly dramatic, but my primary goal has been to stay alive. I ignored you first up when you and Mayflower tried to contact me, but then, when I started to hear things that potentially linked you to Esme, I decided life had to be about more than just running and I tried to contact you. I'm still ducking and diving, nothing's resolved there, but I knew I had to find a way to meet you to see if the rumours were true. Maybe I'm hoping that some elements of my past can finally be resolved before it's too late.

"Hey, look at me talking ten to the dozen and not letting you get a word in edgeways. I haven't even really told you any detail about Esme and me yet."

He grinned ruefully. It was a warm grin—affectionate, self-deprecating, somehow familiar. Based on that smile, Holly felt she could trust him, but what he had said made so little sense to her, that she didn't know if it was wise of her to feel that way.

"But, I don't understand. I know Esme went missing for a while, sort of, but it's really her mother who did the full-blown disappearing act. Esme's been living in Ninanna's cottage for ages. You could have seen her at any time. You could see her now, if you really wanted to; you've managed to catch up with me."

"Yes, I've finally met with you, but look how long it's taken me. As for Esme…at the time I didn't know if she had disappeared because she'd wanted to, because of me. I didn't even know if she was still pregnant or, later, if the baby had survived. Because I didn't know, I didn't look, or at least, not for as long as maybe I should have. I thought she was gone and I'd lost her. Then a couple of years ago I met someone we both knew, back then. We got chatting. He had memories of Esme after she had left me, and he recalled her being heavily pregnant. That opened old wounds, but also got me thinking again. I even went to the Coven to ask about witchlight births, but there was nothing linking a child to Esme or even any suitable infants without named parents. Despite their ponderous systems, the Coven was no help. They didn't even mention that Esme was back. So, there was nothing positive to hang on to, but I think someone must have seen me there.

"I'd had one or two nasty 'accidents,' warnings if you like, before my Coven visit, but afterwards the 'accidents' became less accidental and more open in their aggression. They were more focussed, as if the perpetrator knew precisely where I was. Before long, they were open attacks. I couldn't afford to follow up my visit to the Coven with any further research and, as much as it hurt, I gave up looking for Esme's and my possible child. Then, I started to pick up on the gossip about you and your recently discovered witchlight, including the sheer power with which you passed your DEF. Esme's witchlight was always incredibly strong, like a throwback to the old times. You appeared to have the same sort of power, but had had an abnormally late illumination and apparently hadn't known about your witchlight until recently. That would have fitted with being abandoned or adopted into mortal society. Also, you had been trying to see me. That's when I first tried to make contact. I failed, but then I heard more news. You had apparently met up with Esme and had taken her name and bloodline. That decided it. I had to find a way to meet up with you."

"Yes, but I still don't understand why you didn't just contact Esme herself. If I'm your and her daughter she'd have told you, wouldn't she? She still could, come to that."

"She hasn't told you, has she?"

"She told me a different story."

"Such as?"

"Look, I like you, Apple. You seem open and friendly, but seeming and being aren't always one and the same, particularly, it appears, in eldritch circles. Your version of events doesn't match Esme's. You claim to have loved and lost her, to have missed her, but you won't even go to see her when you can. It doesn't make sense to me. On top of this, you want me to believe you are on the run from a person or persons unknown. If it's as bad as you say and you have to be on the move all the time, isn't there a possibility you might be putting me at risk by meeting up like this? You imply you feel some sort of primal need to connect because I am your daughter, but yet you are prepared to jeopardise my safety? You've told me stuff, but you are also keen to ask lots of questions before you have offered up all the answers from your side. I am starting to ask myself if I'm inadvertently risking anything by answering you. I like you Apple, but it comes down to whether I can trust you, too?"

"You trust Esme?"

"Ye-es."

"You don't seem convinced."

"I trust Esme to be Esme which, as you must know, is rather distant, formal and…calculating. She likes to have her own way and can be…difficult…if she feels she's not getting it. She can also be a bit…underhand in getting what she wants, but at least I know that."

"That description sounds more like Ninanna than Esme. I guess women do become like their mothers as they grow older."

"You'd have known if you'd met her. Plus, how sexist is that, anyway?"

"Possibly quite a bit, but I know I've become more like my father as I've got older. So it cuts both ways."

"But the point is…"

Whatever else Holly was about to say was drowned out by a sudden gust of wind, which turned almost instantly into a steadily increasing roar. Twigs and dead leaves lying sedately on the grass started to jig around, then jive, and then take to the air. Whorls of natural debris were swiftly forming and reforming. Appledore Ashwell was clearly alarmed. He yelled at Holly over the crescendo of wind.

"Something's wrong. Go. Transport yourself somewhere, but don't go straight home. It's happening again. Go. Go now." And with that, he vanished, transporting himself elsewhere and leaving Holly alone and uncertain as the wind continued to increase in velocity, whirling leaves, sticks, larger chunks of wood and stones into a localised cyclone, a small but growing cone of abrasive air and debris. Larger and larger items were getting sucked into it. Their potential for a grinding impact on flesh and bone did not bear thinking about for long.

Holly needed no further prompting and transported herself out of Kew Gardens and to the first place that came into her head and wasn't home.

Chapter 16

The lounge was warmly golden with afternoon sunlight. Dust sparkles hung lazily on the still air and above the well cared for, but somewhat dated, furniture. There wasn't a single draught in the room, let alone a wind. Holly stood motionless in her parents' house in Croydon. She was listening for something, anything, but the house was still and silent. Holly breathed deeply. All seemed well, and her instinct was to head straight back home. With her father over in Canada, there was no point hanging around an empty house. Appledore's shouted warning not to go straight home, however, was still echoing around her head. So, instead of the flat, open, wind-blown fields of Cambridgeshire, she took herself to the enclosed spaces of the ladies toilets at St. Pancras. Having emerged from their murky depths, she walked vacantly around the station for a bit, peered into one or two shops, and then transported herself in rapid succession from the station back to the house in Croydon, to Jake's empty home, and then to the field behind her own house. From there she walked briskly across the grass, levitated over her garden fence, walked through her immaculate winter garden, and let herself into the house via the back door. She locked the door behind her. It made her feel safer, though she recognised the stupidity of thinking that a locked wooden door could keep out the magic that had been deployed in Kew Gardens. Nor would it be able to keep it in, come to that.

Holly knew she had a good deal to think about and a fair bit to absorb. She'd had more than enough unanticipated drama for one day. She walked round the kitchen table to fill the kettle for a much-needed cup of tea with which to aid her thought processes and almost fell over a bedraggled mound of fur she barely recognised as Barny. He was crouched half under and half out from the table. His fur was matted and blood stained, and his eyes had the glazed, all the internal blinds have come down, look that traumatised cats develop. Worryingly, he let her scoop him up without the slightest complaint, which is when she saw the deep gauges running through the flesh on his left side and flank and the dark, dried blood thickly clogged in his fur. Without a second's hesitation, she transported herself and Barny to their customary vets, where a surprised receptionist looked up to find a fraught woman carrying a badly injured cat, where only seconds before she could have sworn there'd been an empty waiting area.

The vet was swift and efficient and said it looked as if Barny had been mauled and shaken by a large dog, although the scratches along his side more closely resembled those caused by a very, very big cat. In any event, Barny needed to stay at the vet's for emergency treatment and round the clock observation, and Holly returned home to the third deserted house she had visited in just under two hours. This time she didn't bother to fill the kettle, but just pulled a freshly made and very strong cup of tea from out of the air in front of her and sat down heavily on the nearest kitchen chair. She now had almost too much to think about, let alone absorb.

Where to start? That in itself presented a problem. Merton and his issues seemed paltry in comparison to later events, although Holly still wanted to know, eventually, what Esme's involvement in the Merton fiasco had, or had not, been. First things first though, tornadoes in the States and then suddenly in Kew Gardens were matters to be considered carefully and from all angles. So, too, were attacks made against Jake and a man claiming to be her biological father. Then there was poor Barny and the fundamental issue of whether he would survive the next twenty-four hours. She didn't really want to go there. There was also the underlying question of whether what had attacked him was linked to the other attacks, or was no more than heart-rending, but random, evidence of nature red in tooth and claw. This last question was beyond Holly. In truth, as she sat at the kitchen table with a cup of cooling tea in her hand

and the same blinds-down look in her eyes that had recently been in Barny's, right now, everything was beyond her.

Three cups of cold, undrunk tea later, she was little better. She had, however, looked at things from every likely angle she could think of, and there was only one obvious link between all three incidents: herself.

It was possible whoever was after Appledore had come after her too, but got Barny instead, but that wouldn't explain Jake's twister, which had happened well before Appledore had even contacted her. If, on the other hand, someone was trying to get at Holly via the people and things she loved, ignoring the fact she could think of no one who might want to do such an appalling thing and no reason for them to do so, that would explain Jake and Barny, but not Appledore; despite their alleged relationship, she hardly knew him, let alone cared for him. There was only one clear link to all three of them and it was a link she knew could create and manipulate winds and who was capable of subconscious magic she didn't know she was doing. That link, of course, was her. She had been upset with Jake prior to the cyclone when he hadn't returned her calls and because he wasn't there when she needed him. She was annoyed with Appledore for spinning her a cock and bull story about himself and Esme that didn't make sense when she had needed it to, but Barny—she hadn't been annoyed with Barny. She loved him. He was her boy, and she'd had him since a kitten. He was loving, responsive, and a sweet, uncomplicated comfort to her. The last thing she wanted was for any harm to come to him, but then, despite her temporary annoyance with Jake, didn't she really feel that way about him too, or had her then fears for the future of their relationship got the better of her? Even then, though, she was fearful because she was scared of losing him. She didn't want to harm him. So how could she be responsible for any of the attacks? Yet the one, obvious link sat there staring back at her whenever she happened to glance at a shiny, reflective surface. The kitchen had a lot of shiny, reflective surfaces.

Another thought struck Holly—what about Appledore himself? She only had his word for the fact he was being hunted. He could have caused the Kew whirlwind himself, could have caused the twister that went after Jake (his call had come surprisingly close to Jake's phone call to her). Indeed, thinking about it, it had been Ashwell who had told her not to go straight home. Her jaunting around Croydon and St. Pancras would have given him the time to come to her house. He might have been searching for something, and Barny had simply got in the way. His story didn't match Esme's, and Holly hadn't been entirely happy with all his questions when she felt she should have been questioning him, so perhaps Appledore Ashwell was the link to all the incidents, but why? The more questions Holly asked herself, the more questions there seemed to need answering. She reached for her fourth cup of tea.

In summary and a fifth cup of tea, which she actually drank, later, Holly decided a significant unknown was Appledore Ashwell and any connection he genuinely had to her and Esme. A sensible way forward, therefore, might be for her to investigate Ashwell's story in greater detail than he had chosen to provide. The next issue was how she might go about doing just that. Ashwell's file in the Coven records had been unhelpfully empty, which was suspicious in itself, so there was little point in looking for further information there. Holly didn't want to approach Esme at this stage because of the contradictions between her and Ashwell's versions of events. Partridge apparently didn't know any more about Appledore Ashwell than Holly did and, anyway, they were no longer talking, and the thought of that set another hare off running for its life: Partridge's parting shot the last time they'd met. Could it have been a threat that he and the Coven were now following through? Getting at her through those she had connections to? It was a chilling thought. In her gut, Holly didn't believe it could be Partridge, but she knew she couldn't be certain, not totally. She really needed to talk to someone about all these possibilities, or at least get hold of some more facts to contribute to her deliberations. It was at this point Holly realised, not for the first time, that she had precious few contacts in the witching fraternity. In fact, the number of witches she knew could be counted on the fingers of one hand: Partridge, Esme, Appledore, and Merton. The last name made her pause.

She didn't particularly like Merton, but she figured he owed her after the fiasco in the back of the limousine. More importantly, he had claimed they were distantly related, and he obviously knew something about Esme and Ninanna. Perhaps he, or one of his family might know something about Esme and any possible candidates for the role of her biological father, including Appledore Ashwell. It was worth a try. Which was the reason why, three and a half hours and a rather strained conversation with Merton later, she found herself sitting in a grand, somewhat overheated and stuffy, Victorian-styled lounge with Sister Abigail Holmfirth, Merton's aunt on his mother's side. The old lady was, much to Holly's discomfort, in the process of pouring out two cups of tea. At the same time, she was explaining why she chose to look like a wrinkled old dear of about ninety.

"At my age and with the knowledge that Brother Death could be knocking on my front door anytime now, it seems pointless to try to look like a young gel like yourself, but…well, I still have some vanity, and ninety was a good age, as I recall. This way, I get to look younger than I am without having to maintain the sham of youthful enthusiasm."

"How old are you, if you don't mind me asking?"

"I don't mind, dear. I'm quite proud of the fact that my next birthday will be my one hundred and fortieth. It's a pretty impressive innings, though I know a couple of old battlers who've played the game for a few years longer."

Holly stared at Abigail Holmfirth in amazement. She knew Partridge was old and had told her you could extend life even further via witchlight. Esme had even explained the basics to her, but to meet someone who had actually done it for so long a period was something else entirely. She responded with the usual trite phrases that are habitually offered to the very elderly.

"Gosh, that *is* a good age. You must have seen a lot of changes in your time?"

"Oh yes, dear. You'd be surprised. When I was a gel, one aspired to have a little cottage for just you and the cat." She gestured in the direction of a sleek British Blue curled up asleep on a black velvet cushion. "These days one is expected to display one's illumination with wealth and ostentation. I don't really need a house this big, but the family insist I make the effort. Still, there was something to be said for the old times. They were less showy, but the power you had meant more. As a witch, you could do what others couldn't, but now ordinary people light up their houses at a flick of a switch and fly through the air to other countries. You get realistic moving coloured images in a box in your parlour, and people can see and talk to others instantly half the world away. Witchcraft isn't as special as it was. The mundane world's even learning to postpone the ravages of time, although that's one thing that magic can still do better, I feel." She patted her thin hair coquettishly and laughed, although to Holly's ears it sounded disconcertingly like a cackle. Perhaps there was a good reason why witches avoided looking old.

"Anyway, dear, enough of my mental meanderings. Young Merton said you were looking into your family history?"

"Ah, yes. I've, um, been illuminated rather late in life, having been adopted, and though my mother's told me a little about things, I wanted to play catch up, as it were, and get a broader picture of the family."

"Merton said you are Esme Beldam's gel. Quite a turn up for the books, though I'd have known from just looking at you—absolute spitting image, two peas from old Ninanna's pod. Still, you may not be a baby anymore, but I wouldn't say it is late in your life. Still time to have a few witchlings of your own, eh?" Abigail definitely cackled this time.

"I guess so, but I'm not exactly youthful in that department, either."

"Oh it's amazing what magic can do for you. Hecate only knows how old your grandmother was when she finally got around to producing Esme. Never did know who the father was, either. Ninanna had a touch of the black widow about her."

"So what else can you tell me about Esme and Ninanna?"

"About Ninanna? Not a great deal. Kept herself to herself did that one. She'd occasionally put in an appearance at the welcoming ceremony of a newborn, but that was about it. Some said she was broody, but she took her time producing Esme, so I doubt it."

"What about her disappearance?"

"What about it? It wasn't anything unusual. She came and went quite often, sometimes for years. This time's been the longest, though. Must be coming up for almost forty years. She was rumoured to be older than I am now before she went. So, I guess she'll have gone for good now, even with her old knowledge."

"Older than you are now?"

"Oh yes, though no one knew for certain. She was only very distantly related, though those who hanker after the old knowledge like to suggest a closer lineage. No parents living either, or other close relatives that I knew of. But, she'd been around the peripheries of things for a long time. So, yes, an oldie like me, though she kept herself youthful, didn't choose to run to seed and stone like I have." More cackling.

"And Esme? What can you tell me about her?"

"Poor little lass. It can't have been a happy childhood. Ninanna kept her close. I doubt she had any friends. She wasn't even allowed to play with the family children when her mother deigned to make a visit. I'm sure Merton must have said. He tried to make friends once, and Ninanna drove him away with a flash of witchlight. So amazingly rude and quite unnecessary when it's witchlings."

"So, Merton is roughly the same age as Esme?"

"Close. I think he might be a decade or so older, but he tried to involve the poor little thing and got yelled at and worse for his pains."

"What about boyfriends?"

"Ninanna never bothered about gentlemen callers and after Esme, I doubt there was a need."

"No, I meant Esme."

"Oh, I shouldn't think Ninanna permitted them. If she didn't allow little play friends, she'd not be tolerant of more intimate ones."

"Merton said there was a rift between Esme and Ninanna just before they both disappeared. Could that have been over a boyfriend?"

"Not that I ever heard. Esme apparently only went away for a year or so, you know, so I don't count that as a proper disappearance. People confuse her with Ninanna, but she turned up again shortly after Ninanna went her way. Now, forty years gone, that's a genuine disappearing act, but at her age I'll doubt she'll be back. Did I tell you she was already older than I am now when she went off?"

"Yes, you did mention that."

"Oh good. I forget so much these days. I need a little memory jog from time to time. I have a few photos. Would you like to see them?"

"Yes, please."

Abigail stretched out both her hands in front of her, and a heavy stack of photograph albums suddenly appeared in them. For a minute, Holly thought she was going to drop the lot, but Abigail was obviously less frail than she looked.

"Here you are, dear. You have a little browse through these while I go off to make myself comfortable. Advanced age weakens the bladder, you know. Did I tell you that I'm one hundred and forty next birthday?"

"Yes, you did mention that."

"Oh good. I'm quite proud of the fact, you see."

"Yes. So you said."

"Did I?" A slightly confused look crossed Abigail's heavily lined face, making it seem momentarily blank. "I'm probably getting a little tired. I don't have that many visitors these days. Anyway, must pop off. Amuse yourself with the photographs whilst I am gone." And with that, Abigail disappeared. Holly breathed a quiet sigh of relief and turned her attention to the photo albums.

Not surprisingly, some of the albums were extremely old, although others seemed to belong to more recent lifetimes. Right on the top of the pile was an electronic photo frame displaying a small selection of recent baby photographs in rotation. Abigail had apparently succumbed to some recent mundane innovations, even if the frame's power source was a little more eldritch, judging from the plug hanging down unattached to an electrical socket. Holly started with the oldest looking albums.

There were a few stiffly posed, early photographs of an attractive young woman who, in bone structure and appearance, resembled Abigail and whom Holly guessed had to be her. There were a greater number of later, slightly less formal photographs of the same young woman who time seemed to have passed by. Later still, there were an increasing number of snapshots featuring the same young woman and a random cast of others, who were presumably family and friends. It was noticeable that many of these individuals also appeared untroubled by the ageing process to any serious degree. Holly noticed Merton in a number of these snaps, maintaining the appearance of being in his twenties during the nineteen fifties, sixties, seventies, eighties, and nineties. Only the fashions and hairstyles changed. There were a number of photographs of large groups of well-dressed people, presumably taken at formal gatherings like weddings or newborn welcomings. It was one of these photographs that seriously confused Holly when she came across it. To the left-hand side and to the front of a large group of people was her nine- or ten-year-old self. Standing directly behind her, with one lightly be-ringed hand gripping her right shoulder and looking much as she looked now, albeit wearing nineteen fifties' style clothing and with apparently slightly blonder hair (though with a black and white photograph it was difficult to tell) was Esme. This was clearly impossible, but it was what the picture showed. She was still trying to make sense of it when Abigail reappeared.

"I see you've found a photograph of your mother. It would have been taken at the welcoming for one of my sister's younger children, or possibly one of her few grandchildren. Amy was surprisingly fertile for a witch. Comes of having a mortal husband, I suppose. The rest of the family line is largely childless, that's for sure. Such a shame."

"I was trying to make sense of the photograph—work out how it was taken and when."

Abigail looked confused.

"With a normal mundane camera, I expect. There's no point in using magic if mundane means can achieve the same goal as easily. As for when, mid-fifties I would guess, though it could be a bit earlier." She pointed at two very young children to the right of the child that looked so like Holly. "They look like Emma and Nathanial, who I think were born in the early fifties."

"What about me?"

"You dear? I doubt you would have been born then, would you? No, you can't have been. See. Here's Esme and she's far too young to have had you yet." Abigail was pointing at the child who looked so much like Holly did at that age.

"That's Esme?"

"Well yes, of course. Who did you think it was?"

"So, who's that?" Holly pointed at the woman who looked so much like Esme did now.

"That's your grandmother, Ninanna Beldam. See the Beldam family ring on her hand? A rare sighting. She hated having her photograph taken and was invariably suddenly absent at the crucial time. Something must have distracted her."

Holly herself was now distracted by the photograph. She let Abigail chat happily away while she stared at the images of Esme and Ninanna. Did her family always grow up to look like their mothers, or was there something else going on? Esme obviously manipulated her appearance to maintain her youthful looks. Had she also manipulated them to make herself look more like her mother? Holly was so perplexed by this she almost didn't pay attention to the two snapshots that Abigail was now pointing out to her. They were of an open-air party, which had taken place sometime in the sixties, judging from the clothes. Abigail was there, as was Merton, looking just as he had looked the other week, although his hair was somewhat longer in the photograph. There was no sign of Ninanna-Esme, but an older looking Esme-Holly was there, and she seemed to be enjoying herself if the broad smile on her face was any indication.

The second photograph was of the same event, but taken from a slightly different angle. Holly glanced quickly at it, then noticed the profile of a short young man standing less than two feet away from Esme. Age him twenty or thirty years, put a bit more flesh on the face and a few specks of grey in the hair, and it could be Appledore Ashwell.

"Who's that?" Holly pointed at the potential Appledore Ashwell figure.

"Sorry, but I can't help you, dear. He looks familiar, but I can't put a name to him."

"Appledore Ashwell, perhaps?"

"Well, that name is familiar too, but I can't visualise its owner, I'm afraid."

Holly tried very hard not to let her frustration show.

"Is there anything you can tell me about him? Any fact or snippet, however small, from the party?"

Abigail seemed very doubtful, but screwed up her eyes to peer more closely at the image.

"No, I really have no idea who that young man is, but I do have a feeling he was as young as he looked, so perhaps you could ask Merton about him. He was closer to the young'uns back then." Abigail rubbed her eyes. "Is there anything else, dear?"

By now, Abigail was clearly becoming tired and starting to look every one of her displayed ninety years. Indeed, Holly was beginning to see telltale signs of even greater age weighing her down. Holly thanked her profusely and genuinely for a very informative time, made her excuses, and left. Clutched in her left hand were hastily and magically created copies of the three photographs of Esme, including those with Ninanna and the possible Appledore Ashwell. Other than a whole new set of questions, they were amongst the few concrete things Holly had gained from the visit.

Chapter 17

It was setting itself up to be a good day. Barny was back from the vets, sore and very sorry for himself, but basically on the mend, and Jake was coming back from the States. Holly had spoken to her father in Canada, and he had sounded happier than he had done in weeks. The change of country and associated environment was doing him good.

Jake's plane wasn't due back until late afternoon, which gave Holly plenty of time to have a chat with Merton Holmfirth about past times. She wasn't convinced it was a chat that either of them was particularly going to enjoy, but if she was going to find out any more about the photographs she had seen at Abigail Holmfirth's, it was a chat they were going to have.

Merton was taking his ease in his large and expensively furnished City office when Holly popped in. She had decided it would be simpler to adopt a direct approach and arrive without bothering Merton's PA, or indeed any of the building's staff, including the doorman. Merton did not seem unduly surprised by Holly's unannounced arrival in a puff of faintly lavender air. He simply swung his chair away from the panoramic view of the City he had been gazing at through the spotless plate glass window of his twenty-fifth floor office suite and turned his sky blue eyes to Holly.

"Sister Beldam, good morning to you. You should have let me know you were planning on dropping in."

"What can I say, Brother Holmfirth? I have a tendency towards spontaneity. If it's any consolation, I'm not planning on a prolonged stay. I just need you to tell me about these."

Holly placed the two photographs of Esme at the outdoor party on the empty, richly French Polished desktop in front of Merton.

"It was a long time ago. They are old photographs."

"And you so youthful. Do feel free to try past life regression if it'll help. Bottom line though, I need to know when, where, and who."

Merton shrugged.

"Summer 1968, Ashwell House in the Scottish lowlands, and the cast included me, Aunt Abigail, Ash Greyweather, Landel Hawthorn, Esme Beldam, and Hazel Winthrop. There were others present—it was quite a sizeable gathering—but they're not in this photograph, though I think that's Apple Ashwell in this one."

"You've a remarkable memory for someone who wasn't even born then. I'm impressed you have remembered all the names."

"Leaving aside the issue of my miraculous pre-birth presence, it was quite a memorable house party for a select group of the illuminated. Even your grandmother put in a token appearance. It was easy to get to know everyone, which was, I think, the intention."

"So, you knew Esme pretty well?"

"Perhaps I should have said, nearly everyone."

"Why not Esme?"

"She wasn't exactly a party animal."

"She seems to be having a good time in this photograph."

"Sister Ninanna had left by then. While she was around, Esme's behaviour was somewhat circumscribed. Once she had left, it was a different story."

"You didn't get to know Esme better then?"

"No, despite Sister Ninanna's wishes. Esme was focussed on getting to know someone else better."

"Sister Ninanna's wishes?"

Merton had the grace to look embarrassed.

"Sister Ninanna was kind enough to indicate she considered me a good match for Esme, despite my family's, erm, difficulties in producing heirs."

"'Indicate,' as Esme more recently did for me?"

"There are similarities, yes."

"Did you try to play tonsil hockey with Esme, too?"

"No."

"Are you sure? Because your seduction techniques do leave something to be desired, you know, and that may be why she was feigning interest in someone else."

"I did not get as far with Sister Esme as I did with you. She wasn't interested in me at all. She'd already set her sights on someone else at the party."

"Who?"

"I'm sure I couldn't say."

"Do you have any idea?"

"Not for sure, no. There were two or three contenders, but nothing definite that I could see."

"So, who were the possibles?"

"Landel Hawthorn for one, Apple Ashwell, and some other guy who's not in the snapshots."

"Name?"

"I'm thinking."

"Well, think harder."

"Corey, Hoxton Corey."

"Hoxton? You're sure it was Hoxton, not Coxton or Cox?"

"I'm sure it was Hoxton. I don't know anyone called Cox, or Coxton for that matter."

"What else can you tell me?"

"What else do you want to know? I've answered the questions that were on your bottom line."

"What happened at the party?"

"It was a good party. I had fun. I don't need one of you Beldam girls to have a good time. I'm not exactly a small man, you know. There are plenty of ladies and more than a few beefcake-flavoured hunks who find me attractive for my own not-inconsiderable attributes."

"Provided, presumably, they're not in the back of a limo with you. So, what did you think when Esme pimped me out to you exactly the same way her mother did to her forty years ago? Have you no shame?"

"Not when it comes to witchlight as pure and powerful as the Beldam rays. In that case, I am totally shameless and postpone any embarrassment until later. Sister Esme rang to suggest I might escort you for the evening and, at the time, I felt nothing but honoured. It's possible she thought she'd missed out, you know. Now, if I've answered all your questions sufficiently, I'd like to spend some time indulging my delayed embarrassment on my own, if that's alright with you?

"Hang on to your embarrassment for just a little while longer, can you? Tell me about Apple Ashwell. What's he like? When did you last see him?"

"I haven't seen Apple for ages. We were never exactly close. We had a social connection, but then he seemed to go off the rails for a bit, and we lost contact. God knows where he is now."

"So what was he like back then?"

"Nice enough chap, seemed solid, but it's rumoured he got involved in some decidedly dodgy stuff after he lost it—the sort of stuff you don't want to talk about too much, you know?"

"Actually, I don't."

"Time you learned, then. Now are you going to go? Please." Merton fell silent with a rising tone to his voice that indicated he wouldn't be saying anything else.

Holly felt she had got all the information she was going to and, indeed, in some instances, rather more than she wanted and was more than happy to get back to Barny. She left Merton Holmfirth in peace and went home to prepare for Jake.

Barny was safely curled up asleep in the kitchen when she arrived back. Since his return from the vet's, Holly had made sure that Barny in particular, and the whole of the house in general, were covered by a strong Old Magic warding spell. Nothing magical, other than Holly herself, should be able to penetrate it, and if anything did, including anything emanating from Holly, Holly would know immediately. She still wasn't totally sure if all the security was necessary, somehow it all seemed so unreal, but she wasn't taking any chances—not with Barny and especially not with Jake. Barny was also draped in his own personal protection spells, and Holly intended to do the same for Jake just as soon as he walked through the front door or, she reconsidered, as soon as she met him at the airport in just over an hour's time, which seemed so much the better idea she was surprised she hadn't thought of it before.

While she waited for the hour to pass, she spring cleaned the house in honour of Jake's return. She also ensured it was full of flowers, regardless of season. As that took under two minutes, she wiled away the remaining time by making a huge fuss of Barny and scrutinizing, yet again, the three photographs she had replicated from Abigail's albums. Staring at them unblinkingly for ages didn't make things any clearer, however. The photographs couldn't tell her how the solemn-looking Esme, in the grip of her mother in the first photo, became the laughing young woman in the second photograph or the unbending and acerbic woman of today—a woman who now bore more than a little resemblance to her apparently stern and unbending mother. Things had come full circle. The photo couldn't tell her if Apple Ashwell was on the point of having an affair with her mother, had already embraced just such a relationship, or was merely fantasizing about it while Esme had been, or was about to be, swept off her feet by a man called Cox. Other than the completion of inexorable circles, there was nothing to explain to Holly why she still hadn't formed a proper child/parent bond with the current Esme and why, despite looking so much like the earlier Esme, she now felt isolated from the older one. Was the relationship between Ninanna and Esme the key to it all—the firm, well-manicured, and be-ringed hand clamped uncompromisingly on the child's shoulder preventing her from engaging with people, both then and now? There was no sign of love or even affection in that grip. How can you pass on love if you've never known it?

Holly realised she could spend pointless hours staring at the photographs and decided to give up before any more time passed. Instead, she used the remaining minutes more constructively to make herself fresh and presentable the old-fashioned way, by using water and a hair brush and simply adding a finishing touch of witchlight before transporting herself down to Heathrow, where she was waiting at the arrivals gate when Jake emerged bruised and with his arm in a sling, but otherwise remarkably well considering his run-in with the twister.

She managed to throw herself into Jake's one good arm without any damage to the one in a plaster cast and kissed him vigorously. She was delighted to note he kissed her back with equal passion, as were the rest of the disembarking passengers who rewarded the heated public display with an appreciative round of applause.

Untangling herself from Jake, she admonished him for carrying too many bags and proceeded to take change of them. She ignored his protestations that he still had one perfectly good arm and was a good deal taller and stronger than her. She similarly ignored any guilt on his part that such a small woman should have to struggle with so many heavy bags without, of course, telling him that, having decided, willed, and directed, as far as she was concerned, his bags collectively weighed no more than her handbag. It was no bad thing for him to think he owed her. She also insisted on driving them both back up to Cambridgeshire in his car.

It was a good journey. Alone together in the car, they talked as they hadn't done for months and as they used to do before things became awkward. Having said that, the drive couldn't finish too soon for either of them. They both wanted to get the other home as soon as possible to rip their clothes off.

As soon as they were through Holly's front door, Jake grabbed hold of Holly with his one good arm and kissed her deeply. She kissed him back, long and hard and unhesitatingly.

"I love you. I've missed you. I want you," she said as she unbuttoned and peeled off Jake's shirt for him.

If the removal of clothing was somewhat impeded by the sling and plaster cast, neither really noticed. A trail of clothes from the front door to the bedroom was swiftly abandoned, giving Barny plenty to sniff, pat, and play with and eventually curl up and go to sleep on.

In the bedroom, both were already naked. Holly had a few delicious moments to remember the positive effect of veterinary work on Jake's physique before they were both sprawled across the bed. Then she didn't need to remember that his hands were firm and strong and not just his hands, come to that.

Holly felt Jake's familiar weight pressing down on her, his mouth pressing hotly against hers. Their lovemaking was fierce and desperate. Holly lost herself to the moment, letting go of all control. It felt as if they were one body, one mind, rising higher and higher on the pounding wings of passion and then plunging fast and deep into the dark, wet satisfaction of lust until it swallowed them whole.

As Barny slept soundly, curled up in the hallway on Holly's best blouse, and Holly and Jake lay wrapped around one another on a love-crumpled bed, all three were unaware of a large and solitary ginger cat curled up under a bush in the field behind the house, his eyes unblinkingly fixed on Holly's back door. Similarly, they were happily oblivious to the tail end item on the television news that night, where the incident scene reporter was given to wonder what would make a young and highly successful City broker hurl himself through his office plate glass windows with such force that his body flew up and then horizontally away from the building, out into the chill, blue, winter sky, before plunging straight down onto the pavement several hundred feet below. The broker himself was no longer in a position to answer that question. The dark, wet impact of his fall had already grown cold and congealed.

Chapter 18

Jake and Holly were lying side by side in bed. Holly was looking worriedly at Jake. Jake was just looking extremely bemused. The morning cup of tea that Holly had recently produced for him was growing cold on the bedside table while he watched a small circle of iridescent hummingbirds flutter around the bedroom ceiling light.

"So, this is all real?"

"Uh huh."

"Absolutely, don't punch me because I'm not dreaming and it will hurt, sort of real?"

"Yes."

"Do something else."

The hummingbirds disappeared, and three goldfish in three water-filled glass bowls gingerly circled the light fitting in their stead.

"Do something else that can only be done by magic."

"You normally see goldfish and their bowls floating widdershins around your lampshades, do you? Right you are. Something else. You choose this time, or you won't accept it."

"Like what?"

"You choose. That's the point."

"I wouldn't know where to start."

Holly thought. "What super power have you always secretly wished you could have? As a little boy did you want to be invisible, have x-ray vision, fly, walk through walls, or..."

"Fly. I always wanted to fly. Sometimes I'd dream I actually could."

"Well, let me see if I can make your dreams come true. Get out of bed or at least lie on top of the covers."

"I'll get cold."

"Wimp." But, Jake was suddenly wearing a thick, warm, towelling dressing gown he hadn't previously known he'd owned. He lay down on top of the bed and for reasons best known to him, shut his eyes.

"Okay, I'm prepared. Whenever you're ready."

"Too late."

"What?"

Jake opened his eyes and found himself staring close up at the ceiling. He tentatively turned his head and looked down at Holly, who was still lying in the bed.

"How do I move?"

"Slowly and carefully, because this is rather a small bedroom. Try kicking off gently, as if you are floating in water."

Jake obliged and floated, a little too fast for Holly's liking, across the room.

"And how do I get back down?"

"As if you are diving down under water."

Jake was back on the bed beside Holly and with only a little bit of a bump.

"Wow! Can I do that again?"

Holly sat propped up in bed drinking a fresh cup of coffee while Jake floated around the bedroom. He had already been up and down the landing six times, much to Barny's entertainment, and was now contentedly floating with a broad grin on his face. Just like a six-year-old, thought Holly, a big, gorgeous, grown-up six year old.

It had been important to Holly that, as part of their rediscovered closeness, Jake should be aware of what she was. She had decided to come out to him that morning, as soon as they had woken up and before their attentions had wandered away from one another or been sucked into the day-to-day mundanity of life. She had almost told him the previous night, but after their return from the airport there had been obvious distractions, and Holly had wanted them to spend some, simple, uncomplicated time together. She knew things would inevitably become complicated once she had admitted to being a witch. She hadn't anticipated Jake's childlike wonder at the situation, however. All things considered, Jake had taken her revelation surprisingly well. Yes, he had initially laughed at her and then, after she had produced that first charm of goldfinches, he had gone into a mild state of shock, but after that, and once she had cleared away the broken crockery and spilt tea, made him a fresh cup, and Jake had discovered the simple joy of flying, it had all gone remarkably well. She wasn't planning on coming out to her father until he was back home from Canada, but given Jake's response, she was hoping that telling her father would be an equally pain-free experience. She felt good she had managed things all on her own, without Partridge's interference and his much-vaunted three-step plan for coming out without tears.

Flushed by her success with Jake, Holly had given herself another task this morning. She planned to carry it out just as soon as she had persuaded Jake to come down from his aerial manoeuvres (with hindsight she wondered whether a grown man with one arm in a plaster cast should really be playing at being Superman quite so vigorously) and packed him off to his own house for a little while. Not for too long, mind. Just long enough for him to unpack, check his post, do a bit of washing, and sort out some fresh clothes while she went to visit Esme.

Tomorrow, both she and Jake had to be back at work, but today they had the opportunity to spend some quality time together, just as soon as Holly had confronted Esme about her alleged matchmaking antics with Merton and told her to back off from her love life because Jake was the only man she wanted. Despite everything, or perhaps because of everything, it felt like the right time to make her position unequivocally clear on the matter. She was also debating with herself whether she should raise the matter of Appledore Ashwell in relation to Esme's assertion that her biological father had been called Cox, but she couldn't help feeling one thing at a time might well be the best way forward. Plus, she was still hoping to find a way to work out the contradictions in their stories by herself.

After a bit of persuasion, Jake reluctantly came back to earth. Holly made sure she draped him discreetly and thoroughly in high-level protection spells before he walked out of her front door. She decided not to tell him about the spells, nor her worries about the possible nature of the twister that had hit him. Had he mentioned it, she reasoned, she probably would have said something, but the morning's distractions had occupied him totally, and he didn't know enough about witchcraft or the extent of Holly's abilities to make a potential connection. Holly remembered her own innocent fun at first discovering her magical abilities and didn't want to deprive Jake of the same sort of feeling. Besides, she didn't know for certain that his tornado was a magical attack and there was no point in alarming him unnecessarily. There would be time enough to tell him if she needed to. Of course, had she known of Merton Holmfirth's brief, but very final, appearance on the evening news, she might have felt differently.

Esme went through the usual polite rituals of enquiring after Holly's health and pouring her a cup of tea. Holly hadn't visited Esme since before the debacle of the limousine ride with Merton. So, she used the excuse of thanking Esme for arranging such an initially splendid evening as a way of easing into Merton's advances and what he had said about Esme's encouragement of the same. As soon as Holly made reference to Merton's disclosure, the tone of the conversation markedly changed.

"He told you this on the evening in question, or on one of the other occasions you have since spoken with him? You two have had so much contact recently, I was beginning to be hopeful for the pair of you. I'm really rather surprised that you're only now telling me the evening was such a disaster."

Holly wasn't sure if she should be surprised or angry at Esme's unexpected and unexplained knowledge about her recent meetings with Merton. She decided to keep her options open.

"He's family, I gather. Sometimes, one ends up forgiving family. I thought you'd be pleased I am getting to know some of my relatives, as well as getting out and about a bit more in the witching community."

"Why should that aspect of things please me? Barring young Merton and, of course, you, I haven't been in contact with the remaining family in years, and Merton's barely a relative. I can see little benefit in socialising. I invariably have more productive things to do."

"You were the one encouraging me to socialise."

"It was a special occasion. I hadn't realised you would be seeking such extended contact with the family."

"Yet, you were happy enough to pimp me out within the family."

"That's a very harsh phrase. I shall do you the courtesy of pretending I have not heard it. The witchlight that flows through your blood flows in mine and should be respected. In this shabby day and age, it is almost certainly unique in strength and purity. I would only be doing right by it, and by you, yourself, were I able to secure you a mate with the appropriate aspects of lineage. If you continue whoring after a man with no illumination whatsoever, you will only end up weakening our heritage, and I would be failing in my duty if I did not point this out to you and highlight other alternatives."

"And you have the effrontery to say I speak harshly. 'Whoring'! What do you call 'whoring' after a man with no power? How is that any more acceptable than my accusing you of pimping me out? If there's any whoring taking place, then it's you who's encouraging it. The bad news, Esme, is that I'm in love with Jake and am planning on having a long-lasting relationship with him, so just back off with your insulting, antiquated opinions and your outdated bloodlines talk. I'm not a bloody racehorse and this isn't some past century."

"So, how do you intend to manage a long-lasting relationship, may I ask, when the longest you've been able to keep a man is ten years, despite any slatternly tricks you may have picked up?"

"What? How dare you? You may technically be my mother, but…"

Enough was enough. Furious, Holly found she had run out of words capable of doing justice to the way she was feeling. She couldn't finish the sentence, and in the belief that actions spoke louder than words, attempted to transport herself directly out of the cottage and home, but something went wrong. Instead of reappearing in her own kitchen, she found herself in the hall of the cottage. In the muffled distance, a dog was barking frantically. Holly strode towards the front door, but the hallway appeared to distort and stretch, and the door grew further away the faster she walked towards it. She stopped walking and wiped her hand across her eyes. The distortions remained unaltered. Turning back to face the way she'd come, she found the entire cottage, and not just its hall, had expanded. Whilst still recognisable as Esme's home, extra doorways now lined the hall and several dark corridors jutted from it at unlikely angles. As Holly started to walk towards them the hall seemed to contract until, by the time she was standing directly outside the door to the lounge, the hall was its normal size and shape again. She attempted to transport herself once more and this time ended up on the upstairs landing, except things were further distorted and the hallway she had just left now seemed several floors and a long run of staircases away. A third attempt to leave the cottage brought her back to the strangely proportioned hall at exactly the same spot she had first transported to. The barking dog was getting louder and then suddenly it stopped.

The door to the lounge began to open, and the hall flicked back to its original size and shape. Esme walked calmly into the hallway with Regal at her side. The hand with the least number of rings on it was firmly clamped around his muzzle. Holly's attention was drawn to the large, ornate moonstone ring on her mother's middle finger. She had seen it on her hand before, of course, but this time it seemed different, whilst being oddly familiar in an unexpected way. A frozen image of Ninanna Beldam gripping the child Esme flashed into her mind. The hand that had gripped her shoulder so tightly, even more tightly than Esme was currently clutching Regal, boasted only a few rings, but one was large and ornate. Abigail Holmfirth had pointed it out to her as the Beldam family ring, Ninanna's ring.

Esme noticed the direction of Holly's gaze and looked down pointedly at the ring and then at Regal.

"Hush, boy. She's one of ours." Looking back at Holly she said, "I am sure I have told you it is dreadfully impolite to transport directly in and out of someone's residence. Nurture has clearly bested nature in your case. Fortunately, I constructed this cottage to discourage poor etiquette."

"What do you mean, you constructed the cottage? You've always claimed it was Ninanna's."

"It was. It still is. I think we had better return to the parlour. There are some pressing matters of importance that it appears I need to impart to you."

Chapter 19

Holly had thought her relationship with Esme had produced all the surprises and understated heartbreak it was going to and maybe, in some convoluted way, it had, because the unbending woman seated in front of her was now claiming to be Ninanna Beldam, rather than Esme.

"Do you understand what I'm telling you child?"

Holly bridled at the use of the word "child," whilst recognising that to someone of Ninanna's age (though exactly how old Ninanna was still a point of conjecture) even the Pope would seem a mere infant.

"You're telling me you've been spoonfeeding me a steaming concoction of lies for the last five months; that you are not my birth mother, Esme Beldam, but her mother, my grandmother, Ninanna Beldam; that you have lied to me about the identity of my biological father; and that all of this unadulterated shit has been in my best interests. On top of all of this, you would have me believe it will continue to be in my best interests if I sustain this charade and go on pretending you are Esme. What you haven't told me is why I should accept any of this shit, or why you lied in the first place, or what happened back there in the hall when I tried to transport or, even, why you have suddenly decided to fess up, when it would appear you have been maintaining this deception with the world at large for years. Does that cover everything, or would you also like me to tell you what a cold, callous cow you are?"

Holly's face was flushed with anger, disbelief, and held-back tears. Ninanna's composure, however, was as smoothly controlled as normal.

"I think that covers nearly everything, albeit in an unnecessarily emotional way. You have, however, omitted one or two cogent points, either through pique or because I have not yet communicated them clearly enough to you. In case it is my fault, though I doubt that it is, I intend to rectify any issues of miscommunication swiftly."

"Well communicate away then, because I'm all ears."

Ninanna fixed on Holly with a stiffly unwavering stare.

"These are matters, not surprisingly, to do with the Coven, as unenlightened a group of bigoted, small-minded individuals as you could possibly hope to avoid. Their witchlight shines dimly, believe you me. Just over thirty-eight years ago, I chose to disappear because of their childish persecution of those of us who have mined the rich depths of Old Magic. I had planned a short-term disappearance, but when I returned, I found my only daughter had also disappeared and was quite possibly dead because, I believe, of their intransigent petty mindedness. Having failed in their endeavours against me, I thought there was a real possibility they were trying to get at me through her. I took on the persona of Esme in order to conceal my own identity and to flush out the truth surrounding her disappearance. I believed that if certain people knew of her fate, they would know my impersonation to be false and come after me. In that way, I would soon have proof of their perfidy. I was, however, wrong.

"I have waited. Over the intervening years there have been intimations, possible leads, but nothing concrete regarding Esme. For years, I did not even know if the child she was carrying when she left had survived. When you and the Coven lackey turned up on my doorstep, I felt I had to maintain my pretence, but you looked so like my Esme that I knew, I just knew. Afterwards, when I heard of the strength of your illumination and, subsequently, the story of your abandonment and adoption, it was clear to me that you were my granddaughter, Esme's girl-child. That Coven lackey, Mayflower, was still influencing you, however, so I maintained my pretence of being your mother. I had to. I am sorry for the lies, but they were necessary."

"But, what about after I'd ditched Partridge? Couldn't you trust me then?"

"The arrangement continued. I had become accustomed to it. I thought I might lose you if I told you the truth and after all the years of waiting, I didn't want that. You are all that is left of my bloodline. Also, I could not be certain you would not tell Mayflower, regardless of what had passed between you."

"And then what about the lie that my father was someone called Cox?"

"You wanted to know who your birth father was—it was only natural. I could hardly tell you I didn't know. I had my suspicions, but I couldn't prove anything. It seemed better to make a name up."

"And those suspicions are?"

"There are two who apparently could be your father: Brothers Hoxton Corey and Appledore Ashwell."

"Not Landel Hawthorn?"

"Brother Hawthorn, I believe, is deceased."

"And how does being dead now prevent him from being my father then?"

"It doesn't, but the death of a very close relative causes ripples in the witchlight of those nearest to them. There would have been repercussions, but you have never mentioned any such."

"How would I even know? When did he die?"

"A while back, before you were illuminated. Had he been your father, I believe his death would have uncovered your witchlight that much sooner. The ripples would have been noticeable."

Although her eye contact held firm, the woman in front of Holly stopped talking and showed no sign of continuing. Holly felt a further prompt was required, although deeply resented having to do it.

"So, why are you telling me all this now?"

"I felt I had to, that I owed it to you. Once you had stumbled across the true interior of the cottage and, apparently, had recognised the Beldam ring, you were bound to ask questions. I was not willing to lie to you anymore."

"You've been happy enough to do so solidly for five bloody months."

"There was a need to. I've explained. The Coven could not know I was here. They might come for me and, inevitably, for you. To think otherwise would be foolish."

Holly shook her head in disbelief.

"Why? Old Magic is not illegal. This isn't the old days. Partridge knows you've been showing me things. He may not like it, but he's done nothing about it. They never came for you when they thought you were Esme. Why would they come for you as Ninanna, and, regardless of who you actually are, why should they come after me?"

"Ask Partridge Mayflower. And whilst you are asking your questions, talk to Appledore Ashwell and Hoxton Corey. One of them knows more than he is saying. Now, though, I need to rest. This has been too much of a strain for me. Please leave the house via the front door. Regal will see me to my bed. I am too old for such upsets."

Ninanna didn't sound upset and this was the first time Holly had heard her refer to her age as a limitation. It came as a surprise, therefore, but when Holly looked closely, previously unseen signs of aging were present in Ninanna's face. Her skin looked stretched and had taken on a dry, parchment-like tone. There were growing shadows under her eyes that emphasised the skull beneath the skin.

Holly wasn't really ready to go so soon. Many of her questions hadn't been answered, and the woman in front of her did not seem to have recognised the impact of refuting everything she had said and claimed to have been for the last five months. Yet the drawn look of Ninanna's face pushed Holly to leave. As she reluctantly got up to go, Ninanna raised the hand that sported the Beldam family ring.

"Say goodbye properly, dear. There is such a thing as Witchery etiquette. Now I am revealed as myself and the true Head of the Beldam family line, it would be fitting for you to kiss the family ring before you take your leave."

Holly stood still, dumbfounded. This was the final straw. Ninanna continued to hold out her hand and waited. Holly returned her cold gaze without blinking.

"You may or not be my grandmother and I have no idea, and could care less, if you're the head of the family; there have been so many lies from you that I no longer know who or what you are. In recognition of the apparent effects of old age on you, although that's another new story as far as I am concerned, I am going, despite still wanting the full explanations I really feel are due to me, but there is no way, no bloody way, I am going to kiss your sodding ring like some medieval vassal. I'm going, on foot, out through the front door, as requested. Eventually, I may come back the same way, when and if I choose, but then I will want some proper answers. Do you understand?"

Holly turned on her heel and strode to the front door, opened it, took a step outside, and slammed it firmly behind her.

Inside the cottage, Ninanna Beldam, Holly's maternal grandmother and absolute Head of the Beldam family, stared in unconcealed anger and contempt at the air in front her. The air retreated, leaving a hole of cold, pale blue light. Dust motes floating in the air were drawn to it, but on contact burned, creating an outer circle of scorching white flame.

Outside the cottage, Holly transported herself, with a slight waft of purple streaked lavender air, straight back to her own kitchen and burst into tears. It was in this position that Jake found her hugging a concerned Barny and still sobbing her heart out, well over an hour later.

Chapter 20

Jake sat next to Holly, his arm around her shoulders. He didn't know what to say, which was par for the course. He hadn't really known what to say ever since Holly had told him she was a witch. Sure, the flying had been amazing fun, but it did not involve an extensive grasp, or even a miniscule comprehension, of the phenomenon of witchcraft. As for the latest development, he couldn't even begin to understand Ninanna's revelation or the effect it must be having on Holly, but that was people for you; just, in this case, they were people who happened to wield incomprehensible magical power. He held onto Holly while she cried and then listened as she tried to talk. Now, she appeared to be waiting on a response, but he had no idea what to say.

"I don't know, Holly love. In fact, I'd go so far as saying, I haven't got the faintest idea. Have you thought about trying to talk things through with your old mentor? Partridge? He might be able to put things into a witch perspective, explain some of the things she's said, or at least suggest how best to react to them—from a witch point of view, that is, not a personal one."

"But, being a witch is personal."

"I know, Prickles, but there may be things that need doing in witchcraft terms, rather than from your personal perspective. From a personal point of view, this must all be incredibly hurtful, but from a witch point of view there may be other or different implications? Possibly?"

"Partridge may not even want to talk to me. We didn't exactly part amicably, and I haven't seen him for almost a month. We're not really on speaking terms."

"Didn't he say he'd be watching over you?"

"Yes, but it wasn't clear if it was a threat or a promise."

"Alright. But what are the alternatives if you don't talk to Partridge?"

Holly went quiet and thoughtful, and Jake decided to answer his own question, "If you don't go to see Partridge, who isn't family, won't have any emotional baggage, will be able to analyse the matter clearly and without bias whilst understanding the witchcraft element, you could try to track down this Appledore Ashwell. He, of course, you're emotionally confused about because he may be your biological father. He may be emotionally screwed up over the Esme thing, could be a dubious character, possibly has a magical hitman after him and, oh yes, you can't find him for love nor money. You could also try to track down Hoxton Corey, whom you don't know from Adam, but who also may or may not be your real father, may or may not be trustworthy, may or may not be easy to find. There is always the option of doing nothing—spending your days crying and fretting about the basic inhumanity of a woman who you thought was your birth mother, may now be your grandmother, but has always been colder than a deep-frozen leg of New Zealand lamb. You will never fully understand the vague, veiled comments she has made because they are vague and veiled, are unlikely to get answers to the questions she has so far declined to answer or know the truth about the Old Magic that is apparently lurking in her cottage. Finally, of course, there is the matter of the Coven, which allegedly hates your grandmother with a vengeance, may have been implicated in the presumed death of your birth mother, and may not be too happy with you because of your Old Magic leanings. You need to know what they're thinking, if nothing else."

"And if Partridge is working for the bad guys?"

"Then you need to know that, too."

Jake stopped.

There was a silence until Holly said, "I'll go and see Partridge."

Partridge was not as readily available as he used to be, and it was not until Holly's lunch break several days later that he deigned to make an appearance. In the meantime, Holly had fretted and worried. She had had second, third, and even fourth thoughts about seeing Partridge, made up her mind to cancel their meeting, and then changed it back again without actually doing anything. Because Holly was still not sure their meeting was a totally wise way forward, she felt that a public location was the safest option. So when they did finally meet up, this time, for variety's sake, they met on the concourse at Waterloo Station and then found a café table at which to sit down. Partridge seemed as prickly as he had ever been, and Holly struggled to explain her concerns, particularly those in relation to the Coven and, therefore, Partridge himself. Eventually, however, she got there. As issues became clearer, Partridge's tone noticeably softened and he stopped referring to Esme as "Mummy Dearest."

"I mean, technically she's your Nanny Ninanna or even your Ninanny."

Holly choked back a sob, which might, just, have almost been a giggle. Partridge looked ashamed of himself, and they got down to talking in earnest.

"I don't know; a month without your fairy godfather and look at the mess you're in. I'm not sure there are any instant fixes, though. Families are such messy entities. That's why I disowned my children aeons ago before I turned them all into chickens and wrung their scrawny little necks."

Holly looked horrified, and Partridge continued,

"It's a joke, sort of, but anyway, I can't make Ninanna Beldam a more loveable granny or generally a nicer person. The woman was seemingly known for being anti-social and had been a worry to the Coven for a long time. It was always her we had concerns about, not Esme. In fact, it looks like Esme had her concerns too. That statement she made—the one in the archives? I did some digging and finally spoke to the Sister who took the statement. She reckoned that Esme was probably trying to drop her mother in it with the Coven, or at least give it a heads up about her practice of Old Magic. Not so much love there, after all. That, however, is as far as things went between the Coven and Esme and whatever caused her to disappear, I would assure you it wasn't the Coven."

"You're sure?"

"Would I lie to you?"

"You have done."

"But apart from that?"

A thought hung heavily in the air.

"The Coven was not involved in Esme's disappearance, I swear to it on my witchlight, but it *will* be interested in Ninanna's return." Partridge saw the look on Holly's face and hurriedly added, "But no more than that. We may not be comfortable with the practice of the old ways, but these days we are tolerant of it. Just look at you."

"That's part of what I don't understand. Why were you all so fearful of it, and if the fear was that strong, how come you are suddenly all so hunky dory with it now?"

"If truth be told, we are still afraid of it, but there are so few of you left who are able to practice it that we can afford to be tolerant, or at least more tolerant than we were. The fear lies in the uncertainty of what you might be capable of and also, I think, in the memory of what the rest of us have lost. That's probably more regret than fear, but regret can be close neighbours to both guilt and resentment. Not necessarily a happy combination. Still, what's gone is gone. I can't help you with the Old Magic angle on things and neither can the Coven. That's your area of expertise, now. The distortion you experienced inside the cottage is almost certainly Old Magic. It is theoretically possible to make things bigger on the inside than the outside with standard magic, but it would take a whole lake of juice to distort an entire cottage to the size you have indicated, let alone link it to a transportation block and redirection spell. That's complex stuff and definitely one for you.

"You might also want to look into that family ring and, in the meantime, I'd be careful of kissing it, if I were you. It may just be grandiose affectation on Ninanna's part, but it does rather smack of arcane ritual. You hear stories of thrall rings and the like, though not usually as a tool to be used on other witches."

"What else do I need to think about or know?"

"Your Appledore Ashwell's an interesting guy, but whatever he's got himself into, it's nothing directly to do with the Coven."

Holly couldn't hold back her comment.

"Seems like there's a lot of stuff that's nothing to do with the Coven, these days."

"Too true, I'm afraid. Bogged down in bureaucracy and without a real leader amongst us. We administer rather than rule. Not that we ever did, rule that is, but once upon a time we at least used to harbour delusions of grandeur."

So, is there anything else about Appledore?"

"I've been trying to find him since that time he made contact with the both of us, but when that man chooses to stay hidden, hidden is what he stays. I didn't even know about your meeting him in Kew. I'll be having words with the ginger one over that. As for the mini tornado, I don't know. If it carried on gusting after he'd gone and while you were still there, it feels too long distance and impersonal for you to have been unconsciously calling the shots. I guess it could have been Ashwell himself, though why is beyond me. Make sure you keep your boy Jake well protected and tell him about your concerns in relation to the twister that got him. Keeping him in the dark won't keep him safe if that Yankee wind was more than natural. On the plus side, though, you've got more than enough juice in you to protect both yourself and him. You'd be wise to be on your guard, but I can't see there's reason to be unduly fearful, unless it's you, yourself, who's behind it all."

"Thanks. Should I do anything about Hoxton Corey?"

"Check him out. Why not? If nothing else, you might be able to eliminate him from your list of fathers, or ink him in more strongly on the list, if need be. It'd be no bad thing to have a clearer picture of your lineage. It might cast some of those shadowy uncertainties into sharper relief."

"Will you come with me?"

"What? To see Hoxton Corey? Yes, if you want. Are you sure you want? It seems a bit unlike you, if I may say so, girlie."

"I know, but…" Holly felt in need of moral support following Ninanna's recent disclosure. She also wanted to avoid being in a one-to-one situation with a stranger on unknown territory, though whether that was for her safety or theirs, she wasn't quite certain.

"When would you want to go?"

"Now?"

"Do you have the time? I thought you only had an hour for lunch."

"I can always bend things a bit."

Partridge raised his eyebrows, but said nothing.

Five minutes later they were both standing outside a large mock Tudor mansion in Surrey. The only part of it that was mock was the Tudor; it was most definitely a mansion.

"Where do we start?" queried Holly.

"Try knocking at the front door? It often works for me."

Holly knocked, but nothing happened. She knocked again and then rang, making sure the deafening peal of church bells she had created echoed in each and every room and was followed by a clear announcement that two people were waiting at the front door. It was impressive, but unproductive. The front door remained resolutely shut.

Without any external sign of having cast a spell, Holly announced, "I've run a more detailed tracer spell, and it tells me that Hoxton Corey is definitely in the house, or possibly nearby in the garden. Does a house this big have a garden, or should it be grounds?"

"Who knows? Shall we try round the back?"

In wafts of mauve and turquoise air, they disappeared from the front of the house and reappeared in the grounds at the back. There was no obvious sign of Hoxton Corey, but to one side of the mansion Partridge noticed a swimming pool.

"Let's try over there."

"It's February. No one in their right mind is going to be using an outdoor pool."

"Use your imagination, girlie. Just because its February doesn't mean the pool or the air around it has to be cold. Such is the joy of witchlight."

Holly said nothing, but felt annoyed at herself for missing the obvious.

The pool was a considerable distance away, and they both transported over to it rather than walk. The first thing to hit them was the air temperature round the pool. It was tropical. The second thing they noticed was the body floating in the pool. It belonged to a blond man, apparently in his mid thirties. He was stark naked and very dead.

They levitated the body out of the water and laid it on a lounger beside the pool. The eyes, an unusual watery turquoise, were wide open, but whether it was in fear or surprise, it was difficult to tell. Partridge worked the tracer spell again. Apparently the corpse had once been Hoxton Corey.

"Shit! Talk about a flow of bad witchlight. That's the second brother to go in dubious circumstances this week. Hopefully we can keep this one out of the national news."

"There was another death? On the news?"

"Yeah. It wasn't good. Didn't you see it? A guy only twenty or so years younger than me, though mundane authorities and the media insist on placing him in his twenties. A City high flyer, in more ways than one, by the name of Merton Holmfirth. Made a nasty wet mess on the pavement. Hey, Holly girl, are you feeling okay?"

Holly had turned very pale and was giving serious consideration to throwing up in the pool. Her hazel eyes, wide open in shock, reflected back the turquoise tint of the water.

It was quite some time before she felt able to go back to work. Fortunately, her aptitude at bending a little bit of time here or there meant she was only actually two minutes late for her first appointment of the afternoon. It would later come to light that time had also been bent for just a little while to permit Hoxton Corey to enter his own swimming pool and drown in it.

Chapter 21

In a mountainous part of a large Greek island, best known for its ancient ruins and the ruinous effects of alcohol on young British tourists, an old but still functioning monastery was stoically resisting the buffeting of strong February winds. It would be a good few months before sinfully scantily clad woman started to squeeze themselves back into the towns and villages lower down the mountains and into the resorts of iniquity along the coast. At this point, and just to be on the safe side, the monks would lock their doors and close the shutters against the distractions of supple, sun-tanned flesh lying in wait below them. Now, it was the wintry weather they had locked their doors and shutters against. God was good and had thoughtfully provided them with heavy doors and stout shutters to protect them against the wide variety of evils that stalked the outside world.

Not surprisingly, as a community, the monks tended to keep themselves to themselves, but occasionally the heavy oak doors would be pulled back to admit a visitor. More often than not, it would be a destitute man begging aid and shelter, very occasionally a father seeking to offer up a younger son as a novice and, rather more rarely, a penitent man seeking to purge both body and soul through spiritual retreat. It was not a place men came to lightly or on a passing whim, and very few chose to visit it in the harsh winter months.

Surprisingly for the time of year, the monks currently had a lay visitor on retreat with them. He claimed to be a poet and rock musician in need of peace and solitude. The brothers didn't hold with rock music, but the man was prepared to pay his way and donate a tidy sum to the monastery's coffers. Moreover, as they had neither televisions nor radios at the monastery, they were none the wiser as to his past, and he was free to forget himself. He contributed to the day-to-day life of the small community with honest hard work. He participated willingly in their religious observations and at other times commendably kept himself to himself. With his collar-length hair and abundant brown beard, he even blended in physically until, as the weeks accumulated, the brothers almost forgot he had not always been one of them. Appledore Ashwell knew how to blend in. He was a master of it.

Jake was currently trying to master his fear. He was conscious he wasn't doing it very well. Holly had recently finished telling him of her worries and suspicions concerning his Stateside brush with the whirlwind. She had also been more forthcoming about her subsequent tussle with a similar force of nature (or otherwise) at Kew, her doubts about Appledore Ashwell, and her anxiety regarding her own potential involvement in events. Somehow, this last point got to Jake more than the other revelations. The fact that his little Holly thought she could be capable of such a thing—had the raw power to be able to do such a thing—was more than disconcerting. He hadn't realised; who would?

Holly, on the other hand, felt better for telling Jake. She had convinced herself she was keeping things from him for his own peace of mind, but secretly had come to wonder if it was her own she was protecting. It turned out her own was better served by coming clean. Having things out in the open made life less complicated. She was, however, somewhat concerned by the effect of her telling on Jake. He was looking bemused again and more than a little bit scared.

"Are you okay? Are we okay?" Holly suddenly needed to know.

"I guess so. I mean, we're alright. It's just the rest of the shit that's doing my head in. I'm a vet. I do animals and science. Suddenly, the world's a whole lot more complicated and unscientific than I thought. I'm dealing with that—at least I think I am—but then there's more shit, and I find out I may be a moving target and it may be you who's pulling the trigger. That's where I'm really struggling, Prickles. The Holly I know wouldn't, couldn't; but you're saying maybe, so perhaps

I don't know you as well as I thought, just like it turns out that I don't know the world as well as I thought. It can't really be you, can it?"

"I don't know. I don't want it to be, but I do have the power and the ability, and I have worked magic subconsciously. I have to be mindful of that."

"But, why would you have killed this last guy, Hoxton Corey? You didn't know him. You didn't even know where he lived until you and Partridge worked your mojo and turned up there. It doesn't make sense."

"No, it doesn't, but I knew Merton Holmfirth. I knew where he worked, and I was there not long before he died. I'm not going to pretend I liked the man."

"This is silly. There must be another reason for all of these things. I don't think you did anything; I can't believe you did, but then that means that maybe someone else is out there doing this stuff. That's more than terrifying in its own right."

"I know. I'm sorry for alarming you. Are you sure we're okay, really okay?"

"I'm sure." Jake pulled Holly to him. "I'm confused and a little bit scared, but I'm very clear on one thing and that's that I love you. I understand now why you were distracted a while back. You had to deal with all of this on your own, but there are two of us now, so you don't have to cope on your own and neither do I. We are going to be strong for one another and carry on loving one another no matter what, and that means we will always be absolutely okay from here on in, and I'm starting to ramble, aren't I?"

"A little."

"Sorry. This is all very new, and I don't really know how to deal with it. I love you though, that's for sure. I also know I want to be with you, so the sooner we can resolve all this other crap, the better. In fact, once it is resolved, will you marry me?"

"Pardon?"

"You heard me. Will you marry me?"

"This is all a bit sudden, isn't it?"

"Not really. We've known each other for almost six months, and people have got married and divorced in that time. Not that

I'm planning on the divorce part, thank you very much—just the married bit.

"I truly believe the tornado in the States was nothing more than a freak of nature, but whatever it was, it was the closest to my own mortality I've ever come. It made me think about what I really want from life; what really matters to me. You really matter, and with all this shit currently taking place, I am not going to let another day pass without me telling you so. I love you. I want us to be as secure as possible, so we can get through things together and as soon as we're out the other side of the current confusion, I want to make it formal. So what do you think? You're not going to make me ask again, are you?"

"No, that would be cruel. So yes, I think I would like to marry you, if that's still alright with you?"

At which point, Holly kissed Jake and all conversation ceased for a while.

Later, they talked about when they might announce their engagement and whether Holly should tell Ninanna.

"Well, I'm going to call Dad just as soon as the time in his part of Canada means he'll be awake. Then I'm telling Sarah. Ninanna is my biological grandmother. I ought to tell her something, oughtn't I? Given her attitude last time, I want her to know how solid we are. You're going to be family, and she needs to come round to that. I want her to hear it from me. If she gets to hear it some other way… well, it doesn't bear thinking about."

When Holly said it, it sounded sensible and brave. Now she was standing in the early evening dusk, on her own, outside Ninanna's cottage, she wasn't quite so sure. They had discussed the possibility of Jake going with Holly, but had decided against it for the news-breaking visit. Maybe another time. Maybe.

Holly took a deep breath and started to walk towards the front door. Though not exactly a woman to back away from an argument, she wasn't looking forward to this. The blood ties, the knotted emotions, and the convoluted history complicated things.

Even before she reached the door, Regal had begun to howl.

As she started to knock, the door opened. Ninanna stood in the doorway with Regal at her side.

"Yes?"

The drawn look of the other day had gone, and Ninanna looked much as she had when she was calling herself Esme, except the light brown hair was a shade nearer blond and gone were the pastel and primarily casual clothes. Ninanna was dressed from head to toe in black, and it was crisp, Armani black.

"Yes?"

Ninanna's tone of voice made it clear it would not be a good thing if she had to say yes a third time.

"I came back to see if we could bury the hatchet and to tell you, as family, my good news: Jake and I are getting married."

"You had better come in, then."

They walked down the plain white hallway and into the living room. The internal dimensions of the property seemed normal today and in balance with the outside appearance of the cottage.

Ninanna indicted Holly should sit down. This time round, there was no fine china and freshly brewing tea, or the ritual of polite nothings that usually accompanied them.

"Jake and I have decided to get married. I don't want to marry another witch just because he is a witch. I want to marry the man I love. I thought you should hear this straight from me, in the hope you'll understand just how much I love Jake. He's a good guy. I think you'd like him and, I hope, will one day want to meet him."

"I do not recall doubting your love for this man. I simply did not, and do not, think he would be a beneficial match for you. If you wish to waste the power of your witchlight by marrying only for love, that is down to you. At least one can be grateful you're too old to think of starting a family."

Holly hadn't given the matter any consideration up until now, but her hackles rose at the obvious hypocrisy of the statement.

"Excuse me? No I'm not, and you of all people should know I'm not. Yes, there are often difficulties with having a first baby in your late thirties, but they are not insurmountable, even without magic. With magic, it's easily achievable, as you know. What is the point of telling me otherwise? Are you just prodding me to get a response? It is possible to like people, get along with them, and generally be friendly, you know?"

"I dare say it is, but as your grandmother I am entitled to your respect; liking is irrelevant. As Head of the Beldam family line, your respect for me should be automatic."

"Head of the family line?" Holly snorted. "As far as I'm aware, the immediate family is just the two of us, and we're clearly so dysfunctional we barely deserve the title 'family,' let alone the concept of a line."

"There is your father."

"He's enjoying himself in Canada and, thankfully, you're unlikely to meet him."

"I was referring to your real father, the man who impregnated Esme."

"What a delightful turn of phrase, and it's not as if we really know who he is, anyway. Still, at least the potential paternal gene pool is getting smaller."

"It is?"

"Hoxton Corey's dead."

"How unfortunate for him. I felt no change to the witchlight and assume, therefore, you did not either. At least we can now be certain he was not your father."

"Oh great. Don't feel the slightest bit of human empathy beyond the lack of impact on your prized witchlight. Are you even interested in how he died?"

"If it was noteworthy, I'm sure you'll tell me."

"He drowned in his own swimming pool."

"My, my. How careless."

"I didn't say it was an accident."

"Was it not? I can only assume, therefore, that it was suicide, murder, or an act of a vengeful god."

"The Coven couldn't tell. They just know he drowned."

"Oh dear, what an anti-climax to a dreary little story. Is there any other news of no consequence you would like to share with me?"

"Merton Holmfirth."

"Ah yes, poor lad. I knew about him, of course. It's hardly news. Too unstable for his own good; so many highfliers are."

"You never thought to mention his death to me?"

"I assumed you knew, because of your…growing closeness. You saw him just before he died, I believe?" Ninanna raised her eyebrows knowingly.

"Is there no human compassion inside you at all?"

"Merton's demise was regrettable. As for Brother Corey, I saw him from time to time at the gatherings, but I have not attended one for so long it is well nigh irrelevant. Unless he is embedded within our line of witchlight, he is of little consequence to me and his death even less so. I would encourage you to adopt the same approach. You will find it better for your own peace of mind to bring no one into this world and have regard to no one's departure. As time passes, it makes things easier, believe me. So many are lost along the way, while you are left standing on your own, that you cannot afford to mourn them all."

Holly paused before speaking, seeing, at last, an apparent chink in her grandmother's almost impregnable emotional armour. She was wondering how best to respond when Ninanna's next words brought her up short again.

"If you're not prepared to show respect to me for the family's sake, at least have the courtesy and sense to show it to the witchlight that flows in our veins."

Ninanna proffered the hand with the family ring on it with the grandeur of a Renaissance pope. Holly spluttered.

"You are kidding me, right? I come to try and patch things up and tell you about Jake and me. I break the news about Merton and Hoxton Corey, or, anyway, at least one of them, and all you can do is sit there, like some Grande Dame from way back when and demand I kiss your ring."

"You said you wished to bury the hatchet."

"Yes, as in the pair of us apologising to one another and making up on equal terms. Not as in I do obeisance to you in some antiquated ritual. This is the twenty-first century, you know and I am supposed to be your granddaughter, allegedly."

Ninanna continued to sit, unmoving, with her hand held out.

"You can sit like that for as long as you like. I am not going to do it. This is becoming a decidedly unfunny farce. We're just repeating what happened the last time I came here. I'm not staying for that."

Holly stood up and started to walk towards the door, but Regal was blocking the way. As she reached out to move him, he growled, showing an impressive set of teeth. From behind her she heard Ninanna say,

"Silence. Now is not the time. Let her pass."

The dog slunk away and, without looking back, Holly opened the living room door, strode down the hallway, opened the front door, and left. She wondered whether this was going to be the last time she saw the interior of her grandmother's cottage.

She transported herself straight back to Basingfield Lane where Jake and Barny were both waiting for her. At least this time she wasn't crying.

Outside the monastery, perched on the steep side of its Greek mountain, the wind was growing in force. Inside the monastery, the monks were having difficulties keeping their shutters shut. They could hear the wind howling like a huge, rabid dog, or a fury of demons, as some of the younger, more impressionable monks were heard to mutter. The older monks said nothing. They were not given to overly fanciful stories and were too busy ensuring that the wind and rain stayed on the outside of the doors and shutters, whilst simultaneously contemplating the extent of the repairs they'd be facing the following morning, to indulge in mindless chatter. If they made time to exchange the odd word it was likely to comment that they'd never known a night like it. At least the lay visitor known to them as Meelo was helping them batten down the hatches and keep them battened down. He seemed to be the ablest and the quickest of them, but even he was having problems, possibly because he always found himself struggling with things where the storm was strongest.

It was while Meelo and one of the younger brothers were in the oldest wing of the monastery, trying to lash shut a pair of man-high shutters, that the external wall of the building took a direct lightning hit. The bolt apparently penetrated the three-foot thick stone wall and struck lay brother Meelo full force in the chest and carried on burning. The centuries-old stone of the monastery crumbled, and the outer wall collapsed, plunging down the mountainside and taking with it into oblivion the lightning-charred flesh of Appledore Ashwell.

At home, safe in bed beside Jake, Holly woke up with a start, a searing pain piercing her chest. It felt as if there was a hole where her heart should be and pouring into that hole, temporarily illuminating the whole of the bedroom, were waves of dim, russet witchlight. Then they suddenly stopped, and the room and its occupants were swallowed back into the darkness.

Chapter 22

Partridge hadn't been much help in explaining the witchlight phenomenon the night Appledore Ashwell died.

"It's Old Magic. I don't do Old Magic. That's your thing."

"But, I don't understand what happened. I woke up knowing he was dead, and then there was this light everywhere."

"I know. You've said."

"Did you know Ninanna said you can sense the death of a close blood relative through your witchlight? I hadn't realised it would be like that, like drowning in pain and light."

"I know. You said. If repeating things over and over again brought understanding with it, you'd never, ever, have to ask another question."

"Sorry. I'm just trying to get to grips with things. If what Ninanna said was true, then Appledore Ashwell is, was, almost certainly my biological father. It feels like I've found him and lost him again in the same gasp of breath. Are you sure there's no sign of him, or at least a body, or some remains, or something?"

"I'm sure. The Coven has people searching globally, but unless you can come up with something a little more precise than '*drowning in pain and light across water, fire and air,*' which is very poetic by the way, but not very helpful, it is akin to searching for a needle in a wet, burning, and wind-blown haystack. A poetically described wet, burning, and wind-blown haystack, but unless we get lucky, the poetry won't get us anywhere."

"I thought there might be ways."

"There possibly are, using your witchlight or Old Magic or both, but not by any means available to the Coven, given the global necessity of the search. Have you thought of asking Nanny Ninanna?"

"No way. Not after my last two visits. I'd rather keep experimenting on my own than involve her. I don't know what she's gone through in the past, but I'm sick of her off-loading it onto me in the present."

"Fine. Let me know when you track down the haystack, and then I'll help you look for the needle."

Partridge sipped his coffee and watched the world go about its mundane business. Holly desultorily fiddled with the plastic spoon in her reinforced cardboard cup.

"So how are you feeling in yourself, girlie?"

"Confused. I didn't used to mind not knowing who my biological parents were. Then I find out, but lose them, in effect, almost instantly and without any chance of getting to know them. In Esme's case, it was both instant and retrospective. I feel hard done by. In fact, though I didn't really know either of them, I am now missing them. So, that's not good. Then there was waking up like that, drowning in pain...Yet despite that, I actually do feel physically great, all geed up, full of energy, and with the feeling that almost anything is possible. That's no bad feeling to have, but I don't feel I should have it, all things considering, so I go back to being confused."

"And how's your Jake taking all of this?"

"Not too well. He was struggling with things before Appeldore's death, and to wake up beside me shrieking with pain and then illuminating the bedroom like a low-grade brothel hasn't exactly helped. He's thrown himself into his work with a vengeance, which is great for his clients and their four-footed friends, but not too great for me. I'm getting less of him than I want right now."

Jake was indeed working hard. He'd put in his usual hours at the practice and was now covering an emergency call-out for a colleague who had been taken ill without any warning, other than the thirty seconds necessary to grab the dispensary bin prior to throwing up in it.

The phone call requesting a visit had come from an elderly lady who was concerned that her dog had begun to act strangely. The woman and the dog lived up on the edges of fen country, in an isolated small holding. It was a dark night, and Jake had had problems finding the property, but now at least he was there. The evening was not prepared to give him an easy ride, however.

The house and its outbuildings were in total darkness. There was no physical sign of either the woman or her dog, and the woman wasn't answering her phone. Then Jake heard the barking. It was louder and deeper than he expected. The dog was supposedly one of the smaller breeds and in poor health, but now it was creating a din worthy of Judgement Day.

Jake tracked the noise—it was hardly difficult—to an isolated shed. As he drew nearer, the barking diminished in volume, growing quieter and quieter until, within a short time, it was little more than a whimper. Still holding his torch in his now-bandaged right hand, he had put his left on the shed door handle when the noise ceased all together. He slowly turned the handle and was in the process of gently opening the door when he was distracted by a woman's voice calling from some distance behind him. He turned, continuing to open the door at the same time, to see torchlight making its way towards him. Then, there was a rustling from inside the shed, a rush of hot dog breath, and something large and heavy hit him, knocking him down to the ground. There was piercing pain and claws and tearing teeth.

Holly was almost home from work when she got the call on her mobile: accident, Addenbrookes, please come quickly. This was the third hospital call she'd had in as many months. She wasn't sure how to cope with it, but at least this time she was able to transport herself directly to the hospital.

Jake was already in the operating theatre. There was talk of potentially serious injuries, trauma to the throat and chest and loss of blood, a large amount of blood, but the specific details passed Holly by in a panic rushed blur. At one stage, there was a colleague of Jake's from the veterinary practice there. Then Sarah's Mark turned up and finally Sarah. There were murmurs of consolation and plastic cups of lukewarm tea, but Holly's attention was fixed on the clock in the waiting area, which moved as slowly as if rationing out the last precious drops of life to a dying man.

Eventually, someone in hospital greens came over to the huddled group of two—just Holly and Sarah, now.

"Holly Jepps or, er, Beldam?"

"Yes to both."

Sarah gave her an odd look, but said nothing.

"Mister Wortham's out of theatre now, but I need to be direct with you: it's still touch and go. He's being moved to Intensive Care, and you'll probably be allowed to see him shortly. Amazingly, there'll be no scarring on the face, but the upper torso and neck are in a pretty bad way. He lost a lot of blood and went into cardiac arrest, but we've brought him back. The next twenty-four hours will be the crucial ones, but if he makes it through them he'll be set fair to middling."

"What exactly does that mean?" This from Sarah.

"As I just said, if he makes it through the next twenty-four hours, things will be looking a lot more hopeful, but still not guaranteed. Stable but critical is the standard phrase, but I find most people don't fully understand it."

The doctor disappeared back from whence she'd emerged, leaving Sarah muttering something under her breath about bedside manner. Holly let her get on with it.

It was another half an hour before Holly was allowed up to Intensive Care. Sarah was asked to remain outside.

Jake was cocooned in wires, tubes, and bandages from his jawline down to below his waist. The bed and the medical paraphernalia around it gave the impression of a sizeable sarcophagus cradling its embalmed contents. Holly wished she hadn't noticed the similarity to funeral rites, however ancient.

She sat down beside the bed and took Jake's hand, the one that hadn't been wired and tubed into the modern day canopic jars surrounding the bed. Since she had last sat in a hospital watching someone she loved struggle for life, she felt more in command of her power. The power itself felt stronger. This time she wasn't prepared to just watch and hope.

Slowly but surely, she poured her witchlight into Jake, harnessing it with words she knew and other words that came to her instinctively.

She was oblivious to the world moving round her, but she drew from it and directed its power through her and into him. At some stage, Sarah was permitted to creep in quietly to try to persuade her to go home for the night and come back again in the morning, but Holly was adamant she was staying, and Sarah eventually went home on her own.

Holly continued to sit, framing the power and the words to mend Jake. Some of them were healing words she'd almost had to prise out of Ninanna when she was still Esme. Part of Holly wondered if she'd known them sooner, whether she could have saved her mother, but what was done had to stay done. She had a life to save now, even if she'd lost one then.

In the early-ish hours of the morning, there was an exchange of staff in the unit, and Holly caught snatches of the handover briefing.

"Man with girlfriend sitting vigil…serious mess…surgery… almost eviscerated him, like it was trying to rip out his heart… seriously touch and go."

The unit staff came and went, doing whatever they had to do around her. Holly just sat and held Jake's hand. Eventually she felt herself growing tired, but she just drew down more energy from around her, kept what little she needed for herself, and carried on directing the rest into Jake. Fortunately, the dull glow that by now surrounded them both was lost in the light seeping from the equipment.

Dawn came and went, and when the first consultant of the morning arrived to check on Jake, the nursing staff tried to persuade Holly to go home to get some sleep, a shower, and maybe a bit of breakfast before coming back.

"I'll go, but only after I've heard the consultant's comments on Jake's progress." Holly was adamant, but she knew the night had drained her and she was in need of some solid rest.

The doctor, having finally finished his review of Jake, was obviously pleasantly surprised and whilst not wishing to sound too optimistic, did bring himself to say that Jake was stable and showing signs of improvement. That decided Holly. Whilst desperately wanting to stay with Jake, she knew she was going to have to refill her own energy reserves if she was going to be able to help him any further. If she was honest, she wasn't even sure she was up to transporting herself home. Before she left, though, she used all her remaining power to surround Jake with protection against anything other than positive magical intervention. She couldn't offer permanent protection against mundane incidents, as the dog attack had proved. She'd have to rely on the hospital to keep him safe in the physical world. She could ensure, however, that no one could get at him via magic. How necessary such protection spells were, she still didn't really know, but Jake was either incredibly unlucky or someone was out to get him—possibly the same someone who had been chasing Appledore Ashwell and who had, it seemed, finally caught up with him.

Holly was exhausted and numb. She fleetingly wondered, and not for the first time, how wise she'd been to trust Partridge and didn't know where that left her, but if she had to, she felt she could defend herself. It was those she loved she was worrying about. First though, she really did need to get some sleep.

She headed down to the main reception area in search of a taxi. As she walked past the enquiries desk, the phrase "mauled by a huge dog" leapt out at her from the various conversations taking place. The speaker was an elderly but sprightly woman in green wellies and a khaki gillet, who was holding forth to a woman behind the desk.

"I know I'm not close friends or family, but it was my property he was on when that beast attacked him. I feel responsible, you know. He'd come to see Gilbert, my Jack Russell. The thing must have got itself trapped in the shed, and when he opened the door, well, it was huge. I couldn't see it that clearly, but it looked like some sort of gigantic wolfhound, like they used to…"

The rest of the sentence and the remainder of the conversation evaporated into the general hospital hubbub as far as Holly was concerned. The description "gigantic wolfhound" had triggered a response it was impossible to ignore. An image of Regal, large and imposing beside her grandmother, came into her head and would not go. The more she tried to clear it, the more detailed the picture of Regal became: the way he watched her as Barny would a mouse, his stance as he blocked her exit from the cottage—teeth bared, the deep, rough growling until silenced by Ninanna. The picture grew sharper and fresher until the dog's eyes made contact with her own and his top lip curled back in a snarl, revealing those large sharp teeth. A voice, sounding very much like her grandmother's, said quite distinctly, "Good boy, Regal." And then the image dissipated like morning mist. Holly found herself standing, frozen immobile in the hospital entrance, as the routine life of the hospital bustled on its way around her.

Chapter 23

Holly had managed to get a couple of much needed hours' sleep, a shower, some thinking time, and something to eat. She had fed Barny, made some phone calls, and been back to the hospital to check in on Jake. She was somewhat reassured by his progress, even if the hospital was keeping him in a state of drug-induced unconsciousness for the time being. She laid more healing words on him, along with a further sprinkling of raw witchlight, and then, reluctantly, left.

The vivid image of Regal had pinched and gnawed away at her. There was no real reason to think he was responsible, no concrete evidence pointing towards his, or Ninanna's, involvement in Jake's accident, but. The image had become one of those irritations that Holly just knew she had to scratch.

As she walked up the path to Ninanna's front door, Holly was both angry and hesitant. She had no idea what she was going to say to her grandmother. "Excuse me, I know we don't exactly like one another, but would you mind telling me if you set your dog on my boyfriend and had him try to eviscerate him" didn't really sound like a productive opening pitch. She was trying to think of another introductory line whilst bracing herself to hear Regal's usual warning alarm barks, but there was only unexpected silence. She knocked on the door: more silence.

Holly walked around the outside of the cottage. As far as she could tell, no one was home. She probed tentatively with her witchlight, but Ninanna was obviously wary of nosey neighbours, or the prying of the illuminated, because the cottage was magically shielded.

Even if curiosity had killed the cat, the empty property was too much of a good thing. The temptation to get inside the cottage to look around was chewing away at Holly, but if Ninanna had shielded her home from mystically prying eyes, she had almost certainly shielded it against unsolicited transportation and any other forms of eldritch penetration one of the illuminated might come up with. She had implied as much, and Holly's abortive attempt to transport out of the cottage the last time had already proved the limitations of magical movement.

Holly was on the point of giving up and transporting herself back to the hospital when she noticed a small upstairs window at the back of the property was ajar. A random thought occurred to her. In her desire to keep out the illuminated, had Ninanna overlooked the possibility of good, old-fashioned, mundane burglary? Surely not; but Ninanna didn't seem to take much interest in day-to-day life as most of the world lived it. Also, the window was small and would be difficult for any but the most accomplished cat burglar to access, but Holly was able to levitate and, once level with the window, could stretch an arm through the miniscule gap. From this position, she opened the window fully, crouched on the window ledge, and then stepped down unassisted by magic onto the floor of the room. There were no audible warning alarms, barking dogs, or the disorientating distortion of the cottage's interior she had half expected. She couldn't sense any warning spells. It seemed Ninanna had missed the obvious.

Holly moved cautiously through the building. It wasn't a small cottage, even without its hidden dimensions, but it didn't take Holly too long to check through all the rooms. She had been inside most of them on previous visits, but there were still some that were new to her, mainly bedrooms and a box room on the first floor.

She wasn't sure what, precisely, she was looking for, but she had expected to find more signs of Regal's presence: dog leads, bedding, that kind of thing. If she hadn't already known that a large dog lived here, she would never have guessed it from the house itself. His absence from the place seemed peculiar.

The other obvious absence was a personal element to the rooms. Everything was immaculate and, Holly suspected from the look of it, unostentatiously valuable, but there were no individual touches, even in the room Holly assumed was Ninanna's bedroom. There were no photographs, books, or CDs, no ornaments owned because of their meaning rather than their price tag. Holly drew the line at rummaging in depth through every clothing drawer in Ninanna's bedroom, but from a cursory glance there were no personal things like jewellery, bags, or customised accessories. It was all pristinely formal and, somehow, rather bleak.

It dawned painfully on Holly that a further absence was that of Esme. An observer, casual or otherwise, would never know that Ninanna had once had a daughter, that the daughter had allegedly grown up here, and that Ninanna had passed decades of her life masquerading as her. Even the clothes Ninanna had worn as Esme were missing from the cottage. Those in Ninanna's wardrobe were uniformly dark—shades of black, grey and navy—nothing that might be termed colourful, however far the imagination attempted to stretch.

Holly had now run out of cottage to explore, at least in terms of the traditionally sized and normally dimensioned one. Somewhere, though, was a much larger cottage interior with many additional rooms Holly had never seen inside. The absences in the standard cottage drew Holly, like gaping black holes, to the hidden presence of the alternative cottage interior she had briefly experienced that one time. The big question was how to get into it without transporting from the mundane one, because Holly had a strong feeling that any magic perpetrated inside the cottage by someone other than Ninanna would, as a minimum, trigger an alarm all the way back to Ninanna herself.

Holly had been in the parlour when she had first transported into the alternatively sized cottage. She returned to the parlour now and scrutinized it for any signs of something that might help her get into the rest of the cottage, but there was nothing, nada, zip. She sat down to consider alternatives to transporting direct from inside the building, in the hope she could find a way to be diverted into its alternate. She glanced vacantly around the room. The paintings were the same as they always were—no clues there. She felt she was missing something. She looked again. The sampler caught the corner of her eye and then blurred. Every time she scanned the room, it drifted from her peripheral vision. It was only when she stared directly at it that it remained in focus. It was highly coloured and painstakingly worked—surprising therefore, that she kept glancing over it. It was apparently an exercise in alphabetical characters, but now she was really looking at it, she noticed the alphabet was in a somewhat random order and several of the characters were oddly embellished.

She peered at the sampler more closely. The embellishments to the characters were actually small, minutely worked images: a tiny lion, an ankh, twisted reeds, and a miniscule black and white cottage not unlike the one she was sitting in. The more she stared at the embroidered cottage, the more it looked exactly like Ninanna's. Then something happened. The image started to enlarge and come forward out of the sampler, moving towards her. The larger it grew, the more it became like the actual cottage, and the less it looked like a cluster of tiny stitches. Eventually it was like a three-dimensional photograph, and then it grew bigger still—or Holly seemed to shrink—until it was as if she was standing outside a mirror image of the cottage, albeit still within the original. Then it moved forward and through her and swallowed her. Suddenly, she was standing within the alternate version, a building apparently rotated on its usual axis by one hundred and eighty degrees and stretched in all possible directions. The disorientating effects of her first visit were gone, and Holly found she could move round the alternate cottage quite normally. It was time to find out if this construction had the answers that the quotidian cottage so conspicuously lacked.

Many of the rooms seemed just as they were in the originally sized cottage. Holly gave them a cursory glance and moved on. She was more interested in the rooms she couldn't see under normal conditions. Even then, and given that Holly didn't know how much time she had to explore uninterrupted, there were almost too many rooms to look into.

At least five large rooms were filled, floor to ceiling, with books, many of them apparently centuries old. Other rooms were crammed with old furniture and discarded domestic items, as if the results of numerous house clearances had been randomly dumped in them. There were even the sort of personal items glaringly lacking from Ninanna's mundane cottage, though whether they were Ninanna's possessions was another matter. Holly couldn't imagine Ninanna wielding the extra large golf clubs she found leaning in the corner of an otherwise empty room.

One room made Holly pause longer than the others. It was a bedroom up on the second floor. Decorated in shades of sweet shop pink and yellow, with early photos of the Beatles and other singers from the period, it looked like a teenager's room from the early 1960s. There were two teddy bears and a fluffy pink rabbit on the bed. On a chest of drawers was a photograph Holly had first seen in one of Abigail Holmfirth's photograph albums—the one in which a young Esme was enjoying herself at a summer house party from which her mother was liberatingly absent. In the background, a youthful Appledore Ashwell was captured for photographic eternity in the same frame.

Holly could feel a lump rising rapidly in her throat. This was the closest she'd ever felt to Esme, and the irony of it was she was standing by herself in an otherwise deserted room.

Down on the ground floor, she finally found Regal's sleeping area. It was a brutally bare room with a row of hooks at one end, from which hung an assortment of leads, and a large and currently unoccupied dog basket at the other. A rubber pull ring and a well-chewed rag doll lay on the floor beside the basket. There were a number of large, muddy paw prints. Some of them were noticeably darker than others, and she crouched down to examine them. On close inspection, they looked more like they might be dried blood, but Holly couldn't be totally certain. Then she noticed the contents of Regal's basket. Apart from the bedding, there were scraps of bedraggled and well-chewed cloth. Holly looked closer and decided some of the scraps were pieces of cotton, the type men's shirts were often made from and others were the badly stained remnants of a man's tie. With a jolt she realised Jake had a similarly patterned tie. She felt sick. Had he been wearing it the other evening? She pocketed one of the pieces for further scrutiny.

On the opposite side of the building, a number of rooms appeared to have been turned over entirely to storage. Room after room contained nothing but boxes, crates, jars, and nameless containers. Some were almost as big as a man; others more closely resembled funeral urns.

Holly did not feel at ease in any of these rooms. Whether it was because everything in them was hidden and shut away in one of the innumerable boxes and containers, or whether it was the feeling of bleak abandonment that the rooms gave her, she couldn't say, but it was with considerable hesitation she decided to open one of the boxes to see what was inside. She selected, almost randomly, a small plain, cardboard box from the top of a pile of assorted containers, boxes, and storage jars. Gingerly pulling back the lid, she found it filled with an ash-like substance. As she replaced the box and turned her attention to another one, she thought she could hear the hushed rustle of the ash as it settled back down.

A second container also had ash in it and pieces of what, disturbingly, looked like carbonised bone. She shut it again quickly and distinctly heard the dry whispering of ashes as they shifted.

She rechecked all the rooms being used for storing boxes and crates. The age of the containers varied considerably. Some were far older than others—centuries older by the look of them. She opened at least one in each room. Every one contained ash or what looked like pieces of bone. Some contained both. Desiccated, rattling, and dusty sighs accompanied her investigations. Finally, she plucked up the courage to open one of the largest boxes. She was horrified, but somehow not surprised, to find the scorched remains of a complete human skeleton.

Holly's thoughts were racing. In all the rooms she had entered, she could now hear the dusty whisper of shifting ashes. A dry hissing seemed to have penetrated her head and was beginning to muffle her thoughts. She found it difficult to think clearly, let alone determine where those thoughts were leading.

In the last of the rooms she found a box with an animal skeleton in it. The creature was quite large and though she wasn't a vet, Holly thought it had probably been a big dog. She tried to convince herself the previous skeleton she had seen had actually been an animal's, rather than a human's. It was all still pretty grotesque, but animal remains were less alarming than human ones.

Then she caught sight of what was most definitely a funeral urn: a twist-lid container with a pseudo-bronze finish, like the ones occasionally seen in undertakers' shop windows. There was a small plaque on the lid. It read clearly and unambiguously "Esme Beldam, 1944 -1970: End of the Line." The whispering in her head became a roaring, and Holly stepped back. In the process, she almost fell over a large packing case marked with modern Greek lettering. Righting herself, she suddenly caught sight of Ninanna standing in the doorway with Regal at her side. Ninanna had him on a tight leash, and the dog's hackles were clearly up. Ninanna smiled, and the rushing in Holly's head gave way to a sudden and oppressive silence.

"And there was me thinking you'd come to avenge your beloved, when all you were really after was a family reunion. How touching."

The following four things registered simultaneously within Holly's head: Ninanna had basically admitted responsibility for the attack on Jake; they must genuinely be Esme's ashes she was holding; she wanted to kill her own grandmother; and she was trapped in a room with no external windows, no way to transport out cleanly and, therefore, really, no way out. While Holly was processing her reactions to these intensely compacted and darkly disturbing revelations, Ninanna was standing motionless in the doorway with the same strange smile on her face.

"If you're waiting for me to explain myself, you'll have a long wait. This isn't going to be one of those convenient denouements where I explain everything to you before I inadvertently let you get away. There is no getting away, by the way, in case you haven't worked that out for yourself. If you attempt to transport, you'll find, like before, that you can't. This part of the house permits no magic but its own. The only solution is to kiss and make up. We are family, after all."

Ninanna offered up her hand, the family ring prominently displayed on it, with the same grandeur she had demonstrated previously. Holly could not believe she was still trying to get her to kiss the family ring. Part of her wanted to laugh and another part wanted to scream; the pragmatic part wanted to get the hell out of there.

"No? Still not willing to acknowledge my precedence within the family? You do realise this can only end badly? Rather like it did for your father, I guess."

Ninanna pointed to the crate Holly had just stumbled over. In other circumstances, Holly would have found the implications of that gesture deeply upsetting, but right now there wasn't time. She was too busy working out how to get out of the cottage using the one means still available to her; at least, she hoped it was available.

Ninanna adjusted her grip on Regal's lead and collar, and with a rush of hot nausea, Holly realised that any minute now the dog would be unleashed and over one hundred pounds of canine sinew, muscle, and crushing teeth-lined jaws would come hurtling at her, the same way they must have come at Jake. She just hoped her theoretical method for exiting the building was going to work in practice.

Ninanna let go of Regal's collar and yelled, "Go boy. Fetch the heart!"

Holly visualised the embroidered image of the cottage hanging in the air around her and rapidly moved back and away from it towards the outer wall of the room. As the image had once passed through her, she now passed back out of it, away and through and suddenly she was in mid-air, the equivalent of three storeys up, but outside the cottage. Regal, having hurled himself at her, was also outside, his snarling bite only centimetres away from her face as they fell earthwards together. Being outside the cottage meant Holly could use her magic again, and suddenly, she was floating away and up, whilst the unmagical Regal was still plummeting. Holly didn't check to see if Ninanna came to the aid of her loyal familiar, but just before she transported herself away, she heard a plaintive howl followed by a whimper. Then she was gone.

Chapter 24

Holly had transported herself, without even thinking about it, to a place where she felt safe. Her parents' house provided her with temporary shelter and comfort, but she sensed she didn't have long. She also sensed that giving in to natural human fear and cowering away in an apparently secure refuge was not going to work. After the confrontation at the cottage, Ninanna would almost certainly come after her at the earliest opportunity. The why of things might be unclear, but the what had a momentum that felt horribly inevitable.

Ninanna could track her via her witchlight, so the fewer times Holly caused it to shine out, the better. She remembered Apple Ashwell talking about staying below the magic radar, and she thought she now understood what he meant. However, there were some things she still needed to do, regardless. She had to try to get help. She had to find the time to think things through calmly and find the means to work out what had been going on at the cottage, so she could deal with it. While she did this, never remaining in one place for too long and keeping at least a location ahead of Ninanna were going to be seriously important. She also needed to be able to communicate without using magic.

Before she fled the house at Croydon, Holly used her power to summon a simple and anonymous mundane pay-as–you-go mobile phone. There'd be a bit of a hiccup with someone's database and purchase records, but that was neither here nor there. As soon as she had the phone, she transported away from the house and into the relative anonymity of Central London.

In London, she used a combination of magical transportation and the totally unmagical Underground to keep on the move, popping up in different points around the city only to duck back down the tube and reappear somewhere else. Every two or three changes of location, she would phone Partridge to continue the disjointed dialogue she had initiated at the start of her round London tour. Her main aim was to get help and find out what Ninanna had been up to at the cottage, but it was not proving straightforward.

In her imagination, the human and animal remains stored there were still whispering dryly to her. She felt sure they were linked to the deaths of Esme and Apple and probably, therefore, the attack on Jake. There were also the unexplained but worrying deaths of Brothers Holmfirth and Corey, more possible telltales as to what Ninanna was up to, if only she could interpret them. Plus, of course, there was Ninanna's precious family heirloom of a ring and her antiquated approach to it, which would have been laughably ludicrous if matters were not becoming so dark. Holly knew she needed an explanation that combined all of those threads in a way that made sense and gave her a way forward. She was hoping Partridge would be able to provide assistance and some, if not all, of the answers. She was going to be disappointed on all counts.

"I've told you before, girlie, you're on your own. This is Old Magic, and I don't know anything meaningful about it. Nor, before you ask again, does the Coven. This was, is, Ninanna's speciality and now yours, supposedly, to whatever extent she's shared her knowledge with you."

"But, you've got to know something. There are other Old Magic practitioners out there. The Coven keeps records, right? There may be something in the records that can help—something that's happened before that can give pointers to what's happening now. There must be something about the ring, at least. It's old and has been in the hands of the Beldams for generations. There must be some mention, somewhere. It's all got to be connected. You've been around for ages, Partridge, so have the other Coven members, presumably. Maybe one of you knows something from back in the day, an anecdote, a bit of gossip maybe, that could shed some light on what she's up to."

Holly didn't wait for an answer, At this point, she disappeared down into the tube at Russell Square, only to emerge very quickly again at Piccadilly. She rang Partridge back immediately.

"Why are you doing this, Holly girl? If, as you say, the old crow's out to get you, why don't you just get her first? That's the witchcraft way—the way it was done back in the day, as you so quaintly put it and you, sure as Hecate, have juice enough flowing through you to take her on. You can't afford to be squeamish, you know. You're the one with the power."

"You would say that. Given the Coven's love of Old Magic, I dare say you'd be happy if I managed to get myself killed in the process: two feral practitioners gone at one go. They'd be partying up at Coven H.Q., wherever that is. So much for being my mentor."

"Come, come. There's no need to be like that."

"Isn't there? Ninanna is trying to kill me and mine, and I don't see you or the bloody Coven rushing to my aid. I'm on my own, here. You've already told me that. It's got so bad, I don't even feel safe staying in one place for more than a few minutes. So, I'm going to be off again. I'll ring you back in another five to ten minutes. You'd better have something for me then, or I'll believe you want me dead as much as Ninanna."

Holly hung up, realising it had been something of an empty threat. If Partridge didn't respond, all she'd get was proof there was more than one person who'd like to see the permanent back of her. So what? It was those who loved her and were relying on her that were important. She hoped it was more than just luck that nothing had encroached on the warding magic she was using to protect them.

Holly ducked down into the Underground again and risked using magic to check in on Jake. From what she could gather, he was making steady progress and likely to regain consciousness sometime relatively soon. She just wanted to be still alive when it happened. The protective magic she had thrown over Jake was still in place, and she added more to it to be on the safe side. She wanted to check in on Barny too, but thought better of it. She had already used way too much magic. Instead, she reluctantly returned to London and made a couple more trips on the Tube, hoping to distort any trail she was leaving.

Whilst she was down in the Underground, she reflected on her last conversation with Partridge. Why didn't she just "get" Ninanna first, rather than scurrying down tunnels like a frightened rabbit? Back in the cottage, she'd had the will to kill her—why not now? She was justifying her hesitation, at least to herself, on the grounds she needed to know what she was dealing with, before she could deal with it. More importantly, given Ninanna's significantly greater knowledge and experience, she had, somehow, to gain some sort of advantage she could use to defend herself and Jake and beat Ninanna. She didn't know if it was cowardice or a sentimental softness she could ill afford, but she shied away from the thought of actually killing her. You didn't do that sort of thing in real life. Just defeating her and stopping her from harming anyone would be enough, but to do that she needed much more than she had currently got.

Holly emerged at Embankment and walked over to the river before phoning Partridge again. If he still refused, or was unable, to help her, she had no idea what she was going to do next.

Partridge's phone rang just once before he answered.

"Holly? It's not much, but I've got something for you."

Holly wanted to be relieved, but she knew she couldn't afford the luxury of her adrenaline levels dropping.

"Thank you. What is it? What've you got?"

"A wisp of a story and full access to the Coven archives."

"Come again?"

"You said it. We may not have as much knowledge as we should about Old Magic, but we have extensive memories. I contacted one of our oldest surviving members. Brother Gray used to dabble in the old ways, nothing too serious, but enough to know more than the rest of us. He remembers a ring, either the Beldam family ring or one like it: large moonstone, ornate setting, worn by the head of an Old Magic family. He could use it to draw power from all the witchlight in the family bloodline and to ensure family members' loyalty. Once they were fully illuminated, everyone in the family had to swear allegiance and kiss the ring before he would recognise them. Rumours were, it was a type of thrall ring."

"Okay, that may worryingly explain Ninanna's papal tendencies with her ring. What else have you got?"

"Not much more from Brother Gray, I'm afraid. It took me all my time to get that brief reminiscence out of him, but I can give you access to the archives."

"Oh please, not more bureaucratic paper pushing and infantile alphabets. There's nothing there that'll help."

"No, not the records—the proper, historic archives. The Coven has existed for centuries. Over the years it has acquired and collected acres of information and probably confiscated even more, particularly in relation to Old Magic, with which we've always had a love-hate relationship. Texts we've banned got stored down there: grimoires, Old Magic books, instruction manuals, diaries. They're all kept in the old library. If I'm honest, there are echoes of Ninanna's cottage to it. The library is huge and bigger than it was when it was first built. It grows to accommodate the books and manuscripts it absorbs. I'll take you there. You can have the run of the place. Somewhere in it there'll be something that can help you. Meet me at the British Library and we'll go on from there."

Holly was sceptical, but this was all she had, so she took the Tube to Kings Cross. The wait infuriated Partridge, but he understood her desire to limit the use of her witchlight.

"Nevertheless, you are going to have to use it to transport into the archive—it's the only way in."

First though, they went into the British Library on foot, and Partridge took Holly down to the Coven's records using his magic instead of hers. Blue budgie man wasn't there today, but a young-looking blond girl was seated at the reception desk, a Siamese cat splayed out on the desk in front of her. She waved Partridge and Holly through without saying a word. Holly thought she looked nervous—or perhaps it was just her own anxiety being reflected back at her?

Holly and Partridge walked through into the main records storage area, a huge maze of high shelving and narrow rat-run aisles. The shelves were filled with brown files and boxes of what, Holly presumed, were yet more files.

Partridge hurried Holly down a line of rat-runs until they came to an open space with a large pentagram inlaid into the flooring.

"Stand in the centre of the 'gram and transport yourself."

"Where to?"

"Anywhere you choose. It doesn't matter. Wherever your intended destination, you'll end up in the archives. There's only one way in and one way out, and you're standing on it. It doesn't permit alternatives. There's some valuable, not to say controversial, material down there. The system has in-built protection."

Holly stood in the centre of the pentagram.

"You'll come down straight after me?"

"No. I'm going to stay here and watch your back."

"But…"

"No buts. There's a lot of information for you to absorb down there. It won't be a quick in and out. You may or may not be right about your grandmother's intentions, but if it turns out you are right about Ninanna tracking and coming after you, you're going to be a sitting mallard for quite some time. There's only one way in and one way out, and I'm going to be here guarding it. Whilst I'll admit you could well be correct about the Coven as a whole, I'm my own man. You don't have to fight this corner all on your own. Now, off you go, girlie. Uncork yourself and let your witchlight guide you."

Holly was unspeakably grateful to Partridge, but she wasn't too sure about the reference to cork removal; she had a feeling it was anally related. If she responded, they'd only have another spat and that was hardly sensible or appropriate at this moment in time. She transported instead, but there was no expected sudden transition from one place to another. She found herself falling, slowly, painfully slowly, down a dark, narrow tunnel. Up above her, she could see the silhouetted figure of Partridge growing smaller and smaller as she fell towards oblivion. Then there was starlight. It still felt like a tunnel, but the walls were lined with moving star shine, burning with a sharp cold fire, and then it was dark again and she was standing on something solid.

Gradually, the area became illuminated and she found herself in a vast, barely lit circular space, like a large chapter house. Except, when she turned round, she saw that aisles and book shelves stretched out radially in all directions for as far as the eye could see, which wasn't actually that far, given the poor level of lighting and the thick darkness that covered everything beyond the dim glow of the light.

She stepped forward and the same dull glow moved with her. She looked up and saw a dimly lit globe shining, if that was not too optimistic a term, above her head. Some bright spark had written "Toc H" on it with a marker pen.

Holly began to walk down one of the aisles, selected at random. Everywhere there were books and documents. Some appeared quite recent, others undebateably old. She had no idea where to start looking or what she was even looking for. Partridge's comment that it wouldn't be a quick in and out, suddenly had a lot more unwelcome weight.

Randomly, she pulled an old and musty tome from a shelf in front of her. Once she had accustomed herself to the old-fashioned script, she discovered that the entire book, and it was a large volume, was devoted to different ways of dealing with a riggwelted sheep. Who knew there could be so many different methods?

She walked on a bit further down the aisle and selected another book. This one was written in German and, not speaking the language, she had to use magic to translate it. It turned out to be a recipe book for healthy eating during pregnancy.

Holly looked up and down the aisles around her. Row after row, they stretched away from her into the dark, beyond the reach of her self-transporting reading lamp. There were thousands of books and documents, but how many of them related to Old Magic and how many would simply help improve her jam-making or sheep-rearing skills, she had no way of knowing. Even more disconcertingly, she didn't know how she was supposed to identify and separate the individual veterinary manuals and recipe books from the manuscripts that were at least vaguely relevant to Old Magic—and once she had those, how she would ever be able to work out which specific ones would be of direct assistance to her in her current situation.

As the impossibility of the task ahead of her sunk in, she could feel the tension rising in her neck and down her spine. So much for uncorking; every muscle in her body was holding on to whatever it could with a vice-like grip. In her head, the dry sifting of ash that had been there ever since her discoveries at the cottage was joined by the rustling of numberless pages, frantically turning without hope of ever being read. Partridge's parting shot now seemed both uncharitable and impossible.

"Uncork yourself and let your witchlight guide you."

Well, if she couldn't do the first bit, perhaps she should try to do the second—use her witchlight to track down what she needed. The trouble was, she couldn't really envisage how she might go about it, and nothing either Partridge or Ninanna had taught her was of direct help. She remembered the witchlight flowing out of her the first time in the Lakes. Anger and fear had uncorked it then. She was angry and scared now, but not with the same primal immediacy. This was longer term, energy draining, nerve shredding, anxiety. What if she just envisioned the light flowing out of her as it had in the farmhouse and then directed it to identify and collect books and manuscripts that related to Old Magic, the situation at the cottage, the family ring, and Ninanna's strange and presumably murderous ways? It had to be worth a try because it would take a decade and a half of Sundays, and quite possibly all the other days of the week as well, to track down the knowledge she needed any other way.

Holly stood stock still, closed her eyes, and willed herself to relax. She imagined her body letting go of its tensions and releasing the witchlight inside her in waves of light, waves that rhythmically rolled away from her in search of the knowledge she needed to confront Ninanna and resolve things once and for all. As the waves pulsed outwards, she felt them pushing at her tension and the unseen barriers inside her, and then suddenly, in a flood of brightness, scattered ash, and turning pages, the witchlight poured out of her, seeking, absorbing, digesting. She opened her eyes briefly and saw streams of light flooding the aisles, the efforts of the poor little reading globe drowned out by the sheer magnitude of her witchlight. She could see the light stretching away into the distance like probing glacial fingers. She wondered how long it would keep going, but eventually there was a pause and then the light started to return. Wave after wave after wave, until all the waves merged and it became a flood, and Holly was filled with knowledge and sound and light. It was all about the light.

Ninanna was accumulating the witchlight and power of generations—harvesting it from both the already dead and the soon to be so—until it became a huge river of light, flooding through the veins of the remaining family members. Except, of course, with each harvest the flood became stronger and the bloodline became shorter and the power available to the family became greater and greater until there were only two: the head of the family and the end of the line (and there have been two of those, confirmed a dry quiet whisper in Holly's head).

It was also about fire. Burning and consuming. To harvest the witchlight, Ninanna had burned the bones of her ancestors and then the living flesh of her family until the witchlight evaporated and was caught within the moonstone ring, before being poured back into the remaining bloodline. Everyone glowed just a little bit brighter until it was their turn to be harvested. Whether anyone ever realised what she was doing was questionable, but no one asked any questions, and no one objected to the increased power that gradually came their way. Her ultimate goal was to create a vast reservoir of power, pooled between her and the end of the line, with all other tributaries stopped and pruned away. Then, she would eliminate the end of the line. With nowhere else to flow, the power would become uniquely hers.

"That way you create a vast source of power and almost limitless possibilities. No one had been strong enough to try for centuries. Until me, that is."

Holly opened her eyes. The brilliance of the witchlight had flowed away, and the feeble illumination of the little Toc H was spilling a small murky pool of light for a few feet around her. Standing visible within its dull glow was Ninanna.

Chapter 25

"It's rather a waste of time flouncing around the country like a bumblebee on amphetamines, trying desperately to stay out of magical view and then unleashing an accumulated flood of witchlight into the ether, particularly when I am drawn by the wave it makes. Even if I hadn't located you before, all I had to do was follow your amazingly excessive beacon of light back to its source, *et voilà*, here I am."

Confronted by Ninanna's sudden appearance in the archives, Holly instinctively glanced around for signs of Partridge.

"Brother Mayflower will not be joining us, I'm afraid. Simple magic has problems standing up to Old Magic at the best of times, but when the Old Magic has accumulated and matured over centuries, it is rather like sending a sickly baby rabbit to confront a ravenous wolf."

Ninanna smiled thinly, but whatever emotion she was attempting to display, it had lost much of its humanity. Holly saw this, and whilst briefly registering the presence of her own all-too-human shock, guilt, and grief, allowed them to pass and be muffled within the dry and papery rustlings still subtly, but persistently, present in her head.

"It rather puts your love of family into perspective. So, how many centuries of accumulation and how many generations did you engulf in fire in the process?" Holly retorted.

"Truth to tell, I forget. I killed my great grandfather somewhen back in the seventeenth century, and I've not really kept count after that. The more a family spreads, the more tributaries and connections to the bloodline have to be stopped up and cut off. I have had little time to reflect. I've been busy. There's just the two of us now, dear heart."

"Did you kill my mother?"

"Which one? Although the answer's yes, regardless."

Holly absorbed another pang of shock. Dust dry whispers took it away and stored it for future use.

"Esme's was the death that counted, though. She was conceived and born to have been the end of the line—an end I controlled. I thought she'd just run away from me, but apparently it was to have you. She'd managed to keep you secret, and after she gave birth, she muffled your witchlight, cloaking it from prying magics and from you, yourself, apparently. She even abandoned you to the mundane world and did her best to leave behind what poor witchlight she could to make sure you felt no trace of magic and never thought to come looking for her. I have no idea to this day where she left you. By the time I caught up with her at Kew, you were well hidden. I expected her death would be a fulfilment, a culmination. It took me a while to realise why the full power had not flowed to me as it should have. I hadn't known the snivelling child would prove so capable. I guess you never really know your nearest and dearest.

"Even once I knew of your existence, I still couldn't detect you. It seems my daughter inherited more of my traits than I gave her credit for. I wasted a long time searching for you. I had wanted to find you before you grew up, before there was any risk you'd succumb to your own bestial instincts and extend the line yet again, let alone dilute it with human genes, but as time passed, all I could do was splash enough unfinessed magic around to make sure the course and outcome of true love never ran smooth, and the end of the line, whoever and wherever it was, stayed that way. It wasn't actually until Brother Ashwell crawled out of whatever hole he'd been keeping himself in to look for you that my way to you became clearer. Then you came to me, anyway, and it all became so much easier."

Holly's thoughts were focused on one thing. "You killed Mum as well? Why? What did that achieve?"

"I did. She was reaching the end of her flow naturally. I just hurried things along. It isolated and distracted you. Both might have been useful. Distraction slows you down. I have to say, though, ironically, I was a wee bit disappointed it took you this long to get to the source of the matter. I admit I may have underestimated my daughter, but clearly not her ill-gotten whelp. The Ashwell bloodline was always a weak one. Still, the unsought-for blood tie enabled me to augment our witchlight with a little of its feeble emissions."

Anger flamed in Holly, blending with the witchlight and the rasping stirrings of parchment and dust. The urge to give in to her emotions was strong, but beneath the fury, Holly was conscious her grandmother was, in effect, wasting time providing her with, as Ninanna would have it, unnecessary explanations, whilst seemingly trying to goad her. Why? With the power she had harvested over the centuries, a neophyte witch like Holly was no match for her. She could wipe the floor with her…and then it dawned on Holly. The power that Ninanna had homicidally accumulated flowed equally between them, from the head of the family to the end of the line and back again. Ninanna's power was Holly's power, and whatever Ninanna could do, so equally could Holly.

Ninanna, in theory at least, had met her match, and she was being cautious, but to what end? Her experience still outweighed Holly's, but Holly had youth and anger on her side and, echoed the soft whisperings within her, *Us*. Holly finally understood there was more than echoes of dry noise inside her head. It was confused, but alongside and within the desiccated shiftings and mutterings still reverberating from the cottage, there was a presence or presences. She sensed the amassed Old Magic knowledge of the Grand Coven of Great Britain, Ireland and the Etheric Islands; something which Ninanna, as knowledgeable as she was, could still only dream of. Plus, though this was something Holly was barely conscious of, but barely conscious was enough, the attic-hushed scuttle of dust and bone she had carried with her since the cottage was gifting her strength and the knowledge there were worse things than death.

Perhaps Ninanna sensed this, because she had fallen silent and was staring thoughtfully at Holly. Then, without any indication of what she was about to do, a flash of searing witchlight erupted from her hands and flowed at frightening speed towards Holly.

Fortunately for Holly, Ninanna's aim was ever so slightly askew, and Holly was able to dodge the bolt of light. It shattered the little reading globe and rushed on. For an instant, as she watched the familiar comet tail of silvery blue and white pass by, she caught herself wondering, almost whimsically, what she would have been turned into had the light hit her—a frog maybe, or a crow—and then the witchlight smashed into the books and shelves behind her, reducing them to charred specks of paper and sharply penetrating splinters, tearing into her jeans and the soft flesh of the backs of her legs. Any childhood fantasy of magicians duelling in a witchcraft equivalent of paper, scissors, and stone disappeared instantly in the shock and the pain of immediate reality.

Holly dragged herself to one side, smearing the floor with her blood as she did so. She had barely begun to heal herself when another flash of light illuminated the now-dark library. Instinctively and without further thought, she blocked it with a bolt of her own, and the two masses of light exploded together, leaving what looked like a ragged black hole of even darker nothingness suspended in mid-air about five feet off the ground.

From the ragged hole a strong wind began to blow, whipping up paper and wood shards into a lethal, flesh-shredding whirlwind Holly now recognised as Ninanna's trademark flourish. Holly could feel the changed air pressure and hear the rasp of and roar of the wind. This, she could deal with. She had thought about it long and hard since the incident with Apple Ashwell and Jake's clearly now not-so-accidental brush with a twister. As fast as the winds poured out of the hole and attempted to merge, Holly pulled them apart and aimed them outwards radially. That dissipated the whirlwind, but blew debris dangerously around elsewhere. Holly tried focussing the wind back at Ninanna, but Ninanna responded swiftly, and a wall of screaming wind erupted between them, shielding both of them from one another and preventing further attacks from either side.

It was a protracted physical stalemate until Ninanna suddenly dropped her guard and the gale surged towards where she had been, although by now she was no longer there. It was a gamble that paid off, because she immediately reappeared a few feet to the left and hurled another bright blast of witchlight at Holly. The sudden loss of wind resistance in front of her caused Holly to stagger forward, and Ninanna's attack missed her by a hair's breadth, painfully scorching the back of her neck and obliterating the bookshelves at the end of the aisle.

Using the light from the now-burning fires behind her, Holly ran down an adjacent aisle and out of the reach of Ninanna's witchlight. At least she now knew transportation within the library was possible. The rustling in her head tried to tell her she knew a good deal more about what was, and was not, possible within the archive, if only she would listen to what was inside of her, but Holly was too busy hurling an illuminating ball of burning witchlight at Ninanna to pay attention.

This time, rather than blocking the attack, Ninanna dowsed the flames in water. A cascade of torrential indoor rain soaked everything underneath it and extinguished the fires. Holly transported frantically, finding that the library limited her movements to just a few feet in any direction.

Holly finally thought to adjust her eyesight so she could see through the darkness.

Feeling like a rat in a maze, she dodged down another aisle and waited for the opportunity to launch a further attack against Ninanna, but when the time came, Ninanna blocked the blast with almost feline agility, ripping yet another dark hole in the air between them. The hole briefly fascinated Holly. She wanted to know what lay beyond it, within its peacefully comforting blackness. Something seemed to be telling her that oblivion was an attractive option. The dry rustling in her head grew louder, but whether it too hankered after oblivion or was frantically trying to tell her to ignore the voice of despair, she couldn't tell: she still wasn't listening hard enough to hear.

The fight went on and on, but the outcome of every attack was the same—a fierce and furious counter attack resulting in deadlock. Time and time again and then again. Holly could no longer measure how much time had passed or was still passing. It could have been minutes or hours. It felt like forever. She realised the conflict could drag on indefinitely until one tired slightly more than the other or the archives were obliterated. Despite the vast amount of damage they had already caused, the shelves still seemed to stretch on without conclusion. Holly couldn't begin to imagine how long it would take to destroy the entire place, and even then, there was no guarantee she and Ninanna would have ended things. A different strategy was needed because raw power alone was not working, but whoever took time out to think through a different approach was leaving herself open to further attack, perhaps fatally so. Apparently neither was willing to take the risk.

And so it went on for another period almost beyond time. Attack and counterattack. Attack and counterattack. Another hole cracked open in the stale library air. The moves were becoming so instinctive, Holly could feel herself slipping into an almost trancelike state. That was dangerous. She risked losing speed of response and....

Suddenly she felt the telltale signs of time being bent, just a little, but enough. The air distorted in front of Ninanna, and then for a brief moment there were two of her standing a few feet apart and any minute now, two bolts of witchlight would be hurled at Holly from two different angles. One she could deflect, but two?

Instinct took over, urged on by the hiss of her subconscious. Without thinking of any consequences, Holly leapt into the nearest hole still suspended in the air between them and disappeared.

Holly's motivation had been to escape—both the witchlight flares and the ongoing fight itself. She had wanted away from the battleground and out of the library. In her imagination, the conflict had already stretched on to infinity, and she didn't have the stomach for any more, whereas Ninanna clearly had. She got part of her wish, a respite from the fight, but the hole was a tear in the library itself and it took her deeper into the archives, to another level of books and artefacts, away from the destruction and noise of the fight and into almost tangible silence. Within that silence, the noises in her head were unavoidably audible and insistent. This time she had to listen. There was no choice.

She could feel the desiccated sighs she had first heard in the charnel rooms of the cottage, alongside the papery rustling that had come with the flood of knowledge from the library. But now, she truly heard them and knew them for what they were—the residual imprint of passing humanity. In the case of the library, it was centuries worth of thoughts and opinions and knowledge, mixed with spent witchlight and built up organically over time. The voices from the cottage were more disturbing. Ninanna's unnatural containment of the witchlight had caused it to stay anchored to the living world after its original owners had left it. The ring was a temporary anchorage—the human remains from which the witchlight had originally sprung, correctly magicked, were a more permanent anchor—preventing it from dissipating back into the ether, as it would normally do after death. In the bond between witchlight, ash, and bones, however, a last trace of human consciousness was also trapped. The dead were not permitted to know the full release of death, and their dust was alive with anger and despair. Now, though, they could sense a potential end to their betrayal. With this possibility drawing closer, they yearned all the more for the peace that had been denied them—a peace that would only be claimed through the purifying fury of vengeance, and they didn't care who got burned in the process. They welcomed Holly fiercely as the spark to ignite their longed-for conflagration.

Ninanna was still hunting for Holly. The deep hole the girl had dived into had closed up behind her, but Ninanna could sense her, scurrying about somewhere within the overlapping layers of the library. There was little chance of finding her within the maze they created, but she would have to emerge at some stage, and there was only one way into the archive and therefore only one way out. Ninanna made her way to the pentagram and waited.

Time was variable within the mystic parameters of the library, but it didn't feel as if she had been waiting that long before she saw Holly appear beside the pentagram and step into its centre. Ninanna poured her witchlight straight at Holly, who disappeared beneath it. But then the witchlight itself disappeared, as if being funnelled vertically up into an invisible chimney. Ninanna stopped the flow of light. If the witchlight had disappeared into the exit tunnel, it was possible Holly had too. She ran to the Pentagram and stepped into the centre herself. There was a brief moment when it felt as if time was being bent, and then she was falling slowly upwards through starlight, but the cold light had been replaced with a fiery glow. Up above her, the witchlight she had poured into the exit was rising in tandem with her and burning fiercely.

Holly had left the library before Ninanna had returned to the exit and had slowly risen through starlight and darkness, until she was back in what was left of the records area. Chaos had left signs of its cauterizing presence, and anything once living had been incinerated. Holly averted her eyes from the burnt and crumpled human mass slumped over by the shelving. This wasn't the time either to be horrified or to mourn. Then she noticed a strand of unburnt blond hair and what looked like the charred corpse of a cat next to the mound and realised it wasn't Partridge. Any relief of a sort was short lived. Looking down at the pentagram she was standing on, she belatedly saw the carbonised outline of a sprawled human figure burned into the flooring, but there still wasn't time for real grief. Not now. Tears streamed down her face, but her determination was at odds with her sorrow. Or perhaps not. She made Partridge an unspoken promise and refocused on what she had still to do. The centuries of dry fury in her head were urging her on. Reaching back down through the entrance to the library with her witchlight, she used her own power and the warped dimensions of the library itself to bend time long enough to recreate the image of herself leaving the archive. As soon as Ninanna's witchlight poured into the lower end of the tunnel and started to rise inexorably towards her, she released the chronological fold she had created and allowed time to return to its normal, seemingly linear, flow.

She assumed Ninanna was exiting the library behind her burst of witchlight, but she couldn't know for sure. Still, it had to be done. She just couldn't work out whether she wanted Ninanna to be in the exit tunnel or not and whether her ambivalence was callousness or guilt. No matter. Then the dry whispers briefly retreated, and she was exposed to her raw memories: Esme, Partridge, her mother, the vicious attack on Barny and Jake, vulnerable, bandaged and bleeding and in need of her protection. The dry fury flared and flowed molten. Without further hesitation, she forced her own witchlight into the entrance opening. Because the exit was already in use, the light could not flow down into the library and so, just hung there in stasis, effectively blocking the mouth of the exit. Now all Holly could do was stand above the flames, looking down onto them from the pentagram and wait.

In the tunnel, Ninanna was still rising upwards behind the sheet of witchlight fire she had unleashed. As far as she knew, any minute now the power of her witchlight would erupt back at full speed into the records area, burning everything in its path. Even if it hadn't hit Holly as she left the library, it would catch her at the other end, and then Ninanna herself would be there to finish off anyone the burning light hadn't destroyed. The achievement of centuries was almost hers. She allowed herself a brief moment of elation before glancing up again, expecting to see her witchlight exiting in a blaze. Instead, it seemed to have stopped moving and then, in slow motion, she witnessed the effect of two conflicting currents of witchlight merging and exploding, ripping the air of the tunnel to shreds.

Slowly but steadily, Ninanna was continuing to rise into the chaos. With growing horror, it dawned on her there was only one way in and one way out and it only worked in one direction at any one time. She was continuing to rise up towards the exit, and there was no turning round and going back down. Ninanna had spent lifetimes accumulating vast amounts of power and she was used to relying on it. Without thinking, she unleashed her witchlight in an attempt to halt her rise, pouring more and more power into the tunnel above her, but the tunnel had been constructed to withstand attack, and the third flood of witchlight merely merged with the residue of the other two currents, creating an even bigger slow-motion explosion of raw power, flames, and scorching heat into which she was still inexorably rising.

As Holly waited by the upper pentagram, she sensed rather than heard the explosions and then, without warning, was gripped by a searing agony. She could feel flames, the destruction of flesh, the excruciatingly slow annihilation of everything that had once mattered, and the final hopelessness of consuming despair. Unable to help herself, she fell screaming to the floor, but almost as soon as it had begun, it was over, and Holly opened her eyes to find her entire body bathed in pure white light.

Chapter 26

It was a surprisingly warm day for early spring. In the rural wilderness that surrounded the cottage, two cats were hunting companionably. The fact that they were both male and not fighting over mutual territory was the least unusual thing about them. As they explored what was, to them, new-found land, the local rodent population retreated to the relative safety of its holes and burrows. Anything that squeaked or scampered was planning on staying down there until further notice.

Jake was sitting reading in the cottage's garden, propped up against a cluster of cushions and pillows and with his feet resting on an elegant nineteenth-century footstool. Holly decided she wouldn't tell him the value of the antique piece just yet. It would only make him get up in a panic, and while his recovery had been so fast and thorough that he probably didn't really need to behave quite so much like an invalid, Holly was more than happy to indulge him for a while longer. He had been through a lot, after all, and was still coming to terms with a world that, beneath its ordinary appearance, was full of witchcraft and magic. It would take a long while for him to adjust fully. If only humans were as adaptable as cats.

As far as the mundane world was concerned, Holly was being a dutiful granddaughter, sorting out her grandmother's property and personal belongings after her death. If anyone thought it odd that the woman who had previously lived in the cottage had seemed closer in age to Holly's sister than her grandmother, they kept it to themselves. Holly Beldam was a friendly enough person, pleasant to chat to, but there was something about her, an aura so to speak, that made everyone think twice, and then twice that again, before gossiping about her behind her back.

Holly was most certainly sorting out her grandmother's things, but in witchcraft terms, not by way of standard probate. There was magic to be undone as well as rooms to be cleared. Holly had meticulously and respectfully disposed of all once-living remains found in the cottage, human or otherwise, ensuring that all eldritch links between the deceased and their mortal residue were severed, so the dead could finally lie down in peace.

Only three urns now remained, and Holly was about to scatter the contents of two of them in the orchard at the far end of the garden. It was a suitable setting she thought—peaceful, familiar to at least one of them, and appropriately in the midst of flourishing apple trees for the other.

Holly didn't really know what her biological parents had once felt for one another, but Apple Ashwell had implied it was heartfelt and apparently, for him, long lasting. It seemed right to scatter their remains together, gifting them a companionship in death they had been denied in life. As she poured the ashes from both urns across the freshly growing grass, she felt a strong sense of peace, and the fading whispers in her head sounded like a gentle and final settling of dust.

Holly wiped the tears from her eyes and walked back up towards the cottage. There was still one urn to deal with. Ninanna Pandora Esme Beldam: date of birth unknown; died suddenly March 2009.

The Coven had not been keen on Holly retrieving her grandmother's remains, but as they needed Holly's assistance in reopening the entrance to the archives, there was little they could do about it. Plus, of course, Holly could be very persuasive when she wanted to. She wondered if they had realised the Beldam family witchlight was now anchored to the charred fragments of the one-time Head of the Family's mortal bones.

So, Ninanna had come back to her cottage, as had the family ring—the only thing to emerge unscathed from the fire's purge. Quite why that was, Holly was unclear. It might have been that minerals and precious metals were less combustible than flesh and bone, or that the witchlight within it had saved it from destruction. Not that it mattered. The ring was now on the middle finger of Holly's left hand, and Ninanna's ashes were in a simple urn labelled little more than N.B. It seemed apposite.

Holly transported herself and the urn into what was now her cottage's additional dimensions. All the rooms that had, until recently, stored the family remains were now empty. In the middle of the largest of these Holly had already drawn a large pentagram and added powerful words of containment to its outer borders. She put the urn in the centre of the five-sided symbol and placed a heavy-duty guarding spell on it as an extra precaution.

"You're not going anywhere, grandmother dearest."

If she heard a faint, but frantic rustle in response, she chose to put it down to imagination and calmly ignored it.

Walking back out into the garden and the early spring sunshine where Jake was now fast asleep under the body warmth of two well-fed and very comfortable cats, Holly felt a world of almost limitless possibilities waiting for her. She had no idea what she wanted to do with it all, but there was no rush. She could take her time to explore everything that was out there. She stared at it in anticipation with all the patience of a cat.

About the Author

J.S. Watts lives and writes in the UK. Her poetry and short stories appear in a diversity of publications in Britain, Canada, Australia and the States including Mslexia and Polluto and have been broadcast on BBC and Independent Radio. She has three published books to her name: a full poetry collection, *Cats and Other Myths* a multi-award nominated poetry pamphlet, *Songs of Steelyard Sue,* (both published by Lapwing Publications) and a novel, *A Darker Moon,* a dark literary fantasy, (published in the US and the UK by Vagabondage Press). Further details at: www.jswatts.co.uk and on Facebook: www.facebook.com/J.S.Watts.page

Also by J.S. Watts

Abe Finchley is a damaged man, an orphan with no roots, and no family ties. When he finally meets the woman he has been looking for all his life, he finds not just love and passion, but a dark and violent family history that spans generations into humanity's deepest past.

Eve is the woman of his dreams; but dream is just another word for nightmare, and Abe knows all about those. Amidst a confused web of lies and secrets, Abe is trying to discover who he is and make sense of what he may become. More than just his future and his new-found love is at stake. When he discovers that he has a brother, a man bound by divine destiny to kill him, Abe is going to have to make a difficult choice. A choice that might redeem the world. A choice that just might destroy it.

A Darker Moon is a dark, psychological fantasy. A mythical tale of light and shadow and the unlit places where it is best not to shine even the dimmest light.

From Vagabondage Press. Available wherever fine books are sold.

www.ingramcontent.com/pod-product-compliance
Lightning Source LLC
Chambersburg PA
CBHW050526260626
47157CB00004B/1484